Love is
a time of enchantment:
in it all days are fair and all fields
green. Youth is blest by it,
old age made benign: the eyes of love see
roses blooming in December,
and sunshine through rain. Verily
is the time of true-love
a time of enchantment — and
Oh! how eager is woman
to be bewitched!

FORBIDDEN LOVE

When Bella is just seventeen she is tricked into marriage with a man she has only met once. Ordered to follow Edward to his plantation home in the New World, Bella endures a long, restless sea voyage to Virginia. On board is Adam Tarrant, and Bella realises that this is the man she will love for the rest of her life. Despairingly, she tries to deny the dangerous love, for she knows that a husband waits for her who's good looks hide a cruel, sadistic nature — and that he will never let her go.

DONNA HUNT

◆

FORBIDDEN LOVE

Complete and Unabridged

ULVERSCROFT
Leicester

First published in Great Britain in 1981 by
Macdonald & Co (Publishers) Limited
London

First Large Print Edition
published August 1991

British Library CIP Data

Hunt, Donna *1934–*
    Forbidden love. – Large print ed. –
Ulverscroft large print series: romance
I. Title
823.914 [F]

ISBN 0–7089–2481–6

Published by
F. A. Thorpe (Publishing) Ltd.
Anstey, Leicestershire
Set by Words & Graphics Ltd.
Anstey, Leicestershire
Printed and bound in Great Britain by
T. J. Press (Padstow) Ltd., Padstow, Cornwall

1

THEY were in the church, a small, ill-lit place where the tombs of the dead overawed the living, before Bella awoke from the daze that had held her unresisting for the past two days. She shook her head slightly to clear her mind as they left the chill sunlight of the early April day and entered the dank cold of the stone building. Her companion, interpreting the gesture as a refusal, tightened his grip on her arm and hustled her onwards.

"Oh, no, you don't! It's too late now to draw back. You made your choice and must abide by it. Edward is waiting for you, and an anxious bridegroom he is."

"Choice?" Bella queried scornfully, her spirits quickly reviving. "You call it a choice that you gave me?"

"It's more than most would have done, to have provided you with a dowry and a husband, when you have no claim on me," the man replied with a short laugh. "You and the brat were lucky not to have been turned out into the streets to beg for a living."

"Where is he? Where is Toby?" she demanded.

"Awaiting you, as I promised, with old Alice to take care of him. You can spend the night at the inn before boarding the ship tomorrow. A comfortable bed in an inn is preferable to a ship's bunk for a wedding night."

"You are a fiend, Henry Martin!" she replied, and relapsed into silence as she glanced round the church.

There were two candles on the altar, and some indistinct shapes of men nearby. Bella clutched her cloak round her as she was pushed forward, and scanned their faces anxiously as soon as she was able to distinguish their features. There were three men, but she ignored the parson, a pale, thin figure who coughed apologetically and began speaking in a low voice to Henry Martin. The second of the waiting men was small and elderly, with a straggling grey beard and creased face. He stooped forward, his shoulders were rounded, and he plucked nervously at an elaborate lace collar with gnarled and twisted fingers. Surely even Henry would not have agreed to a marriage with such as he, Bella thought, and turned to the third man who must be the one she was here to wed.

What she saw in his hot, hungry glance made her wish fervently that it was greybeard after all who was to be her bridegroom. The man was tall and broad, with a jutting chin and square face. A long scar crossed his dark-skinned cheek, leaving a thin white line that dragged the left corner of his mouth up slightly. Deep clefts between the nose and the corners of his mouth gave him a cruel, perpetually sneering expression. His bold dark eyes raked her from head to foot in a manner which caused her to flush angrily. She felt as though she were stripped naked before him, and suddenly angry, she threw up her head and gave him back stare for stare. He laughed delightedly and turned to Henry Martin.

"You spoke the truth, my friend. A beauty, as far as I can see. If her form matches her face I shall be well-pleased. Well, Master Parson, be about your business. I can scarce wait for your permission to bed my wife."

Bella gasped in fury, the parson twittered in dismay, and Henry Martin laughed, pushing Bella forwards so that she stumbled and fell against her bridegroom. He made no move to assist her, and it was only by clutching at his doublet that she saved herself from sprawling ignominiously on the ground at his feet.

"Patience, my love," he scoffed. "There are some formalities with Master Parson before you can show me your aptitude on your back. You did not inform me how hot she was," he added, turning to Henry, who smiled grimly but did not answer.

Suddenly Bella realised what she was doing. Her world had suddenly collapsed, she was on the verge of a new life, and yet she had had so little choice in it!

She had always accepted that she would marry where her parents chose, but she had trusted them to select a man she could love. When her mother had died and then her father, her thoughts had been far from marriage. And then the other disaster had overtaken her. It had been on the day of her father's burial.

"Henry Martin wants to speak to you. I've told him it's not fitting, but he won't

4

go away," Alice, one of the maids who had lost her own baby and become her young brother's wet nurse two years earlier, announced disapprovingly.

Before Bella could answer Henry Martin had forced his way into the parlour where she sat. Thrusting Alice aside he came to stand menacingly before Bella.

"What do you want?" she asked, puzzled at his behaviour, for he normally avoided her company.

His position was a strange one. Bella's father openly recognised him as a bastard son, and he had never attempted to presume on the relationship. Now, however, he appeared aggressive and determined.

"What is mine by rights!" Henry replied. "Look at these."

He thrust some papers into her hands, and Bella, puzzled, glanced at them.

"All these years I've had to bear the stigma of bastardy. Men have laughed at me behind my back — they dared not to my face. All to protect you and your damned brother. Well, it's over now. These papers show that my mother was wed to my father, but she left him: and she's still alive. It's you and the squalling brat who are the bastards. And I am the rightful heir!"

Bella had tried not to believe this incredible revelation. How could her gentle, courteous father have married her own beautiful, loving mother if he had a previous wife still living? But Henry Martin had brought lawyers from London who had told her that the papers he possessed undoubtedly proved him legitimate, and as such her father's heir instead of her brother Toby.

Shattered by this calamity so soon after the death of her father Bella had been threatened with destitution. For herself she did not care knowing that she, young and strong, could soon begin to earn her bread. It was another matter for her brother Toby. Henry threatened to place him in a foundlings' home where if he survived the rigours of such a life he would become a labourer or be sent to sea. There was no way that Bella could earn for them both, keeping Toby with her.

It was when Bella had finally admitted the reality of this desperate plight that Henry had offered her an alternative.

"I've a friend bound for Virginia. He wants a wife. He'll take the brat too. But

6

you'd best decide now, he leaves England in a few days."

Faced with this ultimatum Bella had been forced to agree, but as she now looked at the man in the church who was to be her husband she wondered whether the alternative might not have been better for both herself and Toby.

Nervously the parson directed them where to stand and Bella, seething with fury but utterly helpless, forced herself to say the words that, incredibly, made her the wife of this detestable man; a man whose full name she only then discovered to be Edward Sutton; a man who had never previously seen her, but who was to take her and Toby away from England for ever, to face danger and quite possibly death in the new lands far across the seas.

The parson mumbled his way hastily through the service, avoiding Bella's eyes, and peering down at the book shortsightedly. He backed away nervously when he had done and Edward Sutton, holding the hand Bella had been forced to give him in an unyielding grip, pulled her to him and encircled her waist with his other arm, crushing her against his chest in a cruel hug. His mouth, unexpectedly wet, covered hers as she opened her lips in a gasp. She writhed to avoid him, but was imprisoned so securely that there was naught she could do but endure his hateful embrace as best she might.

It was Henry Martin who ended it.

"Come, Edward, it is time to leave."

"Are you so anxious to thrust us into bed together?" Edward replied, releasing Bella and laughing down at her as she instinctively dragged her hand across her mouth to wipe away the stain of his kiss.

Her cloak had fallen away from her shoulders during the rough embrace; he looked appreciatively at her slender waist and the curves of her breasts under the thin silk gown she wore. Bella flushed and pulled her cloak about her, but her heart was bleak. The old way of life was ended suddenly and ruthlessly, and in two short weeks she had lost almost everything. Only her small brother, whose birth had cost their mother's life two years ago, was left to her, and it was for his sake that she had agreed to this match. From now on Edward Sutton, of whose very existence she had been happily unaware but two days ago, had complete dominion over her and could do with her as he wished. It was clear already that he would be no gentle husband, and she shivered as she thought of the days and months to come when they would be trapped on a small ship along with others voyaging to the new colony of Virginia. She reluctantly refused to think of what lay in store for her during the hours of darkness, knowing that if she permitted her fears to gain an ascendancy over her determination she would long only for death. And that, for little Toby's sake, was unthinkable.

Meekly Bella followed her new husband out of the church and Henry Martin, possibly afraid that she might make a sudden bid for freedom, again grasped her arm. The older man, with a look that she thought was of pity, muttered a few indistinguishable words and hurried off towards East Cheap, leaving them to turn back to where the huge white pile of the Tower reared up beside the river.

Beyond that fortress lay the Pool of London and the ship which was taking the colonists across the seas. Many times in the carefree past Bella had watched similar ships sail up the Thames, setting off on what she had then thought enviable voyages, or returning laden with exotic treasures. Little had she expected, as she rode on the Kentish banks of the river, that she would one day leave those green hills and sail on one of the ships.

The two men led Bella to a small, shabby inn huddled close by the walls of the Tower. Here a parody of a wedding feast had been set out in a small private parlour.

Alice sat on a settle beside the fire, rocking her nursling who was so soon to be sent away from her. She was a blonde, buxom woman about ten years older than Bella. Daughter of one of the older servants, she had been with the Cliffords all her life until she had married a groom. But he had been killed soon afterwards when he had fallen under a wagon, and Alice's baby had died a few days after his birth. She had gladly returned to nurse Toby, and since his own mother had died of a fever regarded him as her real son.

Toby, with chubby arms that clung tightly to Alice as he sat on her ample lap, looked at Bella hopefully as she entered the room. There were the streaks of tears on his fat rosy cheeks, and his vivid blue eyes were swimming with more unshed ones. His dark curls were rumpled, and he pushed away all the tempting morsels Alice offered to him, burying his face in her bosom as he hid from the loud voiced, large men.

Bella sat beside her new husband, numb with the detestation she already felt for him, and despair at her plight. She nibbled at the wing of a chicken while he and Henry ate and drank their fill.

Her distress, however, went unnoticed by Alice, wrapped up in her own misery at the impending loss of Toby. She had little pity to spare for Bella. Apart from the scar, Edward was a strong, broad, not unhandsome man. Doubtless once Bella had recovered from the shocks of the past few days she would grow to love him. There was little else she could do, and she tried to convince Bella of this when it was time for her and Henry Martin to leave.

Bella nodded, blinking back her tears, and then busied herself consoling the little boy, who wailed as he sensed the strangeness of the moment.

"For the Lord's sake, stop that!" Edward ordered.

"He's tired and frightened," Bella protested.

"Then he's best in bed. Our room is through here. See to him."

There was a cupboard bed in the room, and Bella saw her brother tucked in. With an occasional sob shaking him, he fell quickly asleep, and she nerved herself to go into the next room.

Edward had been drinking as he waited, naked on the side of her bed. He glanced up at her.

"Get undressed," he ordered brusquely.

When she hesitated he rose to his feet. He was somewhat the worse for drink, she realised, horrified, and involuntarily stepped backwards.

"Come here!" he shouted, strode towards her, and seizing her by the arm, threw her across the bed.

Before she could move his hands were fumbling at her gown. Impatient at the fastenings, he suddenly dragged the bodice from her shoulders and ripped it down to the waist, exposing her firm breasts.

Bella, suddenly furiously angry, struggled to escape from his groping hands which were fondling her as they tore off the rest of her clothes. She fought, scratching and biting, but was no match for him. Indeed the opposition appeared to stimulate him. He laughed triumphantly as, capturing both of her hands and holding them imprisoned above her head, he straddled her body, his weight driving the breath from her.

"You're my wife, you'll do as I wish," he panted, forcing her legs apart. Helpless to resist, but too angry at his savage brutality to consider begging for mercy, she endured the humiliation in silence, sobbing once only as he penetrated her roughly and the searing pain tore her apart.

When he was sated he rolled away to the side of the bed and fell asleep, sprawled negligently on his back, snoring with his mouth open.

Bruised, shaken, and furiously angry at this merciless initiation into the rites of love — 'Love!' — Bella whispered scornfully to herself, she gently eased herself off the bed, wincing at the pain. Then she ineffectually tried, with the small jug of water which was all she had, to feel clean again.

Among the possessions which Edward had thrown onto the floor when he had discarded his clothes lay a short, wicked-looking dagger. Briefly Bella looked from it to the unconscious form of her husband, wishing that she had the courage to use it and rid herself of him. It would not serve. She would be caught and hanged. She was married to him, and he could do as he liked with her. A great sense of bitterness came to her as she saw endless years of harsh misery to be endured at the hands of this brute, and she suddenly determined that, although she could not murder him, she would escape from him. He would not again use her for his selfish pleasure.

With new hope she dressed speedily, thankful that her cloak would conceal the tatters of her gown. A purse heavy with gold lay on a small table; cautiously she lifted it and slipped it into her pocket. Then, praying that Toby would not cry out when she wakened him, she went into the next room. Fortunately the child was sleepy, and she dressed him and carried him out of the inn before he could begin to chatter. No-one saw her departure, and, keeping to the shadows, Bella began to

14

walk westwards, away from the forbidding Tower.

Throughout what seemed an endless night, Bella crept through the streets of London, hiding in doorways from those who roved in the dark in search of helpless victims. Toby had fallen asleep in her arms, and his weight forced her to rest often.

Soon after dawn she ventured to approach an inn and hire a horse. She had no other family who might help her, but in these last few desperate hours she had thought of one of her father's old friends who lived near Canterbury, and who would surely give her shelter and advice until she could think of some way of making a living for herself and Toby.

She never reached him. When she paused for food at an inn near Greenwich she discovered, to her dismay, Henry Martin in the stableyard.

"What the devil? How do you come to be here?"

Too exhausted to attempt to escape Bella glared at him.

"I won't go with that fiend!"

"That is what you think! I've not paid him to take you to Virginia to have you

15

back on my hands. Ostler! My horse, at once!"

The weary return to London began. Bella almost fell from her horse when they eventually reached the inn she had left so short a time before. She went dully with Henry as he pushed her into the taproom.

"Mr. Sutton," he demanded loudly.

The landlord shook his head.

"He's gone. The ship sailed first thing on the tide."

For a second Bella's hopes revived. Her hated husband had left England, he had not waited for her, or wanted her enough to stay behind and try to find her.

"Are you Mr Henry Martin?" the landlord was asking. "I remember you were with him last night. He left a letter for you. I was to send it on."

He proffered a sheet of grubby paper and Henry, tight lipped, nodded his thanks as he tore at the seal. He scanned the contents quickly and swore softly and fluently.

"Damn him! He's gone, and says you may follow or not as you wish. The coward, they'd not have caught up with him so soon. You'll go on the very next ship and

16

don't think you can escape me," he added, swinging round to Bella, who had slumped wearily against a table. "For the moment you'll have to return to Clifford Manor but I'll see to it that you don't have any opportunity of getting away again."

"He's gone?" Bella asked, ignoring his threats. All she could understand in her weariness was that she was safe for a while from Edward Sutton's lusts.

"Yes, the fool! He was afraid that the Carters would be after him. He's bold enough when there's no danger, your precious husband, but he won't risk his neck. Come, you've cost me enough time. We'll return to Clifford Manor and you can see what changes I intend to make there."

2

THE Boar's Head, a small and decrepit-looking tavern, crouched beneath the walls of the Tower of London, a few yards away from the river itself. It was a place where seamen snatched a respite from their rigorous duties on board ship, and where travellers, wishing to sample just once more the comforts of home before embarking on the dangerous adventure of a sea voyage, halted for a last tankard of ale. Travellers disembarking at Tower Wharf, after one look at the unprepossessing exterior of the Boar's Head, usually shuddered and made their way further into the City before halting for refreshment in surroundings more congenial for celebrating a safe landing.

Adam Tarrant and his servant rode slowly through Aldgate, past the gallows on Tower Hill, towards the tavern. They were on the verge of departure from England, a fact that caused Daniel Fletcher considerable satisfaction, while his master

18

hovered between regret for a lost way of life and anticipation at returning to the new one he had carved out for himself on the far side of the Atlantic Ocean.

They dismounted and Adam handed the reins of the horse, a sturdy but ancient hired beast, to Daniel.

"Come and join me when you have stabled them," he said. Daniel had served his master for almost twenty years now, since Adam was a lad of fourteen, and was more friend than servant. Such invitations were commonplace.

Adam stood for a moment looking up at the massive walls of the Tower, a wry smile on his handsome face. It had been the threat of incarceration in that forbidding fortress which had originally sent him overseas. He had thought at the time that if it had not been for his mother's pleas, he would have risked remaining in England, but now that she was dead he could review his decision. And he realized that it was not fear of King James's wrath that had persuaded him to return but an anxiety to resume the task of wresting a fortune from the lush soils but difficult new colony of Virginia.

He turned to enter the low doorway of the inn, but paused again. Another party of travellers had arrived and a man of about his own age was assisting a woman carrying a child down from a horse where she had been riding pillion. Another woman sat on her own horse, drooping in the saddle and taking no heed of what went on around her. When the man turned and brusquely bade her dismount she raised her head to look about her as if aware of her surroundings for the first time.

Adam's eyes narrowed appreciatively. She was a vastly pretty creature, he thought, and if her figure, at the moment concealed by the green velvet cloak she wore, was in any way comparable to her face she would be the loveliest visitor this wretched tavern had ever seen. About seventeen years old, she had big brown eyes, slanting upwards in a fascinating way and fringed with thick curling lashes. Her creamy-complexioned face was oval, framed in ringlets of a rich red-brown shade, and one look at her enchantingly red lips made Adam long to kiss them.

Her escort lifted her down from the saddle and as he did so her cloak caught on the pommel. Her figure, Adam noted with satisfaction, appeared to match her face. She had an elegant slender waist, and he caught a glimpse of enticingly swelling breasts, as well as the suggestion of long and shapely thighs under the thin stuff of her gown. A slender ankle peeped from beneath her skirts, and the hand she rested momentarily on her escort's shoulder was long-fingered and delicate.

Adam stood aside while they entered the tavern and then followed them, idly speculating on the relationships of the travellers. The man and the older woman might be married, he supposed, for they were of an age, yet they were hardly old enough to be the parents of the young charmer. The thought that the enchanting young girl might be the man's wife he thrust away from him distastefully, hoping that the similar colouring of their hair denoted a blood relationship.

Smiling a little to himself at his concern he followed them inside, finding a stool a little distance away from where they had seated themselves about a small table. The older woman was occupied with the child, who did not appear to appreciate his surroundings. Adam, looking about him at the low, crowded room, filled with noise and smoke and the odours of unwashed bodies and stale food, silently agreed. It was an unlikely setting for such a jewel as the girl, and the most probable explanation was that they were about to set off on a similar voyage to his own. If by some good fortune they were on the same vessel Adam knew that he would contrive to know the girl better.

Unobtrusively he watched them. The girl appeared listless and apparently unaware of the suggestive remarks made by several of the sailors nearby. The older woman had flushed angrily and said something to the man. Then she shrugged and turned her attention back to the child when he gave her an abrupt and apparently unsatisfactory answer. They were too far away for Adam to hear what was being said over the talk and laughter around him, and he permitted his thoughts to revert to his own affairs.

"It is but a short time and you will come to no harm. Alice is no shrinking maiden to fear the jests of a couple of sailors, and they won't rape you in the potroom," Henry was saying, chuckling thickly.

"You are a villain, Henry Martin!" Alice cut in angrily.

He raised his hand as if to strike her, and then sank back into the corner of the settle, shrugging.

"I've told you a dozen times already that my name is Clifford," he replied through pursed lips.

"So you say," Alice sniffed. "Your mother was a Martin and never claimed aught else!"

Henry flushed a dull red.

"I have explained the reasons for that and they have been accepted by those that matter. Take care, woman, not to miscall me, or you'll go with your precious infant after all."

"He means it, Alice," Bella said quietly, and clenched her hands tightly as Henry laughed in triumph.

In an effort to still the turbulence of her emotions, so tightly held in check, she glanced through her lowered lashes at the man who had been at the door of the tavern when they had arrived. If Edward had been like him she would not perhaps have railed so fiercely against the cruel fate that had so unexpectedly overtaken

23

her. The stranger was better dressed than the rest of the customers, and exceedingly handsome, tall, with broad shoulders and a slim but muscular figure. His hair was blond and his eyes, of an especially deep blue, looked kind. She doubted whether he would treat a woman as Edward had treated her.

One of the inn servants approached Adam and handed him a sheet of paper which he scanned quickly, a frown in his eyes.

"We sail alone," he told the manservant bitterly when Daniel rejoined him. "My so-called friends have changed their minds. I had thought Thomas more reliable, I did not expect him to retract from the venture. One discovers one's true friends when one is out of favour!"

"He must have heard discouraging tales of Jamestown," Daniel replied soothingly. "There's plenty told in England."

Adam shrugged. "It's hard, yes, and many have lost their lives. But we are far more fortunate than the first settlers. We have houses and the town is well protected."

"Safer than here in England," Daniel

muttered, and Adam grinned affectionately at him, his good humour restored.

"You're an old woman, Daniel," he chided. "You've not ceased worrying all the time we've been in England."

"And still am, Master Adam! I'll not rest until we're on board ship."

"The Tower will not hold me this time," Adam replied confidently.

As he spoke the man with the unknown beauty pulled at her arm, forcing her to stand up. Maintaining a firm grip on her, almost, Adam thought, as though she were a felon, he pushed her in front of him to the door. She cast an anguished look at the older woman, who followed with the child, deftly slapping away the bold hand of a sailor who sat near the door.

Adam rose casually from his seat and strolled out of the room, causing Daniel to protest in surprise then, realizing that his master had not heard him, he hurriedly drained both half-empty tankards and ran after Adam who was standing just outside the tavern doorway, watching with an odd expression a group of travellers moving towards the landing steps.

Henry had Bella in a firm grip, but she

25

tried to wriggle free.

"I'll not go!" she gasped, and almost cried out as he twisted her arm painfully.

"You're wed, and your place is with your husband. It's a wonder he's still willing to take you after what you did!"

"His letter said he didn't care," Bella said angrily.

"But I do. I've paid him to take you, and I'll not keep you here. I've allowed you to take Alice, despite the extra cost. Edward can claim more land for her, so he'll not care."

"If I promise not to fight your claim, will you let us stay?"

"I'd not trust you a handspan away from me in England. That was what you intended when you came back to Kent, wasn't it? It was fortunate for me that we met on the road."

"I'd keep out of your way. I could work to support Toby."

"I offered you that choice, and you preferred marriage."

"You said you'd put Toby in a home for foundlings."

"Enough! You are going to Virginia."

Bella subsided, but when they came to

the top of the steps and she saw the small boat waiting below that would finally sever her from England, she halted once more.

"Alice, run," she called, and kicked Henry on the shin, trying to free herself from his grasp.

She almost won free, but Henry was too strong for her, and clung to one arm. Alice, after a startled movement, had paused and was looking on, shaking her head sorrowfully.

"It's to no avail, Miss Bella," she said soothingly, and with the help of the waiting boatman clambered into the boat. Henry pushed Bella into it, and followed, all the while keeping a tight hold on her.

"It'll not be so bad when you're used to it," Alice whispered consolingly. "At least you've got me and Master Toby still."

Shuddering as she recalled her husband's attack on their bridal night, Bella doubted if she could ever again suffer to have his hands on her, but the opportunity for escape had passed, and she was determined to show no more weakness. Somehow, she vowed, either before they reached Virginia, or when they arrived, she would contrive to escape from her detested marriage. She concentrated on the multitude of boats surrounding them.

It was a chaotic scene. A dozen or more tall, brightly painted, three-masted ships towered above them, hordes of sailors clambering about in the rigging and calling to one another as they prepared to sail on the turning tide. Some sails already flapped in position, and Bella's ears were assailed by the noises of canvas slapping against the ropes and the wood, the shouts of the sailors, the creaking of spars, and as a constant background to these more distinct sounds, the muted rumbles of the river itself and the piercing screams of the gulls as they searched for food. Beneath the tall ships darted a throng of lesser boats, carrying passengers and cargo, or delicacies which were meant to entice the voyagers into last minute purchases: boats in continual risk of being crushed between their mightier brethren.

Toby bounced up and down on Alice's lap, pointing eagerly and stumbling over the few words he knew as he strove to express his excitement. Alice herself was uncharacteristically silent and suddenly, as a bigger than normal wave hit their small craft awkwardly she thrust Toby at Bella.

"Take him, Miss Bella!" she gasped, and leaned over the side of the boat in considerable distress. The boatman laughed unfeelingly.

"If that's the way it takes you now, you'd best come home wi' me," he offered, leering. Bella glared at him.

"Be silent, you heartless oaf!" she snapped.

Alice gradually recovered her countenance, although she looked exceptionally pale. She was able to scramble up the ladder hanging from the deck, and assured Bella, anxiously following her, that she felt much better to be on a larger vessel.

"I'd like to lie down, though," she admitted, and Bella turned to Henry.

"Well, you have succeeded. Where is our cabin?"

He laughed. "I paid Edward for your cabins on his ship. This voyage you'll travel in the hold."

He beckoned to a sailor who grinned when he heard the instructions and cast a sly look at Bella.

"This way, Mistress," he said.

"Don't think to disembark, my dear," Henry warned. "I'll be waiting until the

29

boat sails, and this good fellow will know what to do if you are foolish."

Bella turned away with a toss of her head. Carrying Toby, and giving what assistance she could to Alice, she found it difficult to follow the man along the deck which was strewn with coiled ropes, barrels, crates and pens full of noisily indignant livestock. When they reached a narrow ladder leading down to the lower deck she had to ask for help. After he had guided Alice's faltering steps down the ladder the sailor came back and took Toby out of Bella's arms.

Below deck it was cramped and stuffy, but the sailor led them to a hatch and down another ladder, into the gloomy hold. Bella looked around her. It was not so dark as she had at first thought. A few candles had been lit, and she could see that there were dozens of people crammed together. Some sat still, bewildered, but many of them were busy arranging their belongings, contriving islands of limited privacy with improvised hangings attached to the vast beams of the ship. Seeing Bella hesitate, a skinny woman gestured to them.

"There's space beyond us where the three of you could squeeze in," she suggested, and Bella stepped forward with a word of thanks.

Behind the curtaining the woman had already hung up was a small triangular space, awkward to get at because of an enormous rib of the ship which was at an angle to the others. Bella nodded with satisfaction, however. The rib would act as a barrier to prevent Toby from straying, and there was just enough room for the three of them to lie down. The boxes which Alice had packed were brought down by the the sailor who had shown them the way, and while Alice, overcome, sank down to the floor, Bella struggled to unpack a few necessities.

"Oh, Miss Bella! I'm that ashamed. I'll be better shortly, and able to help you."

"Of course," Bella said bracingly. "Father — " her voice broke, but with an immense effort she managed to continue, " — used to say that everyone grew accustomed to the motion of the ship eventually. And doubtless it will be smoother than that ridiculous small boat."

Soon Alice fell asleep on an improvised mattress, and Toby, worn out by the long journey he had had, curled up beside her.

Bella was left with her uneasy thoughts for company. Would she really be able to escape her husband? And how could she and Alice, burdened with a young child, cope in a raw and undeveloped land without a man? Bella gritted her teeth. No man would ever use her again. Instead, she would do her utmost to turn their weaknesses to her own advantage. She would need to be cunning, to pit her wits against theirs, but now, when the sharp grief of her father's death had softened to a dull ache, she would make no more mistakes such as the one which had put her into the power of Edward Sutton.

What would Virginia be like? she wondered. Tales she had heard of the new colony had been frightening. A large majority of the earliest settlers had died, and the few survivors had a hard task to wrest a living from a so far inhospitable land. Some merchants, the Virginia Company of London, determined to win profits from the venture, had offered so much land per person as an inducement to settlers. Edward had agreed to marry her and to take her brother partly because of the dowry Henry had offered, and partly because with them he would be able to claim a larger grant. He had been forced to leave England hurriedly for some reason Bella still had not discovered.

When Bella had once more fallen into Henry's power he, determined that she must not contest his claim to her father's lands, had locked her up until he had been able to arrange another passage, and she had not dared make another attempt to escape while Toby was at his mercy.

At the thought of her home, seen for the last time that morning silhouetted against the rising sun, a lump rose in Bella's throat. She had been so happy there, in that comfortable manor house built just over a century ago. Then her mother had died when Toby was born, and youthful joy had been at an end. The death of her father had been another crushing blow, and before she knew what was happening her half-brother Henry had produced those papers to show that his mother had been married to Sir John Clifford after all, and he was therefore the legitimate heir.

Bewildered, with no-one to turn to, and threatened by Henry with beggery or confinement in a brothel, she had agreed to wed his unknown friend. 'Fool! Fool! Fool!' she berated herself, but it was done, and she was on her way to Virginia and her hated husband.

Suddenly the movements of the ship changed, and instead of rocking gently she began to roll, her timbers protesting and creaking. From far above came an increase in the shouted commands and Bella realized that the anchor had been raised, and the journey had begun.

Many of the passengers went up on deck to catch a last glimpse of home, but Bella, unable to leave Alice who had again succumbed to nausea, remained with her, comforting her and Toby as best she could.

By nightfall Alice had recovered slightly, and she urged Bella to go and take some air, for already the hold was becoming unbearably stuffy. Thankfully Bella climbed up to the deck, and savoured the fresh breezes, watching the outlines of the hills on the southern bank of the Thames, the first evening stars twinkling above them.

As she turned and went down into the narrow passageway below the deck, one of the men passengers, who had seen her come aboard earlier, lay in wait for her and seized her hand as she passed him.

"Be kind to me," he mumbled, clearly drunk, and attempted to drag her into his arms. As he did so the fragile silk of her gown split, and in the glow of a lantern hanging in the passageway he could see an enticing glimpse of white skin and softly curving flesh. Swaying, he attempted to tear her bodice, his wine-sodden breath wafting over her face.

Bella's hands flew out as she clawed and scratched at his face, but unexpectedly a slender rapier appeared over her shoulder and a cool, deep voice from immediately behind her spoke.

"I think you have demonstrated your gentlemanly qualities sufficiently, my friend. Away with you, before my sword slips where it is aching to reach. I would dislike intensely to have to wipe your villainous blood from its noble blade."

Bella turned her head and looked at a tall, golden-haired man whose smile made her heart turn over. Altering his grasp on the jewelled hilt of his elegant short sword, he held the other at bay as he backed away a pace and fumbled at his belt. Then she cried out as her rescuer flung out an arm and pushed her aside, causing her to fall heavily against a door jamb, while he dropped to his knees. Above his head, quivering in the solid wood of a cabin door, a bare few inches above his smooth golden hair and close to Bella's shoulder was a short but wicked-looking dagger.

Before Bella had understood the significance of this her rescuer had sprung forward, grappling fiercely with the man who was dragging his own sword from his belt. In the low, narrow passage, there was little room to move and the two men, both tall enough to be in danger of cracking their heads on the wide beams, swayed together silently for a few moments until the stranger, thrusting Bella's assailant away, brought his clenched fist into contact with the man's chin and snapped back his head with a jerk.

Her attacker staggered back and collapsed against the open door of a cabin, the sword he had freed from its sheath clattering away along the passage. He lay still and Bella looked up at the stranger.

"Is he dead?" she asked, a quiver in her voice.

"It would take more than a blow to kill such a one. I beg your pardon for pushing you so, but there was naught else that would serve."

Adam Tarrant smiled down at her, and thought again that she was the loveliest creature he had ever set eyes on. But Bella was unaware of his admiration. Lost in the horror of what had passed, she looked from the man at her feet to the dagger which pierced the stout wood of the door, and her lips trembled.

"He threw it at you," she said quietly. "He might have killed you. Or me," she added as an afterthought. "I am so sorry, but grateful to you for — for intervening!"

Recalling her torn gown, and made conscious of the admiring flow in the stranger's vivid blue eyes as she finally looked up at him, Bella flushed, the delicate red staining her cheeks in bright contrast with the creamy pallor of her skin.

"I am happy to have been of assistance, Mistress. I am Adam Tarrant. I believe I saw you in the Boar's Head?"

Bella nodded. "Yes, I was there. I recall seeing you. You arrived at the same time as we did, did you not?"

Adam nodded.

"Will you honour me by taking some wine with me? You have been badly shocked, and need a restorative."

Unexpectedly tears came to Bella's eyes, and she angrily blinked them away. To receive such kindness after the brutality she had suffered and the sorrow she had undergone in the last few weeks was too much for her composure. Why, she raged inwardly, could Henry not have married her to such a man as the one now looking down at her? Then she hardened her heart, and recalled her resolve to use men as they had used her. With a cool smile, she inclined her head.

"Thank you, but no. I must return to Alice and Toby. They will be concerned, for I remained on deck longer than I intended."

"You are with friends? I will escort you to them before that oaf regains his senses."

"I shall be safe now," she said and quickly turned to walk away. Adam looked after her thoughtfully. What had made her suddenly change her attitude, which had at first been friendly? Had she been afraid when he had suggested she drank with him? That must have been it. She would not willingly trust any man so soon after such an attack. He smiled, thinking that on so long a voyage he could well afford to take his time. No matter how frightened she was he would woo her, and he was sure that in the end he would win her.

In the hold a few curious looks were cast at Bella and her torn gown as she made her way towards the corner where Alice peered anxiously round the edge of the makeshift partition. One slatternly dressed girl threw a ribald remark at her but Bella was unaware of it, and after staring angrily at her the girl laughed.

"Thinks herself too good to mix with the likes of us," she commented, and returned to the task of spreading out her belongings so as to enlarge the portion of deck she occupied. A scared-looking woman who was squeezed into a smaller space already, and had two children aged about six and ten with her, protested feebly when her meagre possessions were pushed aside, but the slattern threw a mouthful of abuse at her and she cowered back, catching the older child, a boy, to her when he would have tried to protest.

"What has happened? Who tore your gown?" Alice demanded,

"Oh, some drunken oaf. Another man stopped him. Don't fret, Alice, I came to no harm. Indeed, what could be worse than what has already happened to me?"

"Was it that sailor Henry spoke with?" Alice suddenly asked.

"No, a passenger. And it was another one who stopped him. I think he liked me, and at least he was a gentleman. We might need his help, Alice, later."

"What was his name?"

"Adam Tarrant. He saw us at that horrible tavern. A tall, blond man, well-dressed. Do you recall him?"

Alice shook her head, and covertly examined Bella. There was an odd expression in her eyes, and Alice was puzzled. She had counselled the girl to make the best of her hasty marriage and accept what was inevitable. If Bella had begun to show an interest in this Mr Tarrant there could be yet more problems ahead of them in Virginia, for from what little she had seen of Edward Sutton she did not think he would easily give up his wife to another man.

There was little enough time for such reflections, however, for they soon began pitching about on the waves as they met the open sea, and Alice began groaning and retching in misery.

Before the *Virginian* had rounded the North Foreland they encountered strong easterly winds and heavy seas. That night a storm rose, which pursued them for days along the Channel and well past Land's End, not abating until they were off the coast of Portugal. Alice was helpless and needed constant attention. Toby refused to eat and for most of the time sat miserably weeping. Most of the other passengers were in considerable distress, and when she could snatch a few minutes from her attendance on Alice Bella did what she could to assist them.

Conditions in the hold of the ship quickly became deplorable. The stench of vomit and from the buckets which was the only sanitation provided for the passengers, affected even those with strong stomachs, and there were few hardy enough to do anything more than attempt minimal cleaning of their own share of the hold. The sailors appeared not to care, whether from indifference or because they were too busy fighting the elements Bella did not know. A week after the beginning of the voyage two of the children aboard died and Toby, weak from lack of food, developed a feverish delirium, and she decided to make an effort to improve matters.

Bella had discovered that most of the men were poor artisans. The London Virginian Company was helping them pay their passages in at attempt to provide new industries in the colony, and several of them were French or Swedish, understanding little English. The others, accustomed all their lives to take orders, would not face the possible wrath of the Captain by complaining of their conditions.

"Sir Edwin Sandys gave me my passage," one of them told her. "He's head of the Company, see, and if I'm awkward it'll go ill with me."

"I'd be a marked man, and I want no trouble in the colony. I've had plenty o' that before," another said.

"Best leave it. What else can folk like

us do but endure what comes?" asked a third resignedly.

Bella surveyed them, angry at their lack of spirit and yet sympathizing with their reluctance. It seemed that it was left to her, and she turned with no further word towards the ladder. Since the storm had subsided during the night and fine, warmer weather had prevailed, the passengers were allowed onto the decks. Many of them were still too ill to care, but those who could escaped from the hot, stuffy, and foetid hold to sit in the fresh air and drink in the sea breezes.

Emerging onto the deck Bella looked about her fearfully, half expecting to see her former assailant lying in wait for her, but he was nowhere to be seen. She asked a passing sailor where she would discover the Captain.

"On the quarterdeck," he replied, gesturing towards it. "But Captain Tomkins is an old man, lassie. He'd not satisfy ye, I'll warrant. If it's a real man ye want he's right in front of ye now!"

He tried to seize her hand, but she stepped quickly back, then turned and almost ran to the quarterdeck. She glanced over her shoulder as she began to climb the short ladder but the sailor remained where he was, afraid perhaps of creating a disturbance in front of his captain.

Two men stood on the quarterdeck, their backs to Bella. The shorter of the two was clearly the Captain, but the other was Adam Tarrant. He was even more handsome than she had remembered, Bella thought confusedly, looking at his tall, elegant figure, broadshouldered and narrow-hipped. His legs were long and shapely, and he rested a slim hand on the rail beside him. Some noise she made caused him to turn, and he stepped towards her, holding out his hands. The smile he gave her warmed his eyes to an even deeper blue than she remembered.

"I had hoped to see you again before now. Have you been suffering from the weather?"

"No, but my maid has."

"It was an unpleasant storm, especially for those not accustomed to the sea," the Captain agreed.

"Captain, I came to you to ask if something might be done to improve the conditions in the hold? The passengers have suffered more from the stench and closeness than from the sea, and many are in desperate straits. We cannot procure enough water to scrub the place clean."

"Of course, Mistress — I do not think we have been introduced?"

"My name is Cl — Sutton, Captain."

"Tomkins. Now that we have a calmer sea and time to spare I will give orders for the hold to be cleaned."

"May I bring my maid and the baby out on deck? Toby has been feverish, and I am so afraid for him. They will be better sleeping on deck than in that place."

"There is an unused cabin next to mine," Adam said quickly. "You cannot sleep on deck, the nights are cold."

Bella considered him calmly. Was this a trap? And yet for Toby's sake she must accept the offer.

"Is it your cabin?" she demanded suspiciously.

"Only that I paid for it and intended it for two friends who decided, after all, not to join the ship. Come, permit me to show you where it is. I trust you would not object, Captain?"

"But all the others," Bella exclaimed,

suffering a pang of remorse.

"There are not enough cabins for them all," the Captain said sensibly. "I will see to it that they are made as comfortable as possible. If you will conduct Mistress Sutton to the cabin, Mr Tarrant, I will have the baby and his nurse fetched."

He strode away before Bella could reply, and Adam took her arm to guide her along the deck. She trembled at his nearness, feeling shafts of fire where his fingers rested against her skin. No other man who had held her hand or arm when she had danced with them, or accepted help, had affected her in such a way. She had often been aware of rough, work and weather-worn hands, or the soft, effeminate hands of those who neither worked nor took part in sports and hunting, but never before had her flesh tingled so at the touch of long, firm yet smooth fingers. She recalled the horror of Edward's hands on her body, and shivered in sudden disgust and confusion.

Adam went before her down the ladder, and she trembled yet more violently as his arm encircled her waist to guide her down the steps. As soon as she could she stepped away from him, taking a deep breath to steady her tumultuous feelings. He led the way to the cabin and stood aside to permit her to enter first. It was relatively spacious with two bunks and a small porthole, a table and two chairs.

"Thank you," Bella said, stilling the fierce beating of her heart. "Are you emigrating to Virginia?"

"I already own land there. I have been on a visit to England. You have not been before?"

"No. I am travelling to join my husband, who went ahead to prepare for us," Bella said.

She might detest Edward, and hope never to have to submit to him again, but there was no point in concealing his existence. She thought she saw a fleeting expression of regret cross Adam Tarrant's face, but it was gone so swiftly that she could not be sure. Controlling with an effort the trembling of her limbs, she turned her head away from the stern, now unreadable expression in his eyes, and seated herself on one of the bunks. The tension flowing between them was almost tangible; she felt her pulses pounding like a fever in the blood. In a moment, she felt sure, he would move towards her and she would be lost. She heard her own voice from what seemed a great distance saying, "Tell me about Virginia," and then the door opened.

It was Alice, staggering somewhat and being assisted by a grinning sailor. Another sailor was behind her, carrying Toby, and Bella competently took charge, ordering a weakly protesting Alice to lie down and leave everything to her while she took Toby into her arms.

"Soon have your baggage up, Miss," the sailors said cheerfully, and departed.

Adam Tarrant rose to his feet gracefully and took his leave of them. So perfectly cool and distant was his touch as he kissed her hand that Bella could almost have believed she had dreamed the past half hour.

3

THEY were soon settled in the cabin and Alice, declaring that she no longer felt ill, permitted Bella to send her for a stroll about the deck. When she returned, after a very short time, she was shivering.

"Alice, you look so pale!" Bella exclaimed.

Alice shook her head. "I expect it's the lack of food, Miss Bella. The wind's cold out on deck. I'll be better in a day or so. Now, I'd like to lie down."

Bella tucked her up in one of the bunks, and she was soon asleep. Some hours later she woke, and they ate. Even Toby, who had petulantly refused all the food they had offered him recently, was persuaded to take some of the broth Bella heated for him over a small brazier put on the deck for the use of the passengers.

"Go out for a breath of air," Alice urged. "I'll see to the baby, I'm feeling myself again."

Bella nodded, and taking up her cloak,

slipped out of the cabin and up to the deck. Several of the passengers lounged about on the makeshift seats provided by the crates. Some recognised Bella and called to ask how she had managed to leave the hold.

"I — there was a spare cabin," she explained. "I took it for my brother's sake," she added guiltily, looking at the sickly woman who was trying to control one toddler while a babe in arms cried feebly.

"Good luck to ye, lass," the woman said with no trace of envy. "I'd do the same, given half a chance. They've cleaned the hold. That was your doing. I've heard?"

"I'm sure Captain Tomkins would have seen to it as soon as the sailors had time to spare," Bella said hurriedly.

"When a pretty young gal asks a favour, it's usually granted," sneered a coarse-looking girl a few years older than Bella. "What are you paying for your cabin? Is the fine gentleman very demanding?"

A couple of the men guffawed, and Bella turned away, her cheeks burning. Then she thew up her head defiantly. Let them think what they would, she had done her best to alleviate their lot.

She walked to the far end of the deck and stood apart from the others, leaning over the rail. They were sailing into the setting sun and the water gleamed in its rays. The gentle waves provided a not unpleasant motion, and the creaking timbers sounded friendly rather than menacing.

Adam saw her as soon as he came on deck, and went to join her by the rail.

"I hope the cabin suits you," he murmured, and Bella, her thoughts far away back at her lost home, started as she turned to face him.

"Thank you, it is marvellous after the hold, but I feel so guilty when there are others as badly off as I am still down there!"

"I suspect they are more used to such conditions than you are, and better able to survive them. They are tough, remember, or they would not have lived so long."

Remembering some of the stinking hovels she had glimpsed on her way through London, Bella shuddered.

"Will it be better, where we are going?"

"It is dangerous, but wild and free. A place where a man, if he is lucky, can build an empire for himself."

51

"How long have you been there?" Bella asked, curious.

"Some six years."

"You do not seem the usual sort of planter."

Adam chuckled. "What do you know of them?"

"Very little, apart from the people I have met on this ship. Why should a gentleman want to go into danger, and leave his comforts behind?"

Adam was silent for a moment and then calmly picked up Bella's hand, examining it carefully.

"You are a gentlewoman," he said softly. "Why do you go?"

Bella quivered at his touch, and tried to draw her hand away, but he held it just firmly enough to prevent her doing so without a struggle, so, embarrassed, she ceased the attempt.

"I may have been brought up in luxury, but I am poor now," she replied slowly. "I married a planter."

Adam considered her, noting that she apparently did not consider her husband a gentleman. He began to speak slowly, his fingers caressing hers absently as he did so, and sending shivers of a tingling awareness along Bella's nerves.

"There were too many gentlemen when the first colonists went to Jamestown in 1607, fourteen years ago. Too many who thought their mere presence would ensure them a fortune, and too few prepared to work hard enough for it."

"Most of them died, I think?" Bella said, trying to still her response to his touch.

"Nearly a hundred and fifty started, only a hundred arrived, and by the following year two thirds of them had died. The London Company has granted land to those who pay their passage, and send out poor artisans who will work for the Company for seven years, then be free to make their own way."

"Fifty acres for each passenger," Bella said, recalling what Henry had said. "Edward will get two hundred acres, then, with the three of us. Is that large?"

"Not really. Some men have taken several servants, and have much bigger plantations. My own is larger."

"Have you many servants, then?" Bella asked, trying to ignore the touch of his fingers, now encircling her wrist.

"Not houseservants. I knew something of what to expect, and took several men with me who would be useful on a farm. I have a carpenter and a blacksmith, a mason and a thatcher, as well as labourers. They do work for others who would otherwise find it difficult to manage."

The sun had finally disappeared over the water horizon as they had been talking, and as the light dimmed Adam drew closer to Bella.

"Did you hope to make a fortune?" she asked, trying to edge away, but unable to because he still held her hand firmly in his.

"No, that was not my reason for going," Adam replied. "I was tactless enough to disparage young George Villiers soon after he had caught the eye of King James. I was threatened with the Tower, and I preferred the open spaces of Virginia!"

"So you had no choice either?" Bella exclaimed.

Adam's arm slid round her shoulders.

"Either?" he queried softly, his face close to hers.

"Well, I am married," Bella said breathlessly. "I had to go with Edward."

"Why did you not travel with him? If I had been your husband I could not have borne a lengthy parting. Is he blind?"

Bella tried again to draw away, but without appearing to resist her Adam's arm remained firmly about her and she could not move.

"I must go back to Alice and Toby," she said hastily.

"Surely not yet? Is the child better?"

"Yes, I thank you. But it grows late."

"Are you cold? You are shivering."

Afterwards Bella could not recall how it came about that Adam's arm, which had been about her shoulder, had slipped beneath her cloak and round her waist, and drawn her closer to him.

"You are so slim," he whispered in her ear. "Far too slender and far too young to have a baby."

"Toby is my brother!" Bella exclaimed. "Did you think he was mine?" She blushed in the darkness, and bowed her head.

"So that explains it," Adam said, gently turning her head upwards by a firm hand cupping her chin.

"Yes, and I must go back to them."

"They will not come to any harm. The

cabin is warm and comfortable, and Daniel, my man, is next door. He will hear if they need aught."

"Did you set him to watch? Did you follow me?" Bella demanded, suddenly suspicious.

"Do you object?" Adam queried, and bent to kiss her lips.

Bella instinctively tried to avoid him by twisting away her head, but Adam's fingers were still beneath her chin, and he held her firmly for a few seconds, the firm warmth of his lips sending fire through her veins. Then, as he relaxed his grip she pulled away, and stood breathing deeply, her thoughts chaotic.

He was the same as Edward, she was thinking confusedly. He also wanted to use her for his own gratification. She had loathed Edward's touch, but with this man she had almost lost her senses, swept away on some sensuous tide which had almost destroyed rational thought.

Uncertain whether her resistance was due to the memory of her husband, fear of him, or a genuine worry about the child, Adam held her gently within the circle of his arms.

"Do you wish to go back to the cabin?" he asked.

The cabin! She should have known, Bella chastised herself. No man offered favours without demanding payment. The other passengers who had assumed she had become this man's mistress had been right. Then she shivered, wondering whether he would turn them out, back into the wretched hold, if she refused him. She dared not risk that for Toby's sake. Besides, she told herself firmly, it could not be worse than the degradation she had suffered, and the pain she had undergone, on her wedding night.

She took a deep breath and straightened her shoulders.

"Your cabin?" she asked, with a great effort to speak calmly and not permit her voice to tremble. "I am ready to discharge my obligation to you!"

For a second Adam's grip hardened. Then he said coolly, "There is no haste," and pulled her back against him.

Bella stood rigidly, willing herself not to struggle as he bent again to kiss her. His lips, however, were firm and yet soft, forcing her own into a softness and warmth she would have withheld from him if she could. He held her close to him, his hands gentle yet firm against her back and shoulders. When she was gasping for air he lifted his face for a moment, then, as she gulped in a mouthful of air his lips again descended on hers, and the tip of his tongue traced the outline of her own lips before he forced it between her teeth, tantalizing her to respond.

One hand was stroking the back of her neck, sending shivers down her back, while the other pressed her hard against him. Without that firm hold Bella was certain that she would have fallen, so weak did her legs seem. What was happening to her? she wondered, frantic with the effort of remaining passive. With Edward she had been both furious and afraid, there was none of the mind-deadening langor which was encompassing her now.

Just as she thought she would swoon, Adam's tongue hardened, exploring and searching her mouth demandingly. At the same time she felt his thumb, agonisingly slowly, trace the edge of her ribs, from her back and round her side, gradually rising towards her breast as his hand, burningly hot through the thin silk of her gown, spread out over her taut, flat stomach.

She pressed against him, moaning involuntarily, then raised her hands to caress his chest, before recovering her senses and making a feeble attempt to push Adam away from her, but the effect he was having on her made her too weak for it to be other than a token resistance, easily overcome as the arm behind her back tightened.

Now he was murmuring soft words, indistinguishable words, into her ear. She tried to twist away from him, but it was to no avail. The tiny part of her mind that still functioned was aghast at her instinctive desire to accept, to respond to his caresses, and she was astonished to realise that she wanted yet more. Trembling, unable to resist, she clung to him, and her hands slid up and round his neck.

He kissed her long and hard, forcing her head back, and turning so that she was pinioned between his body and the ship's rail. His mouth travelled down to her neck, where a pulse fluttered as he buried his face in her windblown curls, and she whimpered as his hands slowly, tantalisingly, outlined the curves of her hips, travelled upwards past her waist, and coming to rest, as Bella shuddered in total subjection, on her breasts.

She gave another trembling gasp as he raised his head, and her lips sought his, her hands entwined in his hair as she pulled his head down towards her and strained towards him.

For a moment Adam responded, and then he stepped back, firmly disentangling her arms from around his neck.

"You can consider your obligation discharged," he said quietly. "Now return to your cabin, and don't try to thank me for it again!"

And abruptly he turned and walked away.

Shattered both by the strength of her own desires, so unexpectedly aroused, and his abrupt departure, Bella sank against the deck, racked with hard dry sobs. How could she have behaved in so abandoned a fashion? She wondered as her senses slowly returned. Why, when she had loathed the very touch of Edward's hand on hers, had she craved the much more intimate embraces of a man who was a virtual stranger to her?

Eventually the cold brought Bella back to a sense of her other needs, and she crept back into the cabin, thankful to find that both Alice and Toby were fast asleep, and she could avoid questions on her long absence.

She lay tossing restlessly on her bunk, wondering how she could face that detestable man ever again. It would be worse, she suddenly thought, than facing Edward, for his violation of her had been against her wishes, and yet, if Adam had not rejected her when he had done, what would have happened? She had been powerless to offer any resistance, and had actually wanted him to hold her in his arms for ever.

Eventually she fell into an exhausted doze, to be awaken an hour later by Toby's miserable crying. He was feverish again, and Alice seemed to have caught a chill and was shivering convulsively. While insisting that Alice remained underneath the covers, Bella watched helplessly as Toby grew worse throughout the day, his fever mounting and his breathing becoming more shallow and obviously painful.

All night Bella watched over her brother, trying to keep his wasted little body cool and persuade him to sip a soothing tisane. Alice had fallen into a restless sleep, crying out several times in a manner that terrified Bella, but in the morning she was rational, though weak, and her shivering seemed to have passed.

For two more days Bella almost despaired of Toby's life. Alice, recovering somewhat, helped as much as she could, but she was still very weak herself and could do little more than sit beside Toby and bathe his hands and face, offering Bella comfort and advice. Bella dared not sleep except for a few minutes snatched while Alice was awake. She was afraid to stretch out on the bunk, although Alice urged her to, for fear that once comfortably asleep she would not hear Toby. If Alice also dozed the child, thrashing about feverishly, could come to harm. Alice was gradually recovering her own strength, but she was still too weak to manage the restless child, and inclined to fall asleep in the middle of a sentence.

They would have fared badly if it had

not been for Adam Tarrant. He had sent Daniel with tempting morsels from his own table and Bella, not fully aware of where they came from, gratefully accepted the delicacies which tempted her own flagging appetite as well as those of Alice and the child.

As the third night approached Bella wondered desperately whether she could stay awake any longer. Twice she slept briefly, to awaken with a start, and the second time she realised that Toby was quiet and still. In great fear she leant over him, and then let out her breath in a sigh of relief. He was sleeping peacefully, his arms once so chubby and now pitifully thin, thrown up above his head, and a faint smile on his face. Gently she covered him, tucking the covers more firmly about him, and watched him, her own eyelids drooping.

Alice, who had been sleeping for several hours, woke and stretched, and Bella whispered to her that Toby was better.

"The Lord be praised!" Alice exclaimed. "And I'm feeling more like my own self for a good sleep. You can rest easy tonight, Miss Bella, and I'll watch over him. Here, lie down in this bunk and I'll move to sit on his."

"I shall manage," Bella said, but Alice, feeling restored to her own former energy, insisted.

"You're so tired that you would not wake however loudly he screamed," she chuckled. "I'm rested, and even if I do fall asleep again I shall be beside him, and will rouse if he moves, so you're not to be concerned."

"Very well," Bella gave in, knowing that she could not herself endure more wakefulness. "But first I must have a breath of fresh air. I have not been out of here for days. I shall sleep better for it."

Alice nodded and Bella took a cloak and wrapped it round herself, for the nights were chill, then slipped out of the cabin. Further along the deck two figures, close together, were silhouetted against the pale light thrown by one of the lanterns, but Bella ignored them and went quietly to lean against the rail of the ship some distance away.

One of the figures turned sharply and looked at her. It was Adam, and he moved away from his companion, no longer listening to her chatter. Seeking to distract himself from thoughts of Bella, of her fragrance, her beauty, and her response to him which gave promise of a passionate nature, he had sought forgetfulness in the company of another cabin passenger, a woman in her mid-twenties who had made no secret of her willingness to invite his attentions.

Now, tinglingly aware that Bella stood a few yards away from him, he exerted his considerable charm to dismiss his companion. Bella, heedless, was watching the waves as the moonlight glinted on them. A myriad stars lit the cloudless sky, and a faint breath of wind filled the sails which swung lazily far above her.

It was strangely peaceful. Even the inevitable noises of the ship, the creaking of the timbers and whispering of the ropes, were muted and soothing. Bella almost slept where she stood, and when a quiet voice spoke behind her she had to think for a moment before recalling where she was. Then she shrank away, holding out her hand to fend off Adam.

"You!" she exclaimed, and he winced at the apprehension in her voice.

"I wanted to ask how you are faring," he said quietly. "Is the baby better?"

Bella tried to clear her tired brain and think clearly. She had imagined that he despised her. What did he now want? She was afraid to offend him, dreading the effect on Toby if they were again consigned to the hold, but dimly the notion came to her that, if she could retain his friendship and her own self-respect, it would be to her advantage.

"Yes, much better, I thank you. He was so very ill, but now the fever has broken. Alice is watching him while I take some air." She shivered. "But it is colder than I thought."

"Have you eaten today?" he asked abruptly.

She wrinkled up her brow, trying to remember, and then nodded.

"Of course — you sent us a roasted capon. How did you contrive it?"

"Daniel has all manner of tricks."

"And other things. My wits are wandering. I am sorry, I should have thanked you immediately. You have been kind."

"You could do with some wine to warm you," he said. "Will you consent to take a glass with me. Oh, I promise not to molest you," he added drily, as she hesitated.

After a long cool look, Bella nodded, and as if to show that she was unafraid, laid her fingers on his arm. To her fury the same searing sensations she had previously experienced when he had touched her coursed through her blood. It was too late to turn back, however, and she did not have the energy to do other than follow him.

His cabin was softly illuminated by a lamp, turned low. On a small table there was a bottle, already half empty, and some goblets. There was but one bunk, a wide one, she noticed, and the cabin was much larger than her own. There were two chairs beside the table; she sank into one of them and took the wine Adam poured for her.

"Thank you," she murmured, lifting the goblet and sipping the wine.

"This wine comes from Burgundy," he said slowly. "We are taking wines and vintners from France with us on this ship and I plan to start a vineyard myself on my own land. Whether we will produce wines of this quality, though, is doubtful. We might in time when the planters have gained more experience."

"I've never had wine like this," Bella managed to say, and drank again.

He talked knowledgeably about the various crops they had already succeeded in establishing in the colony, and Bella sipped politely at the wine, with a hazy idea that it might help her to stay awake. She had almost emptied the goblet when her arm, too heavy to hold up, fell back onto the arm of the chair.

"Mistress Sutton," Adam began, and then exclaimed in annoyance, "I cannot think of you as that, but I have not heard your given name. What is it?"

"Bella," she answered quietly.

"Bella, the beautiful. A most fitting name."

Bella murmured something too low for him to catch, and he bent forward to listen to her. A faint blush was visible on her cheeks, and she seemed to smile at him invitingly.

He slid his arm about her shoulders, and her head, which had been bent forwards, fell towards him. It was only then that he realised that she had fallen asleep in the chair. The goblet, almost empty, was still clasped loosely in her hand. He rose and gently removed it, then stood looking down at her, a rueful, tender smile on his lips. No other woman had ever fallen asleep when he had been talking with her. He had not previously realised how exhausted she was, but now he could see the dark shadows under her eyes.

He wondered whether to wake her or carry her back to her own cabin while she slept. Tentatively he picked up her hand, but she did not move. When he slid his arms about her to lift her, she lay limply against his chest, her curls hanging down over his arm. Suddenly he made up his mind. The cold night air would probably revive her, and if she returned to her own cabin she would be concerned about the child. She needed to sleep, and had said that Alice was caring for the baby.

Gently he carried her to the bunk and laid her there. She had let her cloak fall off when she had sat down, and was wearing a loose, simple gown. As he took off her shoes she sighed but did not wake, and he swiftly unbuttoned her gown and eased it from her. She wore no stays, and her thin shift revealed a slender though shapely figure. Her breasts were high and firm, and her waist long and narrow. Rounded thighs and long slender legs made him suddenly furiously angry that this loveliness belonged to another man. Hastily he pulled the covers over her, and she sighed in her sleep and smiled.

For some time he watched her, fiercely quelling his urgent desire to take her in his arms. At length he turned out the lamp and lay down beside her, fighting temptation by lying firmly with his back towards her. Many hours later he eventually fell into a restless sleep, and it was daylight before he awoke.

Cautiously he raised himself on an elbow and looked down at the girl still sleeping beside him. The covers had slipped from her, exposing one breast tantalisingly half hidden by her shift. The swelling beauty of it made his already fast beating heart pound urgently in his chest. Slowly he stretched out a hand to cover her again, and as he did so she sighed and moved slightly so that her nipple brushed against his hand, sending shock waves through him.

Bella was still fast asleep and did not stir when he took her hand in his and slowly, lingeringly, kissed the rosy tip of each slender finger, and then the inside of the wrist. Leaning cautiously over her, he slowly bent so that his lips touched hers. She breathed deeply and rolled over towards him, again uncovering the pearly soft orb of her breast, pink-tipped and unbearably enticing.

Adam feasted his gaze on her beauty, the smooth curves of her face, her long thick lashes spread in two half circles on her delicately coloured cheeks. Her lips were curved in a smile, slightly parted to reveal small, even teeth. Her skin was soft and smooth, unblemished, and one brown curl, escaping from the riotous mass spread on the pillow, rested on her neck and nestled between her breasts.

Gently Adam slipped one arm beneath Bella's shoulders, and with his other hand traced the curve of her cheek and jaw. For a brief second her eyelids fluttered and she looked up at him and smiled, then sighed in contentment as her eyes closed again and his lips descended on hers.

Bella, confused and still drowsy, shivered in delight as he kissed her lips, and his arm about her tightened, drawing her close to him. Still only partly awake she did not resist as his lips became more demanding, kindling a new, exquisite sensation in her whole body.

Skilfully, with smooth, sensitive fingertips, Adam began to caress her face and throat and shoulders, sending shivers of delight down her spine. He was murmuring words of love in between his kisses and Bella, responding sleepily, slid her arms about his neck and lifted up her face towards his, mutely asking for his kisses.

Tenderly, gently, Adam's fingers grew more daring as he traced the curve of the exposed breast, feeling her nipple harden in instinctive response. She whispered his name, still in that uncertain state between dreams and wakefulness. He stroked her breast, cupping it in his hand and then, finding her shift obstructing his efforts to reach the other breast, began to ease it off.

He slipped it over her head and lay leaning on one elbow, gazing at her body. As she opened her eyes, finally forced awake by the cool air on her skin, he bent tenderly over her again.

"My love, my beautiful Bella," he whispered

softly, and kissed her urgently, pulling her to him.

Bella gasped and shivered, attempting to turn away her head. Adam resumed his caresses and Bella, her thoughts and emotions a jumbled turmoil, relaxed gradually under his practised skill. His touch on her lips and breasts aroused quivering sensations that gradually drove logical thoughts out of her mind, and caused her to sink into a strange sea of delight where her entire body ached for his touch, poised for she knew not what.

Adam gradually slid his hand across her belly, and she trembled violently as, with his other arm about her, he pulled her close, whispering tender words into her ear. Then, as his searching hand forced its way between her thighs, she cried out in alarm, remembering the terror and pain with Edward, and struggled to free herself from his grasp.

Startled, he released her and she rolled away from him.

"Bella, my love, there's no need to fear me," he tried to reassure her. "I'll not force you."

With a tremendous effort Bella controlled

the tears that threatened to overcome her.

"Not force me? Then how did I come to be here, naked, in bed with you?" she demanded.

"You drank wine with me, and fell asleep last night," he said brusquely. "You were exhausted."

"And so you took advantage of me! I was a fool to trust you again."

She had been looking about her for her shift, and took it from Adam as he silently handed it to her. He reached for a robe to wear himself, while Bella pulled on her shift and then her gown, which Adam had placed over a chair.

"You and Edward are both the same," she declared as, ignoring the unfastened buttons, she pulled her cloak about her and thrust her feet into her slippers. "I detest all men!"

"Do you? I would not have thought so from your response!" he returned angrily.

Bella, about to open the door, looked at him. Her eyes glittered with unshed tears of humiliation. She attempted to speak, but found that she could not. Then she laughed, a high short laugh that was the beginnings of hysteria. He should not see her inner desolation; she would walk out with her head high, though her pride had been brought so low. Squaring her shoulders as if to ease some invisible burden she turned the handle of the cabin door and slipped out.

Adam Tarrant's eyes had been narrowed with disgust and anger as he watched her. But something about that last sad gesture made his heart go out to her.

4

HOLDING her cloak firmly about her dishevelled hair, Bella retreated to the deck until she regained her composure. How could she have been so abandoned, she wondered in horror, blushing as she recalled the feel of Adam's hands on her body. I was tired, asleep, I did not know what was happening, she protested to herself, trying to bury her awareness that for a short while at least she had been awake and willingly submitting to caresses she had never before known.

Eventually she felt calm enough to face Alice, and went down to their cabin. As she had not thought of any convincing excuse for being away all night, it was perhaps fortunate that Alice was fast asleep with the child cradled in her arms. Hastily Bella changed her gown for a clean one of a soft pale blue wool and brushed out her tangled hair. When Alice awoke she was tidied and composed, and since the maid said nothing to show that she had been missed, guiltily remained silent.

During the next few days Bella kept to the cabin as much as possible. Toby was recovering slightly, but was very demanding, yet Bella could not always ignore Alice's injunctions about taking the air on deck. Alice herself, less plump than before, recovered from her own ills and soon struck up a friendship with one of the other women. Joan Bidwell's husband was an ironworker from Gloucestershire, indentured to the London Company for seven years in return for his passage, and Joan herself was expecting their first child in a few weeks. Alice, ever maternal, made it her duty to cosset Joan and gossip with her about other passengers.

Inevitably in a small ship it was impossible to avoid Adam, but Bella, prepared to be haughty when they did meet, was secretly chagrined to have Adam give her a mere polite inclination of his head and pass her by. What did she expect? she angrily asked herself afterwards. He was unlikely to apologise, even had she wished him to. She preferred to forget the whole distasteful incident, for to listen to apologies would be worse than having the man make another attempt to seduce her!

"Did you know that that nice Mr Tarrant is younger brother to Baron Cawston?" Alice remarked one evening when they were sitting together in the cabin.

"Oh?" Bella replied, and feigned a yawn. "I'm so weary! I think I will prepare for bed."

"He's such a pleasant man," Alice continued wistfully. "You'd not think he's from one of the most important families in the west country. He talks to everyone just the same, even passes the time of day with me and Joan. I must say I'm sorry to see that Bolton woman getting her claws in him though!"

Bella tried not to look interested.

"You're an incorrigible gossip, Alice," she said lightly.

"Why not? It does no harm. This Bolton creature would, though, if she had half a chance. After him as plain as anything, even though her husband is right beside her!"

"I expect half the silly females aboard are!" Bella snapped. "All they seem to think of is a handsome face and fine figure!"

"Aye, he's handsome right enough," Alice agreed, casting a quick glance at Bella's averted head.

Bella tried to forget Alice's words, but could not ignore the sight of Adam, the next day, walking along the deck beside a small, dark, pretty woman wearing a striking overgown of bright red, and a gold-embroidered petticoat. The square neck, edged with fine lace, revealed far too much of the lady's charms, Bella thought waspishly, but the men seemed to appreciate the new fashions. The woman, whom Bella knew was Mary Bolton, cast roguish looks up at Adam as she chattered and laughed. He appeared to be amused by her, Bella saw, and she went quickly in the opposite direction to lean over the rail and try to find some other topic to occupy her thoughts.

Mary, although she did not falter in her talk, was conscious of her companion's switch of attention when he saw Bella. Eyeing him covertly she noticed a slight tightening of the lips and narrowing of the eyes. He did not appear to be looking in Bella's direction, but he seemed to avoid approaching that part of the deck.

Her feminine instinct warned her of some mystery, and she determined to solve it. For the next few weeks, as the ship ploughed across the vast ocean, she watched the couple avidly but saw nothing apart from the occasional cool greeting such as was unavoidable amongst fellow travellers. She had discovered that the cabin Bella occupied had originally been paid for by Adam, and she knew that Daniel, his servant, regularly supplied Alice with delicacies from his master's table. But between Adam and Bella she could detect nothing other than a taut, cold awareness when they were together. Nonetheless Adam, infuriatingly, maintained an aloofness towards herself that none of her wiles could break down.

Adam, fully conscious that the presence of Mary's husband would prove no obstacle to a closer relationship with her, was astounded to find himself with no appetite for what he was openly offered. On several occasions he had taken her into his arms and kissed her, but before their lips met Bella's face would come between them, and all desire for Mary ebbed away. Mary herself, puzzled and frustrated, exerted all her charms to no avail, for whenever she imagined that Adam was succumbing to her at last he would suddenly break off his attentions and either begin to talk of Virginia or retreat into an abstracted silence.

Bella spent as little time as possible on deck however. Toby's health was giving her cause for great concern. The child was so weakened after his fever that she sometimes felt he might never recover. He was pale and listless, ate little, and had none of the lively energy he had possessed before the voyage began. If it were not for the fruit and wine which Adam had purchased when the ship put in to port to take on water and supplies at the Canary Islands, Bella thought Toby would have died. She herself had not possessed the means to make such purchases, Henry having left her on board with a very limited amount of money, and also forced her to leave her jewels behind. She could not but be grateful for Adam's thoughtfulness.

Besides these new stores Adam had brought chickens and goats with him, and the eggs and milk thus provided strengthened Toby as nothing else could have done. Occasionally Daniel slaughtered a hen and this provided the only fresh meat they had, alleviating the monotonous diet of tough, dried meat, meal and biscuits, which would otherwise have been unbearable.

Adam wondered ruefully at his own concern for a sickly child who meant nothing to him. Although he rarely saw Toby apart from when Alice sat on deck with him, Daniel gave him regular accounts of the child's health, and he wondered whether all their efforts were merely to prolong Toby's life for a few short weeks. So many had died in the early disastrous years of the colony, and even in the previous two years, when the number of immigrants had been higher than ever before, a majority of them had died of starvation or disease on the voyage or soon afterwards. Toby had only a small chance of survival even if he lived until the end of the voyage.

"Another two died last night," Alice reported gloomily when they had been more than ten weeks on the ship. "That makes twenty, which I'm told is a small number compared with some voyages!"

Bella shivered and looked anxiously at

her young brother.

"Is he better, do you think, Alice?" she pleaded.

"To be sure, Miss Bella. He ate the whole egg this morning, and is beginning to talk, and he enjoys watching the sailors. He'll manage, never fear," Alice replied stoutly.

"He would not have lived so long without Mr Tarrant," Bella said in a low voice.

"We owe him everything!" Alice declared, looking hopefully at her mistress, but Bella appeared to be more concerned with castigating Henry for forcing her onto the ship than thanking Adam for his help.

Conscious of her debt, but unwilling to discuss it with Alice, Bella soon made an excuse to go on deck. It was blowing up for a storm after a long period of calm, and soon the rain began. Most of the other passengers scurried to shelter but Bella, her mood in tune with the elements, found a more secure place amongst some crates and sat with her back against one of them. She lifted her face up to the rain, relishing the cold stinging droplets that the wind blew onto her cheeks, and the wildness of her hair streaming behind her, falling out of the caul that held it neatly coiled in her neck.

"You like storms?" a voice above Bella asked, and she looked up to find one of the sailors, a coil of rope in his hands, standing beside her.

"Not when they are too wild, as when we started," she answered, laughing. "Is this one going to be severe?"

"No, I don't think so, for we're not in the hurricane area yet. Then it can be much worse than it was in the Channel!"

Bella shuddered. "I hope we do not meet any hurricanes then! How much longer will it be before we reach land?"

"Virginia? A se'ennight or more, and we might touch the Bermudas, depending on the weather, then a week more to the mainland."

"You know Virginia? Have you been before?"

He nodded and sat down beside her.

"Several voyages in the last five years. There are many planters going there now."

"What is it like?"

"The James River is long and deep, with sandy beaches and many creeks. There are vast forests, but I've never gone far into them. There are too many savages living wild, attacking the planters! It's been more peaceful of late, though, since the Indian Princess married one of the planters."

"I remember when she came to London four years ago. Po — what was her name?"

"Pocohantas, they called her. Daughter of the Chief Powhatan, who died himself a year after she died."

"That was sad. She was buried at Gravesend, near my home. Do the Indians often attack the planters?"

"Sometimes. But it's been more peaceful of late, I hear. The settlements stretch for miles along the river now."

He talked on and Bella listened, fascinated. The sailor, who, along with most of the men aboard, had been aware of Bella from the first, tried to discover her situation, but when he began questioning her she answered shortly, replying that she was to join her husband.

"In Jamestown, or does he live in one of the other towns?"

"I'm not certain, he's only recently come out himself. I am getting wet now, I had better go in."

She stood up and the sailor, lithe and strong, leapt to his feet and stood in front of her.

"Must you desert me?" he asked, and tried to seize her hand. "There's a snug empty cabin I know if it's too wet out here."

Bella stepped back angrily, but her way was blocked by crates.

"Pray let me pass!" she demanded, but instead the man came closer, forcing her back against the crates as she tried to evade him.

"Have pity on a poor sailor," he said, this time succeeding in catching her hands and pulling her into his arms where she struggled to evade his clammy embrace.

She twisted her head from side to side to dodge his attempted kisses, trying to push him away from her. Then to her relief he released her and turned away, muttering something about only wishing to please her.

Biting back an angry retort Bella thankfully watched him depart then, realising that something had disturbed him turned to see what it was. To her embarrassment Adam Tarrant, eyeing her sardonically, was standing a short distance away.

"You appear to relish stormy weather, Mistress Sutton," he remarked, bowing slightly to her, and she flushed at his contemptuous tone.

"Good morning, Mr Tarrant," she said coldly. "I was just about to go back to my cabin."

"Indeed?" he replied, a question in his voice.

Did he think she had deliberately encouraged the sailor? Bella asked herself indignantly. She tilted her chin defiantly and stepped forward, but was forced to stop when she realised that he barred her way. Adam looked down at her consideringly and she fumed impotently.

"I wish to pass, Mr Tarrant, if you please!"

"I hope that my presence did not discourage your friend," he replied, not moving out of her way.

"Discourage? Friend? He was no friend! He is a vile creature, thinking he is at liberty to attack any defenceless female!" Bella said furiously.

Adam suddenly chuckled. She looked magnificent when she was angry, with her eyes flashing and her colour high.

"Mayhap his previous attempts have met with greater success?" he suggested softly. "Or did not suffer interruptions!"

"Previous — ?" Bella stared at him, only slowly realising his meaning. "I have never spoken to him before!"

"You were making rapid progress then," he retorted.

"It was no such thing! How can you imagine that I wished for his vile attentions!"

"I am in no position to judge your wishes! But a prudent woman does not run risks! I apologise for ruining your amusement. I quite thought that you were complaisant until you saw me!"

Bella gasped. "I did not see you! I had no notion that you were there until he went!"

"Then you had best not encourage opportunities for further attempts on your virtue!" he snapped. "Some storms are not so easily controlled as you appear to think! Stay in calmer waters, Mistress Sutton, and do not encourage tempests you do not understand!"

He turned abruptly and left her, and she retreated to her cabin, seething with anger at the scorn in his voice. She heeded his warning, however, and was careful not to remain alone on deck again, for fear the sailor, or another of his companions, would seek to force their company on her. She saw the one who had approached her a couple of days later and was surprised when, on espying her, he turned and almost ran in the other direction. Several others of the crew eyed her with respectful, cautious interest, and she was puzzled until she overheard one of them challenge another to speak to her.

"Or are you afraid that her gentleman friend will deal with you the same as poor Dickon? He couldn't sit down for two days! And all he did was talk with her!"

Bewildered, knowing that she ought to be grateful to Adam for his protection, yet furious with him for interfering in her concerns, Bella did not know whether to thank him or protest to him. Wanting to complain she could not, for she knew that she owed him a great deal. She resented this, for while she had no hesitation in accepting anything for Toby, she wished that she need not otherwise be under any obligation to the hateful man.

The days passed, and Toby's strength gradually improved. The weather was mild and Bella and Alice often sat on deck. One day Toby was playing with a little girl a year or so older than himself while Alice stitched at a shirt for him. Bella was mending a rent in one of her gowns and when she had finished she rose to her feet.

"I'll take this back to the cabin, Alice. Do you need anything?"

"No, Miss Bella, thank you, except to get off this ship!"

Bella laughed, but as she went towards her cabin she wondered if she really wanted to arrive in Virginia. Edward awaited her there. Try as she might to dismiss him from her thoughts, he appeared in them more and more frequently as the long voyage drew to an end. Soon she must think of a plan to evade him, she told herself, but she knew in her heart that she had already considered and discarded as impracticable all possible courses of action.

She pushed open the cabin door and went in. Shaking out the creases in the gown she hung it on a peg and then, seeing some of Toby's clothes on the floor, began to pick them up and put them away in the chest. She was busy with this when the cabin door swung open and a man stepped quickly inside.

It was the man who had attacked her on the first evening when she had met Adam, but who had ignored her ever since. Bella had thankfully assumed that he had been too drunk to remember her, and tried to forget the incident which had introduced her to Adam. He shut the door behind him and stood there, looking at her in what Bella, her heart pounding loudly, thought was a horribly gloating manner.

"What do you want?" she demanded angrily, forcing down her fear.

"Oh, not what you think, my fine lady!" he sneered. "I've no taste for you, whatever the others may want. No, I've come to pay my debt!"

"Will you get out of this cabin, or you'll be sorry!" Bella ordered, and then gasped as he brought his hand from behind his back and showed her the knife he was carrying.

"You're mad!" she exclaimed. "What do you mean to do? Kill me? Just because you were prevented from attacking me when you were drunk? You'll not escape even if you do harm me!"

"It's not simple murder I have in mind," he sneered, slowly advancing on Bella as she stood at the far end of the cabin. "That's too quick and easy!"

She wondered for a panic-stricken moment whether to scream. Would anyone hear her and come to her aid? Most of the passengers were on deck as it was a fine warm day, there were none likely to be down in the cabins. She backed away and was brought up short by the table. Feeling behind her her hands encountered a pewter mug, and she grasped at it thankfully. It was a puny weapon against a knife, but it was something.

"I'm going to spoil that beauty of yours!" the man continued, pausing to survey her. "It's a snare and a temptation, just like the drink! Oh, I've seen the error of my ways since I've been aboard, and I'm going to cut the out the Devil from your heart!"

"What do you mean? You're mad!"

"You are a temptation, leading on weak foolish men. You led me on when I wasn't in my right senses, and you've been doing it to many another! I've been watching you! They're all sinners, led astray by a vain woman! When I've finished with you you'll have nothing to be vain about!"

As he lunged forward Bella stepped aside as far as the small space allowed and swung her inadequate weapon round, catching his arm as he trust the knife at her face. He gave a shout of rage, seized her right arm in his left hand, and twisted her round to face him, forcing her backwards so that only his grip prevented her from falling onto the bunk which pressed against her thighs.

"How will you like it, my pretty one, when your face is marred? When men shudder and turn away from your ugliness? Then you won't be tempting them as you do now, will you, my fine beauty?"

Bella struggled, clawing at his face, but he was too strong for her and held her easily. He pressed the point of the knife against the bodice of her gown, then slowly drew the sharp blade down across the thin silk, slitting the taut material which covered her breasts. She drew in her breath and he laughed.

"You might still attract men who cannot see your face! All cats are the same in the dark, they say. But not with what I'm going to do to you!"

Suddenly he twisted the knife in the material. The bodice of Bella's gown fell away as he sliced through the waistband, revealing her smooth ivory skin. He licked his lips, then with infinite care stripped away the last shreds of her gown and the thin chemise beneath.

He stepped back to look at her, and as he did so, Bella seized her only chance. She dodged sideways and stooped to grasp the heap of material at her feet. She threw it at him as he lunged forwards, and the knife caught in the folds, distracting him momentarily. With a couple of strides she had reached the door, but before she could drag it open he was after her again. This time he caught one arm and twisted it behind her back, and she could feel the sharp point of the knife pressed against her skin just below the side of her breast.

He laughed triumphantly. "I'm going to carve patterns all over this wicked body," he promised. "It shall never tempt men again. Then I'll start on your face! Don't resist me, or the knife might go deeper than I intend, and I don't want you to die. I want to watch you when you can no longer drive men out of their senses!"

He threw Bella so that she sprawled face downwards on one bunk. She wriggled to turn over and try to beat him off, but he cast himself across her and pinioned her, holding her with his body and left hand while he drew the knife slowly in front of her face a finger's breadth away from her flesh.

"Now, a mark just here, so that you'll never wear these evil gowns which show so much flesh!"

He raised himself slightly so that he could press the knife against the swelling curve of Bella's breast, and as she writhed beneath him to escape it the cabin door burst open. Before Bella realised what was happening her assailant was hauled away from her and his knife clattered onto the bunk beside her.

She looked up to see Adam struggling to force the man's arms behind his back, while he cursed violently and kicked backwards in an attempt to free himself.

"Have you something for a cord to tie him?" Adam asked quickly and Bella, shaking herself out of her horrified shock, seized her torn chemise and twisted it into a rope. Then, following Adam's terse instructions, she bound it about the man's wrists until he was secured.

"I'll be back," Adam said curtly and thrust his captive out of the door before him.

Bella, weak with relief at the narrow escape she had had, and reaction to the frantic terror of the past few minutes, sank to the floor, her head resting on the bunk. From time to time she shuddered as she recalled the hateful weight of her attacker, his rough hands, and the prick of the knife against her breast. Unable to believe that she was still unmarked, she passed her hands over her body, reassuring herself that the skin was whole. She was unaware of Adam's return until he spoke.

"It's all over. You are safe now."

She looked up at him, a wavering smile touching her lips.

"He must have been mad! He — threatened to — carve patterns on me!" she finished with a sob, and then began to shiver uncontrollably.

"You are cold!" he said abruptly, and she looked up at him, uncomprehending, unaware of her nakedness until she saw his narrowed eyes. Instinctively she crossed her arms across her breasts and turned her back on him.

"You are safe now," he repeated, and took a blanket from the other bunk to wrap about her.

She felt its roughness against her skin, took a deep breath and struggled to her feet, clutching it about her awkwardly, unaware that her long slender legs were partially uncovered still.

"Th – thank you! I am most truly grateful! Where is he?" she added, glancing fearfully towards the door.

"Safely locked away until we land! The Governor will deal with him. Come here, you are still shivering!" he ordered, and unthinkingly, responding only to the comfort of his tone, she obeyed.

He pulled her down beside him on the bunk, and holding her tightly against him so that she felt the beating of his heart against hers, he stroked her hair, whispering nonsensical, soothing words. Her trembling gradually ceased and she became aware of his warmth, the soft feel of his breath against her cheek, and the power and the strength of his arms about her. She felt his lips on her closed eyelids and instinctively raised her mouth to his. Gently but firmly he took her chin between thumb and forefinger. "Look at me." Her eyes flew open, startled.

"Are you feeling better now?" he asked.

"Yes," she whispered, shivering, "but how did you know? How did you come to be there?"

"Your maid's friend, Joan Bidwell, saw the man enter your cabin. She thought it was odd and came for me. But she could not move fast, she is so near her time, or I would have been here earlier."

"Thank God!" she murmured. "They won't let him go free?"

"No, you can be sure of that. Do you know why he attacked you?"

"He was mad! He said — " she hesitated, and then went on in a rush " — that I had tempted him, and it was sinful. He did not want me to tempt other men, he said!"

Adam chuckled. "So wine and women are sinful, but attacking you with a knife is not! Shall I send Alice to you?"

Suddenly reminded that she was curled up against his broad chest wrapped only in a blanket, Bella blushed furiously.

"No, thank you! I would prefer to be alone while I — while I find some more clothes!"

"I'll leave Daniel on guard outside, so you need have no fear of unwelcome interruptions." Adam rose and left the cabin.

Still trembling from the shock, Bella looked down at her ruined gown, lying on the floor. It had been one of her favourites, and for a moment she felt a helpless anger against the madman who had so wantonly destroyed it. Turning away from it she sought in the chest that held their clothes for a new chemise, and had just pulled it over her head when Alice came quickly into the cabin.

"Miss Bella, are you all right?" she demanded. "Joan told me, and Mr Tarrant explained what the wretch had tried to do! He didn't harm you, did he?"

"No, Alice, no! Only my gown, my lovely green silk! Thank heaven Joan saw him and had the sense to fetch Adam!"

Alice, helping Bella to put on the dress she had so recently been mending, smiled to herself. It was 'Adam' now, was it?

"He's a proper man, Miss Bella!" she enthused. "I don't mind telling you that if I were only five years younger I'd be making eyes at him myself, like most of the silly girls aboard! Yet he doesn't seem to care for any of them!"

Bella tried to change the subject, but increasingly frequently Alice reverted to it in the days that followed. Adam did not seem to avoid Bella so obviously as before, and soon Alice was hinting that if she would only encourage him life would be better for all of them.

"Would you make me a whore?" Bella demanded angrily when the hints could no longer be ignored.

"He's a deal better than that one Henry forced on you," Alice responded.

"But I am wed to 'that one', and there is nought either of us can do to change that!" Bella pointed out.

"Hm! I'd not be too sure of that. We're going to a new country; who's to force you to stay with a man you hate?"

"I couldn't escape from him! What would we do? How would we live? Oh Alice, I've tried to think of a way out, but there isn't one! I should never have

100

agreed to marry him. At least we'd have had a better chance of making a living for ourselves in England."

"You'd not have had Toby then," Alice said flatly. "That devil Henry Martin would have seen to that, never fear!"

"He's much better now, isn't he, Alice?" Bella asked, seizing on the opportunity to turn Alice's thoughts away from Adam. Alice, however, was not to be deflected.

"Thanks to Mr Tarrant," she said firmly. "He'd look after you both if you gave him just a little encouragement."

"You'd have me sell my body?"

"What else has Henry Martin done? At least this way you'd enjoy it!"

Bella was about to deny this when she recollected the shameful episodes when she had permitted Adam to make love to her, and had felt her willpower dissolve as she lay in his arms and he had caressed her. Had she taken pleasure in such activities? She turned away to hide her flushed cheeks from Alice.

"I'll never willingly submit to that degradation!" she declared. "Edward, I suppose, has a right to use me for his own pleasure, but no other man shall!"

"Why remain with a man you hate when there is a much better one willing, I'd hazard, to do anything you wished?"

"Edward would never permit it!" Bella said angrily. "Even were I to agree, Edward would fight, and have the authorities on his side."

Gradually, imperceptibly, Bella's anger at the idea began to evaporate. The closer they came to Virginia and Edward the more apprehensive she grew about what awaited her there. Alice lost no opportunity of reminding Bella of her fear and hatred of Edward and his unwelcome attentions. At other times she was full of praise for Adam, repeating her gratitude for his many kindnesses and the conviction that but for him Toby, and quite possibly both of them too, would have died on the voyage. She referred occasionally to Mary Bolton, gloating at the frustration she sensed in the other woman when none of her overtures to Adam met with more than politeness.

They were over twelve weeks out of London when one morning land was glimpsed far ahead.

"They say it's Somer's Islands!" Alice cried in excitement, and along with the remainder of the land-starved passengers rushed onto the deck to watch as the tiny speck grew larger during the next few hours, and became separate specks which were gradually revealed to be many small islands.

The following day they anchored near the largest, and the passengers had their first glimpses of previous settlers who had been sent out by the London Company some years earlier. The *Virginian* took on fresh stores, including water which had been collected by the settlers in large barrels from the rain which provided for most of their needs. Apart from the sailors who were busily loading the fresh stores, no-one was permitted to land, and the passengers lined the rails looking hungrily at the lush forests that covered most of the larger islands. Bella, standing with Alice and Toby watching the sun setting behind another of the islands, suddenly found Adam behind her. He casually rested his hand on her shoulder, causing her to quiver with shock as his fingers, in a seemingly accidental gesture, rested against her bare neck.

"Do you see that? It is a canoe such as the

natives use," he remarked, and leant closer, pointing with his other hand across her other shoulder at a small, strange looking craft which had just appeared near the ship. It was long, narrow, and looked rather like a log hollowed out in the centre.

"The islands were originally called the Bermudas," he went on. "The Company discovered them by accident twelve years ago."

"By accident? How was that?" Bella asked, trying not to show her awareness of his fingers, which were casually caressing the bare hollows in her flesh between her neck and her shoulder.

"Shipwreck. The first settlers came to Jamestown in 1607. Two years later the Company sent out another six hundred settlers in nine ships. One of the ships was wrecked on Bermuda, as it was then called, and the settlers spent the winter there while they built another boat of cedarwood."

"Did they escape safely?"

"Yes, and arrived in Jamestown to discover that only sixty of the other five hundred settlers had survived the winter. There had been much disease and starvation."

"How terrible!"

"The earliest settlers were gentlemen who did not care to work! They came looking for gold, not seeing the need to develop their agriculture, and sat around eating their stores. And to make matters worse the Company sent out too many settlers too soon, before there was any provision made for them, such as food and housing."

"Is it better now?" Bella asked doubtfully.

"A great deal so, although such vast numbers of people have been sent out these last few years that there have been problems again. You are perhaps fortunate that your husband has come early. He will have a home prepared for you," he added, and his hand slid down her arm as he moved to stand beside her, his arm now encircling her waist.

"Yes, I expect so," Bella replied, averting her face. She did not wish to think of that home, or of Edward awaiting her with his animal demands on her body. She shivered suddenly, despite the warmth of the evening.

Alice had earlier slipped away, saying that she had better put Master Toby to bed, and they were alone on this part of the deck. Adam regarded her quizzically.

"I still do not know how he could have borne the parting," he said lightly. "Had you been married for long?"

"No," Bella replied briefly. It was the nearest Adam had come to referring to his lovemaking and she wondered whether he meant to attempt another seduction. "Are there many settlers now?" she asked quickly.

"A couple of thousand or so, but there have been many hundreds sent out during the past three years, and many have died, so it is difficult to judge."

"Why have so many come?"

"The opportunity to hold land which they would never have in England. By the headright system each man can hold fifty acres if he pays his passage, and fifty more for each person he brings with him or later. If the Company pays the passage land is available at the end of their term of indenture to the Company."

"That is a new system?"

"At first all the settlers were servants of the Company, and it was intended to form a commonwealth with everyone sharing and holding no property."

"I would not have thought that was popular."

"It did not prove successful," he replied wryly. "Then the King sent malefactors out to get rid of them. But the new men will be successful. They are used to hard work, and have three crafts we need out in Virginia. Your husband is going for the land?" he added abruptly.

"Yes."

"Is he a farmer?"

Bella was at a loss. She knew so little about her husband that she did not even know the answer to this question. She was unwilling to admit to Adam how little she knew, and so she answered ambiguously.

"He can farm. Why do you ask?"

"Then you are not likely to live in Jamestown. I hope that your husband has taken land further up the river, on higher ground. The town is set on marshy land and is unhealthy. The air is heavy and some of us believe the humours are bad. One day, perhaps, when we have found a way of living at peace with the Indians, we can build in a healthier spot."

"Are the Indians dangerous?"

"Untrustworthy. Their Chief, Powhatan, died three years ago and his brother, Opechancanough, although he has sworn friendship, is not so honest a man."

"What strange names. But I suppose they find ours just as odd."

For some time longer Adam talked of Virginia, telling Bella about the early struggles of the settlers. She led him on to talk of his own plantation, and from what he said guessed that it was one of the largest and best run.

Adam discovered her to be intelligent, quickly appreciating the problems of the new colony, and his desire for her, which he had never successfully subdued, became more intense. Had he misunderstood, he wondered, when she had appeared to offer herself to him in return for his help? He had been certain that she had responded passionately at first to his lovemaking that morning in the cabin. Why had she then repulsed him? Had it not been deliberate, as he had thought at the time, when his pride was hurt that she had turned the tables on him? There might have been some other reason. His heartbeat quickened at the thought.

It was strange, he thought, that he did not want her to prove too willing. He knew that if she had succumbed to him in those first few days he would by now have tired of her, as he had grown bored with so many other women. But now, for the first time in his life Adam felt the need to protect a woman.

Bella realised that it had grown dark as they talked.

"I must go," she said quietly, moving from where they had been standing, his arm about her. "Goodnight, Mr Tarrant."

He turned and took her arm to guide her past the cluttered mounds of new stores that lay about the deck, not yet properly stowed in the lower hold. She stumbled as she trod on a loose rope, and for a moment he caught her to him. She felt his lips on her brow, but as she murmured an apology he released her and led her towards her cabin. She was trembling at the brief physical contact and bade him an abrupt farewell as she opened the door and went into her cabin.

The next day she found herself dreading yet hoping to meet him; terrified that he would take advantage of last night's weakness, but dizzy with longing to feel his arms around her again. She did not know whether to be relieved or sorry when he greeted her with the merest bow and a lazy smile in his blue eyes. Alice gleefully aware of the situation, contented herself with scathing references to Edward's lack of chivalry, brutal behaviour, and probably inability to provide them with any home other than a rough shelter. And day by day watched her mistress becoming more restive as Adam walked and talked with her — impeccably courteous, but distant.

It was not until several evenings later that Bella once again found herself alone, leaning on the deck rail, listening to the quiet hiss of the water against the ship's hull, watching the moonlight turn the sea to silver. So exquisitely peaceful was the scene that she suddenly felt overcome by sadness. In comparison her life seemed unbearably ugly, the thought of her future with Edward sordid beyond endurance. Silenty, unheeded, the tears began to slide down her face.

She did not see his shadow, or hear his footfall, only felt strong hands encircle her waist, felt him pull her round — and found herself in Adam's arms as his mouth came down on her own. For one brief moment she gave herself to him completely, then she pulled back in panic, pushing frantically at his chest until he released her and stood there, looking down at her with a quizzical expression in his eyes. Unable to bear his scrutiny, she turned and fled. Later in her cabin Bella tossed sleeplessly, her emotions in a turmoil as she desperately asked herself what was happening to her, what it was she really wanted, and why, when she hated men, so many of whom had treated her evilly, she forgot that in Adam's embrace.

On the following day Alice was sitting on the deck with Joan, who was very near her time, trying to make the girl forget her apprehensions about the coming birth.

"I'd hoped to be in Virginia!" Joan said worriedly. "I did know know the voyage would take so long!"

"You'll do very well with me to help you. I've delivered quite a few babies in my time," Alice said comfortably. "I'm looking forward to when Miss Bella has her own child."

"She must be anxious to be with her husband again," Joan said, sighing. "I don't know how she could have borne to be parted from him."

"She hardly knew him before they were wed. It wasn't a good match. I'd not weep to find Edward Sutton vanished, he'll not do well by my mistress. She could have done a great deal better for herself."

"Mr Tarrant seems very taken with her," Joan commented.

"Aye. More's the pity she didn't meet him before her husband. From what she's told me he's very rich, with a lot of land in Virginia as well as being heir to a baron! His brother's not wed, Daniel tells me, and he's well past forty."

"Mr Tarrant has not paid that Bolton hussy much attention this past week. She's seething mad from what I can see!"

Alice chuckled. "Too forward! It don't pay to make a man think you're too anxious to jump into bed with him. Mistress Bella has too much sense for that! And she's no need to fear Mary Bolton's success! That one lost her chance by being too bold. Make a man sweat running after you, that's what I've always said. Then he'll appreciate what he's had to work for!"

Joan's husband then arrived and Alice said that she would go and see what Master Toby was up to in the cabin. As they walked away Adam, who had been standing a little distance away, concealed from view by a pile of water barrels, looked thoughtfully after them.

So Bella was regretting her hasty marriage to a man of moderate means, was she? Had she, as Alice's words appeared to suggest, deliberately tantalised him by her aloofness? All his doubts, which had been stilled during the past week, swept back. If Bella Sutton was playing a deep game because he was rich and heir to a title she would soon learn that she could not win.

Angry and suspicious, Adam kept to his cabin and avoided Bella for the rest of the day. During the night the weather grew stormy, and by daylight the small ship was tossing wildly on massive waves, lashed by furious winds. The Captain had taken down all but the minimum sails and was attempting to run before the storm. The hatches had been battened down, and the passengers in the hold had no alternative but to remain there, terrified and bewildered in the dark, listening to the thunderous noises above them and being thrown about mercilessly.

Towards evening the storm abated and Adam ventured out of his cabin. The ship was now being lifted up on gigantic surges and then flung into deep black valleys. The motion was more bearable, but just as dangerous since the abrupt movements could throw men overboard or against a bulkhead in a trice. Realising that his presence on deck was one more anxiety for the hardpressed Captain, Adam turned to go back to his cabin. He was just in time to see Bella, who was trying to fight her way to him against the fierce wind, thrown to the deck and roll towards the side of the ship.

The rail at that point had been smashed earlier when a spar had come crashing down onto the deck, and there was nothing to save Bella from sliding into the turbulent, deadly ocean. Desperately Adam threw himself across the intervening yards of the deck and caught Bella about the waist as she hovered, poised helplessly on the rim of the deck. Holding her with one arm clamped hard about her, he clung with the other to an end of a rope that flapped about the deck, the only thing there was to grasp. Praying that the other end was firmly attached, he edged gradually away from the dangerous gap until he could seize a more solid support and then, half carrying Bella, fought his way to safety.

"You utter imbecile!" he raged at her, shaking her in his fury as soon as he set her on her feet. "Have you no more sense than to walk out on deck in such a storm? You could have been killed! You ought to have been killed! What in the name of God were you thinking of?"

"S — stop it!" Bella pleaded, her teeth chattering together from both shock and his roughness. "I — I was going for the Captain," she gasped as he ceased shaking her, though he still kept his hands tightly gripping her shoulders.

"You were going for the Captain! As if he has not enough to contend with! What did you want! For him to stop the wind blowing? Or did you think it a good moment to complain about the conditions in your cabin!"

"You don't understand!" Bella returned,

almost weeping with frustration. "Thank you for saving my life! I do realise that! But Joan — she needs help! Her baby is coming!"

"The Captain cannot deliver a baby!" Adam said more calmly, as his first anguished fury abated.

"Of course not! And neither can I! I wanted to ask if any of the women in the hold could help me! Those stupid sailors would not open the hatch for me!"

"Where is Alice?"

"She is prostrate with sickness again. Joan's husband came for her, but she cannot stand up, and so I sent him back to Joan and said I would fetch help. There must be someone below who is not ill and who could help!"

"Go to Joan and try to keep everyone calm. Babies take a long time to come into the world. I cannot say I blame their reluctance sometimes! I will find a woman to help."

She smiled tremulously at him, tears in her eyes, and turned away towards the small cabin Joan and her husband occupied.

"Are you hurt?" he asked.

"I'm not sure if my head is very securely anchored," Bella replied, glancing back at him through lowered eyelashes, her lips curving into a delectable smile. "Otherwise I am battered and bruised and truly grateful to you for saving me! Please hurry and find someone!"

She went swiftly away, and Adam knew at that moment that even if she had been deliberately tormenting him during the past few weeks, tantalizing him so that she could use him to escape from her detested marriage, it was of no importance.

5

ADAM managed to find Peg, a woman travelling in the hold who had given birth to a dozen children, and during the rest of that night as the ship was tossed about remorselessly, and the wind howled through the rigging, Bella gave what assistance she could to Peg as she tended Joan. As a pale dawn broke, the rain ceased and the wild surge of the waves abated, although the ship was still being driven fast before the wind, Joan gave birth to a lusty, squalling son.

When Alice, loudly lamenting that she had been feeble and unable to help, went to see Joan and the baby, the proud father laughed and hoped that his son would not prove to have a tempestuous nature in tune with his birth.

Bella, exhausted by the efforts of the night, went on deck for some air. She stood and surveyed the havoc wreaked by the storm, shuddering as she recalled her own narrow escape. The rigging was tangled where a spar and part of the mast had broken away, the sailors were already climbing amongst it, splicing ropes and attempting to repair some of the damage. A rope stretched across the gap where the rail had been smashed, but formed a very precarious barrier.

The deck was littered with broken barrels and crates, and Bella found one containing several hens, some crushed by the roof of the crate which had been forced inwards, but half a dozen peering out with rather more than their normally aimless frenzy in the confined space that remained. Incredibly, in the soaking wet, filthy straw pushed into one corner, lay an egg, shiny white, smooth and whole.

Adam was near the bows, helping some of the sailors coil the ropes neatly again and secure a torn and flapping sail. As he saw Bella he spoke briefly to the man beside him and came towards her.

"I trust you were not hurt last night?"

"No, no, of course not! I wanted to thank you for saving my life!" she replied. "I can see the danger better now!"

He laughed. "Aye! But the storm has carried us much nearer to Virginia, so we have not been greatly harmed. I must beg your pardon for treating you so roughly, however!"

"I — I understand," Bella replied.

"I was angry, but afraid too at the thought that you might have been killed," he said softly.

"You have done so much for us!" Bella exclaimed.

"I hope that you will always ask me if there is any way I can help you."

Was that an invitation? Bella was uncertain and Adam did not make it any clearer. She was well aware that his fury on the night of the storm had been caused by his concern for her. Did he desire her enough to fight Edward? That he would be the victor in any conflict she had no doubt, but would he choose to enter into conflict? How would the Governor in Jamestown view such a liaison? Could Edward be persuaded to accept the situation?

For some days she hesitated, and wondered whether she could sell herself to any man, to suffer the horrors of her wedding night again and again. Yet that was what awaited her with Edward. The recollection of what she had endured on her wedding night, of his brutality and total lack of tenderness for her made her shudder with renewed revulsion. She could not bear to feel his hands on her again, his naked body crushing her, and his thrusting invasion of her own body. Surely anything was better than the repetition of that horror.

Yet what alternative was there apart from the protection of Adam or another man? At the thought she shuddered, puzzled. She could not imagine any man's physical attentions being more welcome than Edward's, and yet she remembered the frisson of desire she had felt briefly in Adam's arms. The memory of his kiss made her tremble, and as she recalled the expression in his eyes she felt the old mixture of terror and longing sweep through her.

Yet how could she tell him? What possible reason could she give? How did one tell a man that one wanted his protection, especially after having rejected his lovemaking so vehemently before, and now of all times, when he seemed to have lost interest in her? Whatever she did or said she would feel deeply embarrassed.

Eventually, realising that it was late and she had very little time left before they arrived at Jamestown, Bella nerved herself to approach Adam. Alice was asleep, so Bella slipped out of their cabin and tapped nervously at his door. She would thank him for his kindness, she planned. It was a feeble excuse, but it would have to serve.

Daniel opened the door, and casting a swift look at Adam, invited her to enter. Suppressing his surprise he saw from under lowered lids that his master was gazing inscrutably at his unexpected visitor. With some reluctance he said goodnight and vanished, quietly closing the door behind him.

"We are almost there. Will you take a glass of wine with me to celebrate a safe crossing?" Adam asked, rising to his feet with a lithe movement.

"Thank you, yes, I would like that," Bella replied nervously, moving further into the cabin and sitting in the chair Adam held for her. He poured wine and gave it to her. Bella drank, heedless of the taste, and hoped that it would give her courage for what she had come to do.

"I came to thank you for everything," she began in a low voice. "You have made the voyage so much easier than it might have been, and we all three owe our lives to you. I am truly grateful, and I wished to apologise for the times when I may have been — have appeared — an ingrate!"

"There is no need for either gratitude or apologies."

"Oh, but I am so beholden to you, and will never be able to repay all we owe! Adam, I was so foolish earlier, pray forgive me!"

He eyed her closely. Her lashes veiled her eyes and she looked down at the glass in her hand, twisting it anxiously.

"I do not desire the sort of payment you offered me earlier in the voyage," he said smoothly. "I've never yet asked a woman to submit unless she has wanted it too. If you are offering me the same coin now I do not wish for it."

"I did not know you then," Bella said softly, looking up at him where he stood leaning negligently against the porthole.

"You are married!" he said harshly. "Are you not anxious to rejoin your husband?"

Bella shrugged, and for a fleeting moment her eyes darkened with pain.

"I did not know Edward when we married," she said quietly. "It was arranged by my — half-brother, after my parents died, and I had no choice. I would certainly never have voluntarily chosen him. We spent one night together, and then I ran away from him. Henry, my brother, caught me and forced me onto this boat, as you saw. Edward has no love for me, he took me for my dowry and the land he could claim in Virginia for me and Toby."

Was it the truth? Had she fled from her husband's ill-treatment, which must have been terrifying if it had driven her to run from him. Was it that which had caused her to reject him finally that morning when she had seemed to be welcoming him?

"Are you so distrustful of men?" he asked, coming to kneel beside her and gently taking her hands in his.

Bella shivered slightly. "My brother sold me, and my husband used me against my will. It was not until I met you that I discovered men could be kind and gentle. Do you forgive me for assuming that you had helped me only for your own purpose?"

"Perhaps you had reason. But why do you choose to tell me so now, when I might so easily take advantage of you?"

Why was he making it so difficult? Bella silently asked herself. Did he expect her to say openly that she wished to become his mistress and beg him to save her from her husband.

"I do not now think that you would force me," she replied, turning her face invitingly towards him. Their lips were but a few inches apart as he knelt there, and she closed her eyes and swayed towards him. Slowly Adam slid his hands about her slender waist and pulled her closer, kissing her gently to begin with and then with greater passion. Bella was at first stiff in his arms, but under his practised guidance she gradually relaxed and her lips became soft and pliable while her hands crept involuntarily about his neck.

He kissed her mouth and then her eyes, and then buried his face in her neck, kissing her throat and moving tantalisingly slowly down towards her breasts. The gown she wore buttoned down the front and she felt his fingers warm against her bare skin as Adam very gradually and deliberately unfastened the buttons and gently caressed her, his hands creeping almost imperceptibly lower. Then he pulled aside her bodice and cupped the firm, rose tipped orbs in his hands, while Bella breathed deeply, fighting the rising tide within her that urged her to abandon herself to the same sensations that had almost overwhelmed her before when Adam had touched her in such a way.

Now he was kissing her between her breasts and her heart pounded against his lips as his thumbs teased her nipples into hardening response. When he stood up and pulled her with him she yielded eagerly into a closer embrace, seeking his mouth with her own as he held her hard against his body.

Unhurriedly Adam slipped her gown over her shoulders, and the chemise followed. She stood naked before him, lost to everything apart from the need she had for his hands, supple and firm as they caressed her body, stilling the tumult within her. When he again drew her against him and his hands travelled across her back, he did not need to exert any pressure to mould her form to his, she was clinging to him freely.

The bunk was only a step away and Adam gently picked Bella up and carried her to it. As she lay there looking up at him he smiled and unhurriedly divested himself of his own clothing. Bella's eyes took in the broad shoulders, muscular arms, and deep chest, then he smiled and turned to the lamp hanging from the hook in the ceiling, and lowered it so that it gave out the faintest flow before moving to sit on the bed beside her.

Leaning on one elbow beside her, Adam gently explored Bella's body with his hands and lips. Her thoughts were in turmoil. Adam's lovemaking was so very different from the brutal violence of Edward, and she felt as though she would drown in the sensations his touch engendered in her nerves, responses he evoked which she would not subdue and which she did not, with one part of her, want to control.

For a few panicstricken moments she asked herself how, if she became so helpless with his expert lovemaking, she could ensure that she was using him and not the other way about? He had not said one word about his intentions once they reached Jamestown, and this, she told herself frantically, was her sole purpose in encouraging him.

Unable to think calmly Bella ceased to

care when Adam's lips began to caress her breasts, drawing her nipples into his mouth and gently stroking them with his tongue. Almost without her being aware of it his hands slipped down her sides and he held her tightly to him.

Slowly, careful not to startle her by moving too quickly, Adam caressed her thighs and buttocks, and soon Bella, consumed with a desire she had never before known or imagined, was straining against him. She had ceased to think, to compare this unimagined delight with the violation of her wedding night, or to care for anything apart from the unknown climax which was building up inside her.

When Adam slid his hand between her legs she sighed and shuddered, unresisting as he gently raised himself and crushed her beneath him. As he lay above her she sought to kiss his lips, and her arms were wound about him, pulling him even closer. She moaned softly when at last, controlling his own fierce desire for consummation, he entered her slowly and with murmured endearments guided her expertly to an undreamed of culmination of passion as they clung fiercely together in a prolonged climax.

Gradually Bella recovered her lost powers of thought. She was lying cradled still in Adam's arms, and he was kissing her softly. She emitted a long shuddering sigh and smiled shyly up at him. Why had it been so different with Edward? Then it had been painful and humiliating. Her husband could never, she was certain, evoke the same abandoned response in her. Never, she vowed, would she return to Edward or grant him power over her body. And with that resolution she relaxed, sighed deeply, and suddenly fell asleep.

Adam gazed down at her, a tender smile on his lips. She had behaved quite unlike his more experienced mistresses, almost as though she were still a virgin. If she had been telling the truth and her husband had taken her roughly, it explained a great deal.

The next two days passed with Bella in a dreamlike state. By day she stood at the rail of the ship with Adam watching in fascination the shores of Chesapeake Bay drift by. They were covered in tall trees and lush meadows intersected with many creeks and streams.

"How beautiful it is!" Bella exclaimed when she first saw the forests in the full riotousness of their October colouring. All about them were the green, gold and yellow, the russet, brown, red and bronze produced by the trees in a final burst of defiance before the onset of winter.

"Changeable, like a beautiful woman," Adam said with a laugh. "Dressed in all their glory, but soon to be bare!" He pulled her to lean back against him, his arms about her, for they were on a secluded part of the deck and none could see them. When his hands slipped down past her waist and caressed her hips and then her stomach, she gasped and turned to kiss him.

At night, locked in his arms, she forgot that she had meant to claim his protection against her husband, but whenever she was parted from him the old anxieties rose in her, reminding her that he had not said what he intended to do after they landed. If he did not soon discuss plans it would be too late. Had she, after all, permitted him to use her body merely to satisfy his lust? Was it to be in vain?

There was no time to find another protector, and she shuddered even at the notion. Yet Edward was only a few miles away. In a day or so she would be delivered into his power. Bella suspected that the horror of that first night with Edward would be nothing to her sufferings now that she had experienced Adam's tenderness. And yet she resolutely refused to examine her own feelings for Adam. She went to him at night and accepted his company during the day for one purpose only, to escape her loathsome husband.

Adam, she concluded with despair as they approached Jamestown, had cleverly tricked her. He never spoke of love, had never mentioned the future. She was utterly unaware of the effort this cost him. Longing to reassure her of his love and protection, but never having felt such need for any woman, he too was puzzled. He had been independent for so many years that he hesitated to bind himself, especially to one who withheld from him her full confidence. Did she love him or was she merely using him as a way of satisfying ambition? Until he knew which he would make no commitment.

It was in this state of indecision that they sailed up the James River on the third day after sighting land. At first the river was wide and the tree-scattered shores sloped easily down to the sandy beaches. There were a few habitations, but the voyagers caught glimpses of half naked Indians, watching them from amongst the trees. They never obtained a satisfactory view of these strangers, but were aware always of eyes following their progress along the river. The Captain kept a strong watch at all times, particularly at night, but the tawny-skinned men came no closer, seeming content to view these new invaders of their tribal lands from a distance.

That morning they were about eight miles away from Jamestown, rounding a point of land which Adam told Bella was named Archer's Hope, after Gabriel Archer, secretary to Captain Bartholomew Gosnold, one of the leaders of the 1607 expedition.

"It was the first suggested site for the colony, but Captain Wingfield, who became the first President, resisted it, probably because he resented not having discovered it, and so they went on to Jamestown."

"Was it better?"

"Possibly easier to defend, for it is a long peninsula with but a narrow neck of land joining it to the mainland. Not quite an island, but almost."

Bella looked about her.

"It's beautiful," she said slowly. "It's a lovely country."

They watched together and then, without warning, the ship gave a violent lurch. Tearing noises, followed by terrified shouts and the screams of women and children came from the hold.

"Stay here!" Adam ordered, and went swiftly along the deck.

Bella found that the ship had twisted off its course and now was drifting and listing sideways. With another shuddering jolt it came to rest at a precipitous angle. Many of the less well secured crates and barrels slid protestingly across the deck.

The screams and shouts from below intensified and sailors, nimbly avoiding the shifting deck cargo, scurried towards the hatches. Others clambered amongst the rigging, hastily furling the sails, and Bella realised how dangerous the wind could be now that the ship was incapable of moving. Peering cautiously over the rails she found that she could see the river bed, and realised that they had run aground on a sandbank covered with only a few feet of water. Some of the people who had been in the hold packing their possessions in anticipation of landing later in the day at Jamestown, now climbed up onto the deck. Some of the women were sobbing, others trying to comfort screaming children.

"What is it?" Bella asked, taking one child from a woman who was helplessly attempting to calm three little ones.

"We must have hit a rock, they say," the woman answered jerkily. "It was in the lower hold, mostly, where the stores are, but the water came in onto us too. Hush, Benjy, you're safe now, love! But there were men in the hold, they say, sailors getting ready for unloading, and two of them were crushed. The crates were loose and the movement landed them on top of the men. They may drown if they can't be brought out quickly!"

For a while there seemed to be total chaos, but when all the passengers had emerged from the hold and were assembled, shivering, on the sloping deck, the injured men were carried up and their crushed limbs and torn bodies attended to. Adam was busy organising teams of men to redistribute the cargo while the ship's carpenter made frantic efforts to block the gaping hole.

"We could go no further until proper repairs were made, even if we had not grounded," Adam told Bella when he paused beside her as she was comforting some children.

"How shall we get off?" Bella asked.

"The river is tidal so the ship will be lifted off at the next high tide, but it is not likely that we can take her straight to Jamestown; at least not with all the passengers. Later I am going with a few men in the shallop to fetch help. There are many small boats, for that is the main form of transport here, and tomorrow everyone can be taken off with their baggage. It will be an uncomfortable night, for the hold is wet and useless, and everyone must sleep on deck. I must go now, I will be with you again in the morning."

He was gone, and Bella felt suddenly

bereft. It was the fear that he would not return, that her submission to him was after all to be useless, she told herself firmly, that caused her to feel so lost. But she lay sleepless that night, remembering his arms about her, his lips on hers, and the exquisite sensations he could arouse in her at will. Falling into a restless sleep towards dawn, she whispered his name in her unconsciousness, and on waking unthinkingly stretched out her arms, realising too late that there was no-one there to welcome her.

A couple of hours after daybreak a flotilla of small boats appeared from upriver, and were met with cheers by the ship's passengers. A noisy, cheerful disembarkation began as families were taken on the small boats with their baggage and set off on the last stage of their long, adventurous journey.

It was to be as eventful as the rest. There had been no time for Bella to speak with Adam who, on his return to one of the first boats, had disappeared into the Captain's cabin with a couple of other men. Delaying leaving the ship until the last, she eventually had to scramble down a ladder and into a boat manned by two young men. Alice and Toby followed, and their hastily corded boxes were lowered after them.

The boat was a hundred or more yards from the *Virginian* when Bella's straining eyes saw Adam appear on the deck. He looked towards her, but she could not be sure whether he recognised her, for he turned back and seemed to be supervising the lowering of some fragile cargo into the last boat.

"Those must be the men who were injured," one of the rowers said, and Bella saw that what she had thought was cargo was in fact the sailors, strapped safely onto boards.

They had gone a couple of miles when from the boats ahead came panic-stricken screams, and suddenly a blood-curdling howl erupted from the bank. As Bella and Alice stared in consternation, several of the boats ahead turned round and headed back towards them. On the bank of the river a small group of men were running swiftly towards the river.

They wore only short fringed aprons, but their brown skins were painted with red and black circles and lines. Their hair was black, long and tied back, but curiously shaved from the right sides of their heads. In the knots of hair most of them had fixed brightly coloured feathers. They carried short bows, and almost without pausing would aim and shoot arrows at the boats, howling fiendishly all the time.

Some of the men in the boats dropped their oars and seized guns, and soon a spasmodic fire was being directed at the Indians, most of whose arrows had fallen short or into the water. After the first rush towards the river bank they retreated into the shelter of the trees. The next few miles developed into a running skirmish between the Indians on shore and the travellers. The newcomers after a while took over the guns from the owners of the boats. With practised rowers they were able to make faster time and soon rounded the last bend of the river before Jamestown.

Adam, with the injured sailors and some of the crew of the *Virginian* had overtaken Bella's boat much earlier, but without even appearing to see her. Now she could only hope that he would be awaiting her when they landed.

The town, surrounded by a high pallisade,

stood as Adam had said, on a long peninsula projecting into the centre of the river. It was clear, however, from the two large ships tied up to the trees near the edge of the shore, that there was deep water on that side. By the quay there was a tremendous bustle as people and cargo were landed and and many of the newcomers seemed completely bewildered and lost. A few were already moving off into the town, helped by earlier settlers avidly demanding news from England.

Bella looked about her for Adam but he was nowhere to be seen. The injured men had disappeared too, presumably through the large wooden gates which guarded the fort. As they swung open she glimpsed the houses inside. They were small and squat. One story high, with wooden frames and thatched roofs, wattle and daub walls, they could have been part of an English village.

Where was Adam? Had he deliberately avoided her? Did he want to be rid of her? It was true that he had spoken no words of love, and what, after all, did she know of him and his life here in Virginia? Such a man would undoubtedly be able to take his pick of mistresses even though there were still few women in the colony. His mistress might even now be awaiting him, and even if she tired of his absence there would be others only too anxious to take her place.

Even if by some miracle he preferred her to these unknown women he might hesitate to thwart the laws of the puritanical Council by openly taking another man's wife. It could bring drastic punishment on them both, apart from what Edward himself might do. Although she acquitted Adam of any cowardice, it would be foolish to disregard the laws and customs of his fellow settlers when he needed to live at peace in a law-abiding small community. Only a fool would deliberately court severe legal reprisals.

These thoughts flashed through Bella's mind as she stood on the quayside looking about her. Then she smiled determindly at Alice and started to walk towards the gates.

"Come, we had best discover what we have to do."

Inside the gates there was a crowded collection of buildings, mostly small single storey houses with one or two rooms and a loft, small windows, and families crowding round the doors watching the new arrivals. Round most of the houses, in small and ill-defined patches of garden, grew strange tall wide-leaved plants which encroached even onto the roadway. In the centre of the town was a larger building which appeared to be a church, and before it a wide open space where many of the ship's passengers had congregated.

Bella walked slowly forward.

"Mistress Bella Sutton! What a pleasant surprise! Welcome home!"

She turned, heart thumping — and saw Edward lounging at the door of one of the houses near the church. Two other men stood with him, and they looked Bella up and down familiarly as though she were a piece of merchandise to be assessed.

"Well, my friends, what do you think of my wife?"

"She don't look overjoyed to see you!" one of them said, nudging Edward in the ribs.

"Wonder if a little bird flew out to the ship and whispered secrets?" the other said. "Never mind, mistress, I'll be only too happy to — "

"Keep your mouth shut!" Edward snarled. "Come here!" he snapped at Bella. "I've a score to settle with you, wife; but I'll do it in private! My canoe waits for us!"

Wordlessly Bella shook her head and as Edward strode towards her she involuntarily took a step backwards. He laughed shortly, seized her by the shoulders and crushed her to him before kissing her hard on the lips.

Releasing her abruptly, he turned and took Toby from Alice's arms and without a further word strode off towards the gates. Toby screamed in terror, and desperately but futilely attempted to wriggle out of his grasp. Bella cried out and ran after him, while Alice followed as fast as she could. They caught up with Edward just before the gates and Bella tugged his arm.

"Give Toby to me!" she demanded. "It's all right, Toby, don't cry!" she added urgently as she tried to wrest her brother from her husband's arms.

"Where is your baggage?" was the only reply as Edward strode on and turned along the quay.

"Where are you going?" Bella almost screamed running to keep pace with him.

"Home! Where the devil did you expect me to be going, wench?"

There was no answer. Adam was nowhere to be seen, this brute was her husband, and she could do nothing but follow him while he had Toby in his arms. Bella stumbled along miserably until Edward stopped beside a canoe, a strange looking craft which appeared to be hollowed out of a tree trunk.

"Get in," Edward ordered, and passed Toby down to an elderly man who stood beside it. "We'll leave the other stores for today, Hal, something better has turned up!"

Bella jumped into the canoe after Toby and took the frightened child into her arms.

"Have you no more wit than to terrify him so?" she demanded furiously. But Edward only laughed and held Alice back as she attempted to scramble into the canoe after her mistress.

"You can show me which your baggage is, and come with me. Take care she doesn't overset you, Hal; she's a wildcat! But might be worth the taming!"

The man had already seized the short

paddle and was driving the canoe out into the middle of the river. Edward could be seen, his hand on Alice's arm, forcing her along the quay to where the boxes had been left when they had landed from the small boat. Soon he was following, and rapidly overhauled Bella's canoe. By the time Bella arrived he had helped Alice to step onto a small wooden landing stage some way up river.

The small settlement was similar to many others they had seen lining both banks of the James River on their way from the fort. A few small cottages huddled together a little way from the river banks, and a larger barn-like building stood beside them. There were pens for a few animals, and small vegetable gardens surrounding the houses, with occasionally the beginnings of an orchard. Further away were fields of strange looking plants, and surrounding all, both protective and menacing, was the dense forest.

Edward watched sardonically as Bella clambered from the canoe. During the short journey she had resolved that, despite Adam's desertion of her, she would fight for her freedom. If Edward knew how much she held him in aversion he might permit her to return to England. He could have her dowry and the land, and might consider that and her absence a better bargain than the constant presence of a reluctant, antagonistic wife.

She stood on the landing stage, gazing back at him haughtily, not allowing the fear she felt to show in her face or demeanour.

"Well, where do we go? I assume one of these is yours," she said sharply, waving her arm towards two of the cottages from which thin columns of smoke rose into the clear bright air.

"They are all mine," he answered slowly. "Over there, the largest."

Bella looked where he indicated, and saw that one of the cottages seemed to have two rooms instead of the single square one which was all the others consisted of. It had at some time been enlarged by adding another bay to the original frame. The thatch at one end looked cleaner, and the wooden frame newer, and it suddenly occurred to her that the cottages must have been there long before Edward arrived a couple of months earlier.

"You have not built these?"

"No, some settlers who came here three years ago did that. I — er — acquired them."

"Who lives in the others?"

"My farm workers. They are out in the fields now, you'll be able to play lady of the manor when they return!" he sneered, and then laughed.

Bella shrugged. There was little point in arguing with him. She began to walk towards the largest house and Alice, who had been watching them in silence with Toby's hand in hers, started to follow.

"You'll sleep in the kitchen, wench!" Edward said to Alice. "With the brat."

"I prefer to have Toby with me," Bella intervened quickly.

"What you want has nought to do with anything! Alice will take care of the brat at night, and by day you'll both work in the fields!"

For a moment Bella stared at him, aghast. This was an indignity to add to the horror of sleeping in his bed.

"The fields? I'm no farm labourer! Nor is Alice!"

"You'll soon learn. Everyone here works for their bread!"

"Even Toby, I suppose!" Bella said furiously. "Who is going to care for him while we are so occupied? You? Do you soil *your* hands in the fields? They do not look as though you do!"

For a moment she thought that he would hit her and as he moved forward she jumped back.

"Doxy!" he spat. "I'll tame you yet!"

Bella smiled grimly. He would soon discover his mistake. She was not the ignorant girl he had violated before, and this time he would neither force nor browbeat her easily.

"I repeat, who cares for my brother? He brought you fifty acres too!"

"Mistress Mason, the wife of one of my men. She cooks for us: she's too old for field work."

Bella shrugged and walked past him into the cottage. It was a bare, dreary room, with no soft hangings to brighten the starkness of rough-hewn wooden furniture and mud-plastered walls. The single window was small, and after the bright sunlight the interior was dark, but Bella could distinguish a wide, deep chimney almost filling one wall, and a small door opposite which led to the other room. A polished chest stood against one wall, and on it were some pewter mugs and wooden platters. A few iron cooking pots were slung over a small fire which was making the room unbearably hot, and in front of it was a long table, two benches and some three-legged stools. On one of them sat an elderly woman who looked at them curiously from small eyes almost buried in a deeply lined face. She went back to stirring the contents of a pot hanging over the flames when she saw Edward following them in.

The door to the other room was open and through it Bella glimpsed a high curtain bed, and a steep ladder apparently leading to a loft above.

She turned as Edward followed her in.

"We'd best talk now," she said calmly.

"What of? What is there to say? Put your things and the child's in there and help Maggie prepare the supper today. Tomorrow you can start work in the fields with the others."

"No."

"You'll do as I say! I'll not have idle hands!"

"You can have my money and land for

the three of us. Will that not content you? The three of us will merely be a burden to you. I suggest that you assist us to return to England and we need have no more to do with one another!"

Edward laughed scornfully. "Not so fast, my pretty one! You don't realise that women are valuable out here! There are too few of you! You can work and more than pay your way. With the new tobacco crops we need everyone. There is no time for fine ladies to loll in their parlours. Besides, we need to establish ourselves and breed new Virginians!"

Bella suppressed a shudder, hoping that in the gloom he could not see her recoil.

"You cannot force me!" she exclaimed, but he advanced on her threateningly.

"Cease this bellyaching! You're here, I own you, and you'll obey me! If you don't it will be the worse for you. There's plenty of men in Jamestown without a woman who'd be glad to sample you. I'll hire you out to them. As for that brat, he'll soon be able to do simple tasks and grow up useful."

"You are vile!"

"I'm a man and I will be heeded! Now help prepare the supper!"

There was no purpose in arguing with him, for he was implacable and there was nothing she could do against his brute strength. While Alice tried to comfort Toby, who was plainly terrified of Edward's loud voice, Bella turned towards the woman who had begun listlessly preparing some trout to bake in the ashes of the fire. An appetising smell rose from the cauldron above it.

"What can I do?" Bella asked quietly.

Mistress Mason eyed her apathetically. "Get the platters, it's almost time for the men to come in."

"Do we feed all of them? How many?"

"Six of them, as well as ourselves."

Bella fetched the platters and some roughly carved wooden spoons and put them on the table. She found a half eaten loaf of bread with an old dagger lying beside it in a small cupboard set into the wall beside the chimney. While Toby sat, confused and timid on Alice's knee, Bella hacked off manchets of bread and put them on the table.

Mistress Mason, after her first responses to Bella's questions, had relapsed into silence, busy with the contents of the cauldron and turning the fish. Bella sat on one of the stools at the end of the table and rested her chin on her hands, staring unseeingly into the small fire as she pondered on her strange position and tried desperately to think of a way of escape.

The image of Adam was never far away from her thoughts, however firmly she tried to banish it. He had deserted her, and had never intended doing anything else, she reflected. Like other men, he had lusted after her body, and like a fool she had permitted him to enjoy it, trusting that his desire would be great enough to make him want to keep her with him. Now she was back in the power of her husband after submitting uselessly to Adam, and she raged inwardly, feeding her fury as she recalled the sensuous delights her treacherous body had indulged in.

She had no intention of remaining a mere field hand in the place that should have been her home, and which had probably been bought with her money. But for the moment she had to submit. Soon, she vowed, she would find a way of escaping from her detested husband and returning to England. Her reverie was interrupted by the sound of footsteps outside the cottage, and several men, talking loudly, entered the kitchen. The first one stopped suddenly as he saw Bella, who had risen to her feet.

"Ma'am!" he muttered, touching his forelock and looking enquiringly at Mistress Mason.

She ignored him, stooped to retrieve the trout from the fire, and brought them to the manchets of bread. Without further ado the men sat down at the table. Edward, who had followed them in, picked up the bread and munched greedily at it, glancing from time to time along the table at Bella.

Bella tried to ignore him. A lad younger than herself was seated beside her and she tried to converse with him, but he was either shy or embarrassed at her presence and mumbled incomprehensibly in reply to her questions. Since none of the other men were talking she soon abandoned her efforts and ate in silence.

When they had finished the fish Mistress Mason made to rise, but Edward ordered her back onto the bench.

"Sit down, my obedient little wife can play hostess. Bella, get the cauldron, serve out the stew and do it quickly!"

Bella's head flung up at his tone, but she suppressed her anger and rose to her feet. The cauldron was heavy and she had difficulty in lifting it from the hook, but none of the men volunteered to help her. She was trembling, both with the effort of carrying it to the table and fury at their lack of manners, by the time she thumped it down onto the table. Some of the liquid slopped out of it.

"Clumsy idiot!" Edward exclaimed. "You'll have to learn that we cannot afford to waste food here!"

"Then you'd best see to it yourself!" Bella flung at him and stepped away from the table.

"Serve it out!" Edward shouted at her as she glared defiantly at him.

"Do it yourself since I cannot do it to please you!"

He rose and took a step towards her. Willing herself not to flinch, Bella stood her ground, but she gasped and involuntary tears came into her eyes as his hand shot out and caught at her hair. He twisted his fingers into it and pulled viciously until she was forced to lean towards him.

"Serve it!" he snarled, pushing her head down almost into the cauldron.

The rest of the men sat as motionless as blocks of wood, and Bella reached blindly for the ladle. Edward relaxed his grip slightly, but it was still excruciatingly painful for Bella as she ladled the appetising smelling stew of venison and herbs onto the platters which were held out to her in silence. When she had filled every platter apart from her own Edward suddenly thrust her away from him.

"Get out of here. You will soon learn not to defy me!"

Bella almost ran into the bedroom. She was shaking with mingled pain and anger, and redoubled her resolution to repay Edward for his humiliating treatment of her. Yet she knew that it would be difficult, if not impossible, to escape from her loathsome husband without help. From what she had seen tonight none of the men Edward employed would lift a finger to aid her.

She was attempting to calculate the distance they had travelled in the canoe from Jamestown, and wondering if she could steal one of the strange craft, when

Edward entered the bedroom. Bella was still fully dressed, sitting on the bed. She stood up as he came in and stared at him with a mixture of fear and defiance in her eyes.

"So you waited to give me the pleasure of disrobing you, did you?" he sneered, beginning to unbutton his shirt.

"I'll not submit to you, Edward Sutton!" she cried.

"What of it? I'll have you in the end, and you'll just get hurt. Take off your gown!"

She stood still, her eyes, narrowed, watching him as he shrugged off his shirt and then sat down on the bed to pull off his boots. He ignored her until he had untied his breeches and they had fallen to the floor, then he stood up and came towards her.

Roughly he tore off her gown, breaking the laces that tied it, and although she fought him with all her strength, she was no match for him. By the time he had ripped away her chemise, thrown it on the floor, and was holding her naked to his own body, he was panting and the scar on his face stood out lividly.

The struggle had stimulated his desire, and Bella writhed as she felt his hardness thrusting between her thighs. Her flesh seemed to crawl with distaste, but he was holding both hands behind her, in one of his large fists, and with the other hand was holding her buttocks.

Gradually, despite her struggles, he forced her towards the bed, and threw her down onto it, casting himself on top of her, driving the breath from her body.

He employed none of the gentler tactics that Adam had used so successfully to awaken her own desire. She cringed from him in loathing, but was too firmly held down to escape. As he thrust into her she bit her lip to avoid crying out from the disgust she felt. For what seemed hours he remained inside her, grunting and heaving until his pent up passion was slowly dissipated. When she tried to wriggle from beneath him as the first fierce onslaught grew less, he slapped her hard across the face, and growled at her to be still.

Once he had sated himself she thought that she would be rid of him, and gave a sob of relief as he raised himself from her. But he had not done. Forcing her to submit partly by holding her arms imprisoned, and partly by repeated slaps across the face whenever she moved, he began to stroke her breasts and kiss her, pulling her hair so that she could not avert her face from his wet lips. She shuddered with horror, but he thought that she was responding to his caresses, and gave a low triumphant laugh.

"You'll soon appreciate what a man can do," he said, and let his lips travel across her breasts before cruelly sinking his teeth into the tender flesh. Totally unprepared for the pain, Bella cried out. He chuckled with satisfaction, and bit her again in her breasts and neck, until his desire returned, and he clambered above her once more and sawed away rhythmically until he achieved a second release.

This time he rolled away from her and fell asleep almost at once, while Bella strove to suppress the tears of both pain and degradation that shook her whole body.

It was even worse than she had remembered. Then there had been the pain of losing her virginity to a violent and careless man. Now she had the memory of Adam as a constant comparison. Even though he had never said that he loved her, he had never hurt her, or implied that he scorned her for submitting to him. By contrast Edward's contempt was unmistakable. She certainly did not wish him to love her, but shame and debasement overwhelmed even resentment, and the tears remained wet on her cheeks until long after she had fallen asleep.

6

WHEN Bella awoke the following day, bruised and aching, she found Edward standing beside the bed. Instinctively she clutched the blankets about her nakedness, but it proved unnecessary.

"Get up," he ordered brusquely. "You're not a fine lady to spend the morning in bed. There's work to be done."

To Bella's relief, he turned and left the bedroom. She dressed slowly, then went into the kitchen where she found Toby cowering on the pallet in one corner which he had shared last night with Alice. Alice herself was nowhere to be seen.

"Feed the brat, and get some bread for yourself, then you'll come with me," Edward said coming to the door which led to the kitchen.

"I stay to care for Toby. He cannot be left alone!"

"You'll do as you're told. I need you in

the fields. Mistress Mason will look after him."

Turning away from him Bella coaxed the bewildered child to eat the stale crusts of bread which was all that was available for him, and then ate another slowly.

"Hurry, can't you?" Edward, who had been outside the house, ordered impatiently. "Leave him."

Edward strode towards them and grasped Toby by the arm, causing the little boy to scream in pain.

"Do as I say or he'll suffer!"

Whitefaced, Bella rose and clasped Toby to her, trying to comfort him.

"You devil, to fight your battles with a baby!"

"You can prevent it by being sensible. I'll not tell you again!"

Fortunately Mistress Mason came into the kitchen at that moment. Bella went across to her, trying to disengage Toby's arms from about her neck.

"Softly, love, I'll come back at dinnertime! Mistress Mason, you'll be good to him, please?" she begged.

With the first smile Bella had seen, the old woman stretched out her arms and took Toby gently away. Hearing Edward's impatient shout from just outside the doorway, she hastily kissed Toby, bade him be good, and ran from the room, shutting her ears to his terrified sobs as he called to her not to leave him.

Edward was waiting by the door and he pushed Bella roughly in front of him. She almost stumbled on the broken step outside, and had to narrow her eyes against the brightness outside.

"This way." Edward led the way between two of the other cottages, past the large building that resembled a barn, and along a well-beaten path which rose gradually as it wound away from the river towards the dense forest.

On both sides there were strange plants, almost as tall as Bella, each with a few broad, large leaves. Some of them had clusters of small pink flowers at the top, but most had been cut to remove the flowers. In the distance Bella could see a group of men working amongst the plants; some way to the west was another small collection of buildings and behind it a further group of workers.

"What are they?" Bella asked. She had

decided that if she were ever to escape, she must behave compliantly in order to lull Edward's suspicions.

Now he looked at her sardonically. "Are you ready to be sensible?"

Bella shrugged. "There is little I can do against your strength. Though you seem to hate me so much that I cannot think why you want us here. Would it not suit you better if I took Alice and Toby back to London, and you could find a woman who is more willing to share your bed, and live here in peace?"

"Women are few, and costly," he replied. "And why should I pay for one when I've got you? Besides, there's some spice in taming you. Don't you realise that it would cost me six pounds apiece to send you back? I can get twice that much profit each year from both you and Alice now, and soon from Toby as well. I'd soon sell Alice, there'd be plenty of men desperate enough for a woman to take her, if she weren't more profitable here. If I had to pay to bring out more indentured servants I'd be operating at a loss. Half of them die on the voyage anyway, so their passage money is wasted, and they soon get their freedom. You and

Toby cannot leave me!"

Somehow I will, Bella thought, but she dared not let him see her face, and contrived to shrug and speak normally.

"What are the plants?" Bella repeated, seeing the uselessness of bargaining with him.

"Tobacco. It's what everyone here grows, apart from a field of Indian corn and a few vegetables. They even grow it on the streets of Jamestown. Did you not see it?"

"Yes. What do we have to do to it?"

"It's almost ready for cutting. Until then we have to weed between the rows and search inside the leaves for worms. I see Alice has already been shown what to do. You must by very careful not to bruise the leaves."

They had reached Alice and the men who were working steadily along the rows of the tobacco plants. Apart from a few quick glances at Bella no-one stopped working. Indeed, Bella had the impression that one or two of the men began to work faster as soon as they saw Edward. A man who had been standing behind the others, not working as they were, suddenly turned

163

round and Bella saw with alarm that he held a musket.

He nodded to Edward then glanced at Bella. "Will you stay today, master?"

"Yes, Tom. But we need meat."

"I set traps yesterday. I'll go and see what they've snared."

He turned and strode off in the direction of the woods and Edward beckoned to Bella.

"Work here," he ordered, taking her to the opposite end of the line from that where Alice was busy weeding. "See, this is how you turn the leaves back. When you find a worm, take it out and kill it like this. Show me."

Bella had to comply. The strange leaves were often up to half a yard long and grew close to the parent stem, sometimes even curving round it at the base. She gently drew each one back and opened it out for inspection. The leaves were slightly hairy, and after she had been working for some time she noticed that her hands were becoming sticky from some substance on them. It was not particularly arduous work, but it was tedious and tiring, especially as there was a cold wind that blew the plants about irritatingly. After an hour of inspecting the leaves and disposing of the nasty little worms she was thankful to change to the task of pulling up the many weeds which flourished underfoot.

During the whole of that long, exhausting day, Bella had no opportunity of speaking to Alice. Edward made certain that they were kept well apart. When it was time to finish he sent the man Tom, who had returned earlier in the day with several rabbits hanging from a pole across his shoulder, ahead with Alice and the other men, while he and Bella brought up the rear of the weary little procession.

They had two more days of this, and Bella was growing heartily tired of the worms, the sticky leaves, and the smell of the plants. By night she had to endure Edward's demands, but by a tremendous effort of will she managed to remain calm, only permitting herself to tremble with revulsion after he was safely asleep.

On the following day Edward announced that they would cut the plants that morning.

"It looks as though it will remain fine for some time," he explained. "We have to leave the plants to wilt in the fields, then hang them in the barn."

The men chopped down the plants and Edward instructed Bella and Alice to move behind them, spreading out the plants so as to take advantage of the sun and wind. Tom, who had harvested tobacco for several years, seemed to be in charge, and Edward deferred to his suggestions. The weather remained kind, and after a few days the leaves were hanging to dry in the big barn.

The work did not cease then, however. While two of the men went off into the forests with Tom to prepare the beds where the new seedlings would be sown in January, the rest of them, Bella and Alice amongst them, dug over the ground and prepared the fields for the transplanting which would be done in May the following year. After the roots had been cleared, the soil was piled into regular small hills.

"If it's well prepared, a good planter can set out a thousand plants a day," Mr Mason told Bella as he worked alongside her at the backbreaking task.

"Have you been here long?" she asked curiously.

The men Edward employed still treated

Bella with a great deal of reserve. Occasionally one of them, as now, would pass some remark which was not strictly essential. But if she reciprocated by showing curiosity they would move away from the as quickly as possible. Glancing anxiously at Edward as they did so.

Mr Mason showed signs of behaving differently. "A while," he answered, and then moved away.

Bella sighed. She would never be able to persuade one of them to help her escape. Well, she and Alice would have to do the best they could for themselves. Bella had considered all possible plans, but none seemed remotely practical. They were guarded too closely both day and night. If she tried to run away while they were in the fields, Tom or Edward, who always carried guns, would have shot her or easily been able to catch her. Besides, it would have meant leaving Toby behind, which was unthinkable.

She wondered whether she and Alice could slip out of the house one night, after Edward was asleep, but he always bolted the door of their room, and when she had experimented one night, ready with the excuse that she was thirsty and wanted a drink from the kitchen, he had wakened at the first movement of the bedcurtains.

She tried to persuade Alice to leave so that she could bring back help, but Alice would not hear of it.

"He'd kill you," she said flatly. "He'd take it out on you, Miss Bella, and I'd not rest easy if I brought more suffering on you. We'll go together or not at all!"

"I don't care if he does kill me!" Bella had cried in despair. "That would be better than this life! Take Toby and go. Take him to Mr Tarrant. Beg him to send you back to England. You think he would help, so go to him! You and Toby could creep out one night and take one of the canoes."

"No, I'll not leave you to take the blame, and blame you he would." Alice declared. "Don't worry, Miss Bella, there must be some opportunity soon."

"It will be too late," Bella whispered, unwilling to admit even to Alice her terror that she would conceive a child by her hated husband. Never, she felt, could she endure to carry part of him within her for ever. She would destroy herself for she would not bring to life another monster, a replica of the beast she was was forced to pleasure each night.

Already Edward was beginning to complain that she had not conceived.

"Are you barren?" he jeered when Bella had been at the cottage for a little more than a month.

'I hope so!' she said, but to herself, for she had learned not to provoke him if she wished to be spared his blows and taunts.

"You don't co-operate," he snarled, and that night, instead of going about it swiftly, he took pains to kiss and fondle Bella more gently than he had ever done.

This was even more unendurable to her than his normal ruthlessness. She had schooled herself to lie unresisting while he had his way, forcing herself to think of anything rather than the heavy, hated body so close to hers. But now as he laid his hands gently on her breasts, fondling them until she felt her nipples harden in instinctive response, she had the greatest difficulty not screaming out a terrified denial of her body's betrayal.

Edward laughed in satisfaction.

"So you're not as cold as you appear!" he said, and moved one hand to explore the secret cleft between her thighs.

She tensed in horror and, gritting her teeth, managed to remain silent. Regaining control over her body she fiercely willed herself not to respond, and Edward sensed her withdrawal. He redoubled his efforts to stimulate her, but in vain. Eventually, able to control his own desire no longer, he took her quickly and roughly.

"You're a cold fish!" he complained in fury as he finished and turned away from her. "But I've not finished with you yet. You'll be crawling to me for my favours before I'm done with you."

The only consolation Bella had was that Toby, with the easy adaptability of the very young, had accepted Mistress Mason. She seemed to have developed a great affection for the child, permitting him to play in the kitchen when she worked, and run about outside the house when the weather was warm enough.

There were very few opportunities to talk with Alice, for normally Edward kept them separated in the fields, and was present in the cottage, but whenever they had the chance of a few whispered words they tried to make plans for escaping.

"Where can we go?" Bella would ask. "We've no money to pay for our passages back to England, and we could not obtain help in Jamestown. The authorities would support Edward."

"We can only find help with Mr Tarrant," Alice would say firmly. "His land is not far away, I've learned, on the other side of the river. It's called Fairmile, and is very large."

"He would not want me. He let me go, and it was all for nought."

"Then what?"

"I don't know, but there must be some way out of this horror."

Towards the end of November there was a knock on the door one evening after supper. Bella looked up from where she sat on a stool beside the fire, mending one of Toby's shirts. It was strange to be disturbed so late at night. By day occasionally Indian traders called with meat and furs, but once the men had been fed and they and Mistress Mason had departed to their own cottages, there were never any interruptions. Edward went to the door, unbolted it, and admitted two strange men who greeted him effusively.

"Well, you rascal, it's been a long time since you came to play cards with us!" one of them said.

"I've been busy, as you can see," Edward replied, laughing, and invited them in.

They stepped inside and halted in surprise as they saw Bella sitting beside the fire.

"Busy?" one of the newcomers said, casting her a lecherous look. "You lucky dog! Where did you find such a prize? I'd be busy too, if I had the way with women that you appear to have. But it's selfish of you to keep her to yourself. I'll play you for her."

"She's my wife, Harry, not for sale — not until I tire of her," Edward replied, a note of warning in his tone. "Alice take the brat up into the loft for tonight. There's a spare pallet there. And you go to bed too, Bella," he added.

Bella, only too glad to escape from her lewd comments of the strangers, tossed back her head proudly and walked into the bedroom. Alice and Toby clambered up the steep ladder after her and, with the aid of some spare sheets Bella found for them, contrived a makeshift bed. When they were settled Bella undressed and crept into her own bed. It was a long time before she slept. She heard raucous laughter, the occasional oath, and thumps as her husband and his guests banged their tankards on the table.

Eventually she slept, but uneasily, and was awakened again later as the light from a candle fell across her face, and heavy breathing warned her that someone was nearby.

Bella opened her eyes cautiously as the light moved away. Through a gap in the curtains at the far side of the bed she saw Edward, swaying slightly, holding a flickering candle. He placed it on top of a chest, and knelt down, and from the sounds Bella realised that he was pulling a small but heavy chest from beneath the bed. With a grunt he rose again, and fumbled with the carving on the post at the top of the bed. Through half-closed eyes Bella saw a small section of it prized away, and from the slight cavity behind Edward removed a key.

He unlocked the chest and Bella heard the chink of coins, then the lid was shut again, the chest locked and pushed back under the bed and the key replaced in its hiding place. Edward removed his clothes, clambered naked into bed, and reached out for Bella.

As he fumbled with her breasts, Bella wriggled, and stirred as though just awakened, then rolled away from him. To her relief he was too fuddled with the ale he had drunk to persist, and soon began to snore. Bella lay in the darkness, trying to suppress her elation. Now she knew where he kept his gold. Gold which had probably formed part of her own dowry! And, what was more important, it was easily accessible. All she needed was the opportunity to open the chest, steal some of it, and they could pay for their passage back to England.

Careful not to disturb Edward, who had fallen into a heavy sleep and was snoring stertorously, Bella lay still, wondering why she did not feel happier at the prospect of leaving the hated Edward and this land which had given her so harsh a welcome. Resolutely she thrust away from her the images of Adam which floated before her eyes, and tried to sleep.

The visitors had departed when Bella rose the next morning. Edward, suffering from his overindulgence in ale, was morose and foul-tempered. Bella had no chance to tell Alice about the gold until the following day when, as they were preparing the bare fields for the next crop of tobacco to be sown there, she contrived to work beside her for a while.

"I'll steal some gold, and when we can escape we'll have money to pay for our passage," she said gleefully.

"But how can we know when there is a ship?" Alice protested. "Sometimes it is weeks before one arrives. We'll need someone to hide us until one comes. We'll have to go to Mr Tarrant."

"No!" Bella replied vehemently. "He doesn't want me. We'll contrive somehow."

"Mistress Mason says he'll have to go to Jamestown soon for stores," Alice said thoughtfully. "Normally he spends a couple of nights there, gambling with his cronies, so that will be our best opportunity for taking the gold and escaping."

Concealing her excitement as best she could, Bella waited anxiously for Edward to depart for Jamestown. It was the beginning of December before he announced one morning that he was leaving that day.

Bella tried not to show her dismay when he added that Tom would sleep in the kitchen until he returned. At least they could obtain the gold, she was thinking, and have it ready for an attempt at escape, even if they could not leave that night.

Alice, however, was prepared. "Don't fret, Tom won't wake. I found some basil amongst the weeds some time ago, and that will make him sleep. I'll put it in his drink tonight."

She contrived to slip some of her herb into the ale which Tom had helped himself to in the master's absence. Soon after Bella and Alice retired they heard him snoring heavily.

Bella pulled out the chest and scooped out handfuls of the gold, wrapping the coins in small pieces of flannel and sharing them between herself and Alice. She was puzzled that the chest appeared to contain a good deal more than her brother had given Edward for her dowry, but then she recalled the gambling on the night when Edward had unwittingly revealed to her the key's hiding place.

Bella woke Toby and dressed him swiftly, and then wrapped him in a blanket, for the nights were cold. She crept across the kitchen in her bare feet, carrying her brother. The bolt on the door squeaked slightly as Alice drew it, but Tom remained oblivious. After a few moments Bella let out a sigh of relief and Alice pulled open the door and slipped through.

Bella had walked a few yards before the hardness of the ground reminded her that she was still carrying her slippers. She bent to put them on, and so did not see Edward approaching her along the path from the river.

"So I've caught you, have I?" he demanded, and Bella straightened up just as he grasped her arm. She choked back a cry as his fingers bit deep into her flesh. "You'll not trick me as easily as that, wife!"

Suddenly he released her and unbuckled his heavy leather belt. Before she could run away from him he had swung it round, but she was just able to turn her back and shield Toby from the wicked strap. Again and again Edward swung it. Bella was almost unconscious from the effort of holding Toby as safely as she could, and from taking the blows which fell upon her back in agonisingly swift succession.

Alice tried to cling to his arm, but he thrust her away and she fell heavily. Before she could come again to Bella's assistance Edward had stopped, breathing heavily. Toby's screams had brought three of the men running from their cottages to discover what was going on, but on seeing Edward they retreated indoors again.

Roughly Edward jerked Bella to her feet from where she had sunk to the ground and pushed her towards the cottage. Alice scrambled to her feet and followed slowly with the wailing Toby. Bella could feel the hot sticky blood oozing from several cuts on her back, and her dress was in tatters.

"You devil, Edward Sutton! I'll kill you for that!" Alice turned on him furiously, but was flung aside again and fell against the table. Toby slipped to the floor beside her, still howling, more now with fright than pain.

"Silence! If you want to avoid the same treatment you'll not speak to me. Get water and clean her up!"

Alice rose, swept the little boy into her arms, and deposited him in a corner beside the still snoring Tom, whispering to him to stay quietly there, or his sister would be hurt again. Then she took a pot of water which hung over the embers of the fire and brought it to the table. Gently she bathed Bella's lacerated back, easing the torn fabric away from the broken flesh as carefully as she could, while Edward sat and watched, gloating as Bella's nakedness was revealed.

"I'm not the fool you took me for," he said slowly. "Did you really imagine I would leave you for the night to escape? You're not the only ones who will be punished for this night's work. What did you bribe Tom with?"

Alice tightened her lips and ignored him. Bella bit back the angry words she would have thrown at him, and stoically endured Alice's ministrations. When the wounds had been washed Alice rubbed in some soothing fat, for there were no other unguents available, and assisted Bella to bed.

Bella slept in snatches that night, unable to lie on her back. By the morning she ached so much that she thought she would not have cared if Edward had killed her. He realised that she was unfit either to escape or work in the fields that day and left her alone. By evening she was feeling better, although her back still hurt excruciatingly, and she was able to drink the soup Alice brought to her when she returned from the fields.

As soon as Bella could walk again Edward attempted to force her back to the fields, saying callously that she could just as well sit at the work there as idle her time away in bed.

"Tomorrow morning you'll come with me," he threatened as he prepared to leave the house.

"I doubt I could walk so far," Bella confessed reluctantly. The cuts across her shoulders and back had begun to heal, but any sudden movement was liable to make her catch her breath in agony.

"I'll not take such whining excuses. Another day in bed will put you right."

Bella wearily complied, wondering if her brutal husband had broken her spirit with his violence. She felt so wretched that she scarcely cared whether she lived or died.

That night Edward raped Bella again. He had left her alone since whipping her, but when he came to bed that night he threw himself upon her, ignoring her gasps of pain as he pressed her still lacerated back down into the rough linen of the sheets.

"You're hurting me!" she cried out, but when he still entered her violently she bit back the pleas she had been about to utter, knowing that he would delight in her abasement.

She could not suppress the scream of agony that rose in her throat however, when his thrusting scraped her back, raw and tender, across the sheets. The excruciating pain, and the mortification of having at last been forced to admit her weakness to him, broke down her defences, and for the first time in her dealings with him she wept, permitting a flood of tears to well up, and sobbing helplessly from the stinging pain in her back as well as from the shame of having permitted him to defeat her spirt.

In the morning, after she had slept an hour or so, exhausted, Bella woke to discover that her wounds had bled again, and the sheet was sticking to her back. Alice had to come and soak away the material, and bathe the reopened cuts.

When she left the cottage, she looked grimmer than ever before, and refused to speak to Edward for the next week, while Bella slowly recovered again.

She was taking a few painful steps outside the cottage one afternoon when she saw Alice, carried by one of the men, and followed by Edward, approaching.

"Alice! What is wrong?" she asked fearfully.

Alice opened her eyes and grimaced with pain.

"I made a mess of it, my dear," she replied faintly. "I tried to run for it, but the devil shot me!"

"What? Shot you? Edward? Why, you're no better than a murderer!" she flared, forgetting her own pain and turning on Edward furiously. "You keep us here against our will, and shoot us and whip us when we would escape. One day you'll pay for this, Edward Sutton! Alice, are you badly hurt?"

"My leg, just my leg," Alice replied, and when she had been carried into the cottage and laid on the pallet beside the fire Bella swiftly examined her and saw that it was a clean flesh wound only, though it bled profusely. She bathed it, bound it up, and Alice, accepting a soothing tisane Mistress Mason provided, soon went to sleep, not waking until the men had returned and eaten their supper.

On the following day Bella and Alice were able to converse properly for the first time since they had set foot in Virginia.

"We'll get away soon, don't fear!" Alice said bracingly. "I was lying awake thinking for a long time last night. I'll pretend my wound is worse than it is, festering, so that I can stay with you. Together we should be able to outwit that foolish Tom he's left in charge. He's a bully but has not much wit. Mr Tarrant's plantation is across the river, not very far away, and if we can get a canoe we can go to him for help."

"He won't want me," Bella responded quickly. "I'll warrant he has forgotten me by now."

"We've no gold now," Alice reminded her, for Edward had discovered it when he had whipped Bella, and now kept the key of the chest with him at all times.

"We'll contrive," Bella said, but could not think how.

They watched for an opportunity of

escaping, but none came. Tom kept far too close an eye on Bella for her to secure his gun as she had planned. After Alice had been in the cottage for a week, and Christmas had passed without any celebrations, the deception was becoming more difficult to maintain. Bella was growing pale and thin with anxiety and frustration.

"Have you any more basil? Can we not drug him?" she asked at last.

"You know we can't, we've tried it," Alice returned. "He tasted it before, and he'd whip you again if he suspected we were trying to escape again."

Driven to desperate measures, Bella secured a dagger from the kitchen which one of the men left behind one day, and hit it under her pillow. She knew that whatever Edward had done to her she could not use the dagger on him in cold blood, but she could use it to defend herself when next he forced himself on her, and if they could not escape afterwards she would welcome either her own death or a charge of murder.

"Go to bed and wait for me," he ordered early one evening.

She went into the bedroom, but did not

begin to disrobe. Instead she secured the dagger and held it behind her back in readiness.

"Please leave me alone," she said as calmly as possible when Edward followed her into the room.

"You're my wife," he replied harshly, "and I'll take what I want of you."

He was between her and the candle, which he had placed on a low chest, and his shadow was a greatly enlarged one, enveloping Bella as he approached her.

She tried to evade him, but he clutched at her skirts and the thin fabric split as she pulled away from him. Stumbling, he fell to his knees. By chance his hands caught her ankle and he dragged Bella down to the floor. As she fell the dagger slipped from her hold, and she heard a faint thud as it hit the floor beside her.

Without it she was helpless, and for a moment a blind panic overwhelmed her. Then, wriggling away from Edward as he tried to throw himself full length across her, she felt frantically to try and retrieve the dagger.

Edward was fumbling with her clothes, but her hand fell on the welcome cold steel of the dagger. Swiftly she grasped it, and as Edward raised himself to his knees and tried to seize her hands she swung her arm and thrust with the dagger, feeling the sharp point sink into solid flesh. Edward cried out and rolled away from her, cursing loudly.

"You bitch! What have you done? Damn you, help me! You're my wife!" he gasped.

"Not for much longer, I trust," Bella replied furiously and, easily evading Edward's clumsy efforts to catch her, ran for the kitchen.

"Alice come!" she panted, and struggled with the bolts on the door. Alice, who had been listening appalled to the struggle, seized her cloak and picked up Toby, and together they ran from the cottage as fast as Alice's limp permitted along the path to the river.

Edward was not far behind them. They could hear shouting and cursing as he stumbled after them, and it was only the fact that he fell over a root along the path that enabled them to reach the river before him.

Both canoes were moored at the landing stage. Alice scrambled into one of them and, depositing a wailing Toby unceremoniously in the bottom of the craft, began to use the paddle to edge it away from the mooring, while Bella untied both canoes and dragged the second one after them. She managed to fling herself beside Alice just as Edward reached the small landing stage.

He tried to leap after them, but misjudged the distance, and fell with a tremendous splash into the icy water, catching at the side of the canoe as he did so and almost upsetting it. Bella beat desperately at his hands, but he clung on for some time until the numbing cold of the water, and the weakness from his wound loosened his grip. At last he slipped down into the water, struggled to his feet and scrambled for the bank as the canoes drifted into the centre of the river.

"Thank God!" Alice said fervently, and Bella nodded speechlessly.

It was a cold dark night without a moon, only a few stars gave grey ghostly illumination to the river banks and the occasional darker shadows of habitations lining them. Bare gaunt trees stretched their branches to the sky, their still skeletal shapes oddly menacing. Bella shivered from nervousness as much as from cold and reaction to their narrow escape.

Alice paddled steadily while Bella nursed the terrified Toby. She refused Bella's offer to help, reminding her that the wounds on her back were still not healed. When they reached the middle of the river Bella let go the other canoe and watched as it floated away from them before coming to rest against an overhanging tree on the far bank of the river.

"It will take him a while to find another canoe," Alice said comfortingly.

"We've a good start," Bella agreed. "We'll be able to get to Jamestown, or hide somewhere in the forest for the day if there is any sign of pursuit," Bella said.

"Jamestown? Mr Tarrant's house at Fairmile is nearer."

"I'll not go to him!" Bella protested.

"We've no choice," Alice declared. "I know where to find his house. Mr Mason has described his plantation to me several times. He has heard a great deal about him. Mr Tarrant is quite famous along the James River."

"No!" Bella reiterated vehemently. "We'll go to Jamestown, and demand protection from the Governor. Surely they will help us there?"

"More likely to charge us with wounding him," Alice pointed out firmly. "Think, Miss Bella, you're his wife, and you've stabbed him and run away. They might charge you with murder if he dies. And I'm his servant and I've aided you. We'd have no sympathy from men who don't know how he's treated us, and precious little, I'll be bound, even if they did know. Mr Tarrant's our only hope."

Bella knew deep inside her that it was true, although for some time she tried to argue against it, hoping that she would think of some way out of their plight without having to involve Adam. It was no use, however. In the end, reluctantly, she had to agree, and sat silently watching the silvery river slip by as she drew near once more to the man who had awakened her senses to delights that only he knew how to evoke in her.

7

WHEN Adam had supervised the transfer of the wounded men from the *Virginian*, he hastened into the streets of Jamestown to look for Bella. There had been no time to make arrangements with her after the grounding of the ship, no opportunity for her to ask him for protection. He did not know whether she wanted it. He had to see her again.

"Adam!" a voice called as he passed the church in the central market place. He turned impatiently, to see Mary Bolton walking towards him.

"Well?" he demanded before she had reached him.

"Are you looking for Mistress Sutton?" Mary asked silkily.

"Have you seen her? Where is she?" Adam did not attempt to disguise his anxiety.

"Oh, she went off with a tall, dark man some time ago. I heard that he was her husband. Very handsome, too," Mary added softly.

"She went? Where? Did you see?"

"Yes, I was waiting at the gate and they went in a canoe, upriver. The little boy and the maid were there too, and another man I took to be a servant. The man who told me who he was said that he had quite a large plantation a few miles away."

Adam frowned, then with a brusque nod turned to walk away.

"Adam," Mary persisted, "my husband would like to talk to you. He needs advice about the best land to acquire, and since you know the country, I thought you would be willing to help us."

"The sites down the river are the most suitable," Adam replied quickly. "Forgive me now, I have much to do."

"Oh, but surely you do not intend to leave us like this, when we were so — friendly aboard ship? How can I contact you to let you know where we shall be? I hope, indeed we both hope, naturally, that you will come and visit us when we have a house."

"Anyone will tell you how to send a message to me," he said discouragingly, and made his escape.

On the wharf he found Daniel, and his servant confirmed that Bella had gone, apparently willingly, with a man he also had taken pains to discover was Edward Sutton.

"Was she willing? Did he force her?"

Daniel shrugged. "She didn't struggle, if that's what you mean. She went of her own accord, I'd say. Are you ready to leave for home?"

"Yes. Have you made arrangements for all our baggage to be moved?"

"I've sent on the small boxes, but I'd best stay here and see to the transfer of what was in the hold of the ship. They won't start that until tomorrow. Sam is here, waiting for you."

"Thanks, Daniel. I'll see you when all is organised then."

He walked away to where a young man, smiling in welcome, stood beside a canoe.

"Welcome home, sir! It's good to see you again."

"And good to be home, Sam! How is Fairmile? Is all well?"

"It will be an even better crop of tobacco this year. The corn is doing well too, and we have some fine apples."

He chatted eagerly on the doings of Adam's plantation as he paddled up the river, and Adam firmly dismissed thoughts of Bella from his mind as he tried to listen and make appreciative comments. Sam, who had been a lad on the first voyage with him, had worked enthusiastically and loyally for him ever since and proved to be a remarkably efficient plantation overseer.

During the next few weeks, however, Adam found it impossible to forget Bella, to cease thinking of her beauty and her timid, though eventually fervent responses to his lovemaking. At all kinds of unexpected moments he would suddenly feel a pang of dismay as he recalled her sweetness, and his expression was grim as he thought of that other man, one she had told him she feared, enjoying her favours. Had she been telling the truth? And if she had, why had she departed willingly with him? If it had been only Mary's word he would not have believed her, but Daniel had also seen Bella going apparently compliantly with her husband. Had she intended to do so all along, he wondered? Or, and the thought nagged him worryingly, had she thought that he had deserted her, because his stubborn pride had made him delay too long to ask her to remain permanently with him.

To assuage his restlessness Adam spent more time than usual in Jamestown, discreetly trying to discover what he could of Edward Sutton. He also made many excuses to take his boat past Edward's plantation, but he never caught a glimpse of Bella. Once he thought he saw Toby playing outside one of the cottages, but when an elderly woman came to the door and called the child to her Adam concluded that he had been mistaken.

"Edward Sutton? Came out early in the year." One of his informants told him on one occasion, early in December.

"He's a good sized piece of land for a newcomer," Adam commented. "Did he buy it? The houses are not new, but I can't recall who owned them before."

"Richard Newman."

"Newman? Wasn't he the man who tried to attack the Governor last year?"

"Aye. His wife and all six children died of the sweating sickness, and he blamed the Company for settling in what he said was an unhealthy spot. Crazed with grief, he was."

"I remember now. What happened to him?"

"He promised to behave, but he scarcely went near the house; spent most of his time here, drinking and dicing. Trying to forget. Then he met Sutton."

"Oh?" Adam said quietly, sensing that he was about to hear something of interest.

"I make no accusations, mind. Sutton is a quick-tempered man and would not hesitate to harm me if he knew what I thought. Many others think it too, but we keep quiet."

"I'll respect any confidence," Adam reassured the man, an elderly sailor who had left the sea some years before. "I've no cause to love Sutton myself."

"Well, rumour says that Newman was drunk, too far gone to know what he was about, and Sutton persuaded him into a game. No-one knows what took place, although we suspect, but Sutton came out of it owning Newman's plantation. Newman stayed drunk for a week, while Sutton went off upriver and started to make his weight felt amongst Newman's servants. Then one day Newman disappeared and no-one has heard of him since. He could have thrown himself in the river but his body would probably have been washed ashore, and it has never been found. Or he could have gone to live with the savages. He wouldn't have been the first to take up with them."

"Does Sutton often come to Jamestown?"

"He used to, at first. But now he's got a woman up there. They say she's his wife, a real beauty, came out after him. No wonder he's less interested in what we have to offer!" the old man chuckled.

"Does she ever come?"

"I've not seen her. Sutton has a fellow who comes in for him, a brute like himself, and he was in a week ago buying stores. Said his master's woman was ailing, breeding no doubt, and sickly. It's often the way with the first, and when a gal has too little to do. I'll warrant Sutton cossets her if she's as taking as those that saw her maintain."

Adam nodded his thanks and turned away. Bella with child to that man! The very idea made him hot with fury against

Edward for his enjoyment of her body, against Bella for permitting it, and against himself for caring. Then it occurred to him that Bella could well be carrying his child, and he stopped so abruptly that a man who had been walking behind him cannoned into him. Oblivious, Adam did not respond to the man's apologies, and only after a couple of minutes when his thoughts had returned to some sort of order did he resume his progress towards the canoe which was to take him back home.

Whose child did Bella carry? If it was his how could he leave his son to be brought up by a man like Edward Sutton? And Bella herself was ill and possibly in fear of her husband. Could he bear to think of her as Sutton's wife, mother of a child Sutton would claim as his own? Could he continue to live in Virginia where he was bound, some day, to meet her again?

Adam had never before cared when his mistresses had gone to other men. Usually he had already tired of them and was glad to have them gone, for women had a tiresome habit of clinging to him long after he was bored with them. Neither had he ever cared whether their children were his, so why, he wondered, should he feel so strongly about a girl whose favours he had enjoyed for just a few short nights? Was it the brevity of their association, and that he had not had time to tire of her? Was it because she had resisted him for longer than any other woman he had laid determined siege to?

Despite the violence of his feelings for her when aboard ship, he had expected soon to forget her when she had left him, particularly as her departure was apparently voluntary. Indeed he had hoped to forget her with that part of him which refused to accept his dependence on her, but it had been impossible. Every day he missed her, and the pain of his loss did not diminish as time passed. His workpeople noticed his abstraction, and all but Daniel concluded that either the death of his mother or nostalgia for England was causing his unusually sombre mood.

At last he admitted that he loved Bella totally differently from the way in which he had cared for anyone else. He could not forget her. For some time he hovered on the verge of visiting her and demanding to know the truth about her feelings, then he cursed himself for his inability to forget her, telling himself that he would look an utter fool if he tried to discover whether another man's wife was pregnant by him or her husband. Bella had gone willingly to Edward and had never said she loved Adam, or asked for his protection. Perhaps after all she had offered her body out of misplaced sense of gratitude for all his help during the voyage.

Weary with indecision, Adam welcomed the arrival from England of the friends who had been unable to travel with him on the *Virginian* but who had decided to follow on a later ship. Perhaps in their company, talking of mutual friends and the news from England, he could forget Bella. Thomas Wray was a couple of years older than Adam, a widower whose two young daughters had been left with their grandparents in England. He was a younger son and had few prospects in England, but was determined to make his fortune in the new colony.

"It was a great pity that I could not come with you," he said on the first evening after supper when they sat about the table drinking wine.

"But then you'd not have met Mistress Perry," John Porlock, the other new arrival, a gay young man with dark twinkling eyes and an infectious laugh, reminded him.

Thomas laughed. "True! She almost captured me! To think that I might have married her from sheer boredom if the voyage had taken a week longer."

"I didn't think the lady was particular enough to insist on marriage before granting you her favours," John remarked.

"I find that very few are if I persist," Thomas rejoined, "but that was what the delectable Mistress Perry was after. She only submitted to my attentions because she thought she could find a legal protector before we reached Jamestown. What are the ladies like here, Adam? Have you not been snared yet?"

Adam tried to enter into Thomas's mood.

"There are very few women at all," he said. "If you are anxious to wed you would perhaps be wise to visit this charmer before she finds a better prospect."

"I think I'll look at the savages first," Thomas said flippantly. "If John Rolfe could win an Indian princess I might try to do the same. Did you ever see his wife? They called her Rebecca. Quite a lovely creature. What was her outlandish native name?"

"Pocohantas. But I'm not certain that the new Chief will be as friendly as Powhatan, her father. Still, they have certain generous laws of hospitality."

"I thought they usually fought us?"

"Honoured visitors who are given hospitality in their lodges are also offered companions for the night," Adam explained, laughing. "You had best set out on a journey. But be careful not to come away with more than you bargained for. The Indians are riddled with the pox."

"I'll take heed of your warning." Thomas grinned. "Perhaps I'll be content with such as Mistress Perry."

The next few days were filled with the tasks of showing Thomas and John the land round about, and introducing them to the more important settlers in Jamestown. Several plantations, the owners of which had died, were for sale, and were inspected. Adam met the vivacious and pretty Jane Perry, and a quieter, younger girl, Rachael Marsh, who had also been on the boat with her parents and who was obviously very interested in John.

Feeling it incumbent on him to play the host, Adam arranged a party for his friends, and a dozen people gathered at his house for supper some few weeks after they had arrived to celebrate Twelfth Night. Adam was outwardly calm and affable, but inwardly he was tense, and admitted that it was because Mary Bolton was there with her husband, reminding him unbearably of Bella and their time together on the ship.

He had not invited her. Thomas had made her acquaintance one day in Jamestown and mischievously, perceiving that there was some secret from hints Mary had dropped, took advantage of Adam's casual suggestion that he invited any friends he cared to ask to the party.

Because of the distance from Jamestown the guests were to stay the night either in Adam's house, which boasted six rooms, a very large number for the colony, or in the cottages of his plantation workers. It was late, but the revellers had not retired. Parties were all too rare in Jamestown. The table had been pushed aside in the largest room and an energetic dance was taking place, one of the field hands scraping energetically at a fiddle. Adam, having avoided Mary all evening, was standing at the side watching his guests when he heard a knock at the door. He looked up, frowning. It was far too late for an ordinary caller. It might be one of his workers with news of some trouble. He strode across to the door and flung it open just as the fiddler came to a halt and the dancers, laughing, threw themselves down onto the benches and stools at the sides of the room and energetically fanned their hot faces.

Alice was barefoot and clutched an inadequate cloak about herself and the little boy. Adam's bemused gaze absorbed the fact that Toby was dressed only in a thin nightshirt, and Alice seemed to have no more than a linen chemise on beneath her cloak. Bella, whose hair was tangled, had on a thin blue dress which was torn to reveal the swell of her breasts, and gaped wide from an enormous rent at her waist, so that even though she struggled to hold it tightly against her, an enticing glimpse of her bare thighs was visible.

Then Adam noticed a rapidly darkening

bruise on her cheek and he frowned. Bella, who had been pushed forward by Alice as the door was opened, thought he was angry at seeing her and tried to step back.

"What the devil?" he ejaculated, taking a step towards her with the objective of sweeping her into his arms and telling her that she need not look so frightened. An exclamation from one of the women behind him brought him to a halt.

Bella was aware only of him. She was shivering from the bitter cold, from the reaction of the fight with Edward and their narrow escape, but also with some other emotion as she searched Adam's well-remembered face, fearful that he would resent this demand for his help and reject her.

"I — I am sorry, I didn't mean to disturb you," Bella whispered, as he came closer and bent towards her to hear what she said.

A buzz of conjecture from the assembled guests made Bella tear her eyes away from Adam and glance behind him. When she saw that a dozen or so people were regarding her with avid curiosity she flushed painfully.

"I didn't know you had guests. I'll go," she said confusedly and turned away.

Adam reached out and caught her hand, restraining her.

"Why are you in such a dreadful state?" he asked gently.

"It's that brute Sutton, he did it!" Alice declared, pushing Bella forward.

"Your husband? He beat you?"

Speechlessly Bella nodded.

"But come in. What am I thinking of, keeping you out here? It's cold. Come, we'll go into the other parlour. Thomas, I beg you'll excuse me, my friends clearly need help. This way," he added softly, and with his arm about her shoulder, drew her into the room in order to lead her across towards another door in a side wall.

Trying to ignore the eager looks of the other people, Bella went with him, then turned suddenly as she heard the well-remembered voice of Mary Bolton.

"Why, Mistress Sutton! How delightful to see you again. But has there been an accident? There is blood on your gown."

For the first time Bella looked down at her skirts. A great stain streaked it to one side, and she realised that the blood must be Edward's. She shuddered and Adam, shaking his head silently at Mary, drew her on through a door to a smaller, more comfortable looking room with some velvet hangings of a soft green, and a pair of well made, European-style chairs.

"Sit down," Adam said, guiding her to one of them. "Are you hurt?"

"I must not, the blood will ruin the cushions," Bella replied. "I am unhurt, it must be Edward's blood. I did not realise, it happened so quickly!"

"Would you prefer to go to bed now and explain in the morning?" he asked gently.

Bella blinked back her tears. "I'm sorry, I didn't want to come, but we had no money and I could think of nothing else. Alice said you would be sure to help."

"Of course," he began, and turned as the door opened.

It was Mary, carrying two goblets of wine.

"I thought that Mistress Sutton might be in need of this," she said softly, smiling up at Adam. "Is there anything I can do to help?"

"The little boy, he is exhausted," Alice

interposed. "Is there somewhere I can put him to sleep?"

"In my room. Come I'll show you. I'll double with Thomas tonight. I will return in a moment," he said swiftly to Bella.

Adam handed Bella one of the goblets. But Alice shook her head when he offered the other to her and so he led her through a small door up a narrow flight of stairs to the room above, leaving Bella standing in front of the small fire, staring into the flames and almost oblivious of Mary standing watching her.

Bella's emotions were in turmoil. She was full of relief at accomplishing their journey, and at the sudden freedom from the terror of Edward's pursuit. She trembled with unacknowledged delight at seeing Adam again, and the thrill of his arm about her, slight though the physical contact had been. This joy, however, warred with a curious sort of anger at Mary's presence. She was behaving as a hostess would. Had she succeeded in her designs on Adam after all, Bella wondered. Her familiarity suggested that she had.

Bella, exhausted both emotionally and physically, was not aware that Mary was asking her questions. She did not see Mary's look of fury when she failed to reply. A fury which increased when Adam came back into the room carrying a wrap over his arm, and Bella looked up and gave him a tremulous smile.

"Mistress Bolton, will you be so good as to tell the others that I will soon rejoin them?" he asked, and held the door for her so that she had little alternative but to leave them.

"Take off that gown and put this on," Adam ordered. Bella hesitated and looked at him anxiously. Carefully he disentangled the laces of her bodice, which had become knotted, and as his fingers brushed against her breasts she felt a tremor of the old excitement grip her. But his fingers stilled and he drew in his breath sharply as her gown slipped from her shoulders and he saw the still vivid weals across her back where Edward had whipped her. A couple of them had started to bleed slightly again from her exertions.

"My God! Did that devil do this to you?" he demanded furiously. "I'll see that brute is punished!"

"I — I may have done so already," Bella

said slowly. "I — we fought, and I had a dagger. I stabbed him, that is where the blood is from, I expect, but Alice and I did not wait to see. We have been trying to escape ever since we arrived, but this was the first opportunity we had. He pursued us to the river, but we just managed to get away on the canoe."

"Has he misused you? I heard that you were sick."

"I was ill for a few days after this," Bella replied, letting her skirts fall to the ground and turning so that Adam could fold the wrap about her. "That is all. What did you hear?"

"I heard that you were — with child."

Bella had at last sat down, but at his words she looked up at him, startled. Slowly a blush stained her cheeks, throwing into even greater prominence the bruise on her face. She shook her head.

"I — no. Whoever told you that must have been mistaken."

"Why did you come to me?" Adam asked, kneeling before her and taking both her hands in his.

"I stole some sovereigns, enough to pay for the passage back to England," she said.

"That was earlier, when he caught us trying to escape he whipped me. This time we had no gold, and Alice felt sure that you would help us. It was all we could do. I hope it does not make problems for you. She said the Governor would not help us, for they would not believe, or would not care what he had done, because I am still his wife."

"She is right," he agreed, disappointed that she saw him only as a last resort. "Come, you had best go to bed now and tell me all about it in the morning."

He took her upstairs to where Alice waited, and bade them both a swift goodnight. Sinking into the luxuriously soft bed beside Alice, Bella wondered briefly where Adam would be spending the night, and whether he would find a welcome in Mary's arms, before she drifted into an exhausted sleep.

By the time Bella awoke late the following day most of the guests had left. Only Thomas and John remained and they had discreetly taken themselves off for a day's hunting. A plump, jolly woman who announced that she was the housekeeper Meg, had appeared with an armful of gowns, saying that the master had obtained them from a neighbour who had three daughters, and she hoped that something would fit. Then she whisked Toby off to the kitchen for breakfast. Alice selected a cherry-coloured gown with a black bodice and delicate lace collar for Bella and then, attired in a grey one herself, they went down to the kitchen.

Adam was sitting at the big table, making entries in a ledger, but he closed it and smiled as they came in.

"Did you sleep well?"

"Why, it's the first soft bed we've slept in since we arrived. It was like heaven," Alice declared.

The food was simple, but delicious after what they had been permitted by Edward. Fresh new bread, honey, eggs, goat's milk and cheese, and some crisp apples encouraged their appetites. Meg would have urged them to eat all day if they had been willing. But soon, when she could persuade them to eat no more, she took Alice to where Toby was playing with some other children and left Bella alone with her master.

"Do you feel like talking now?" he asked gently.

Bella shuddered. "It was worse than anything I have ever imagined," she replied softly. "He made Alice and me both work in the tobacco fields where we were always guarded, and could not escape. I tried to, one night when I thought he was in Jamestown, but he caught and beat me. Then he shot Alice when she tried to run away. It was not until last night, when I stabbed him, that we had any opportunity of escaping."

"You stabbed him? Why?"

"I could endure no more. I hated him! I did not want him ever to touch me again!" Bella cried. "I told you, I was forced to wed him, and he always treated me abominably."

"Then why did you go with him when we reached Jamestown? Daniel saw you," Adam said accusingly, "and said that you went willingly."

"He had Toby," Bella explained bitterly. "What else was I to do?"

Adam admitted to himself that it sounded plausible. And yet she now admitted that she had come to him only because she had not the means of returning to England. Was this because she resented his previous lack of decision, or was it because she had quarrelled with her husband, and was using him only as an instrument of revenge? Adam did not know but suddenly decided that he did not really care. She was there, and he had missed her more than he had ever thought he could miss a woman.

"You must stay here," he said abruptly. "I'll see to it that your husband does not molest you. You and Alice and the child will be safe here. I can protect you."

For a moment he thought he read an expression of joy in Bella's eyes, but she swiftly veiled them and murmured her gratitude.

"What if he tries to make trouble with the authorities?" she asked anxiously. "Or if I killed him? He fell in the river; it was icy cold, and he was wounded. He must have bled a great deal."

"We will wait until he tries to make trouble," Adam replied grimly. "The Governor is not able to force everyone to his will, especially plantation owners such as myself, whatever behaviour he may enforce in Jamestown with the help of his kill-joy ministers. I propose to visit him today and inform him that you have sought refuge with me. Short of bringing a troop of men he can do little about it, and in any case I am too valuable to offend, for I have many influential friends both here and in London. As for Sutton, I'll send a man to discover how badly hurt he was. Don't worry, I'll not permit a charge of murder to be brought against you if he's dead."

When Adam returned late that afternoon just before dusk, Bella forgot everything apart from her relief at seeing him again, and flew down the path to the landing stage, just preventing herself at the last moment from casting herself into his arms. Conscious of the curious stares of the other men with him she stopped awkwardly a yard or so away and looked speechlessly at him. He took her arm and walked her slowly towards the house.

"The Governor will not interfere," he said reassuringly. "As for Sutton, he was not badly hurt. You wounded him in the leg, and he is apparently confined to bed. He will soon discover that you have my protection now, and you will be safe. He is a bully but I think that, like most bullies, he is afraid of a stronger man. However,

I advise you not to stray out of sight of the house, and to take one of the men with you whenever you wish to go further. Apart from that, let us forget him."

He would say no more, and Bella was content to trust him, certain that now she was safe.

Alice had, with Meg's assistance, moved herself and Toby into another room so that Bella found herself alone in Adam's room when she went upstairs. At supper she had been introduced to Thomas and John, but they had clearly been told something of her story, for they carefully avoided all reference to it or her sudden arrival the night before. Bella had wished them goodnight and left the three men talking, but she had barely time to realise that Alice and Toby were gone before Adam entered the room behind her.

"It has seemed a long time," he said gently, holding out his arms. Bella, with a gasp that was almost a sob, ran to him and was enfolded in them.

"Bella, my beautiful Bella!" he whispered, holding her gently. "Are you rested now?"

She nodded, and heaved a sigh, and he bent to kiss her lips. Then as he pressed her to him she winced with pain.

"What is it?" he asked, instantly aware of her.

"My back," she answered. "Some of the cuts still hurt me. I'm sorry, you couldn't know."

"Fool that I am! I should have realised, but I forgot in the delight of having you close to me again. Come, let me take off your clothes."

Gently he unlaced her bodice, and Bella felt again a frisson of delight run through her. Yet she flinched when he took her breasts in his hands and bent to kiss them gently.

Adam gave no sign that he had noticed the involuntary movement, but continued to rid Bella of her confining clothes. When she stood naked before him he tenderly traced the marks that Edward's whipping had left on her back.

"This is what that vicious brute did to you?" he asked, controlling his fury with great difficulty.

"Yes, but they are almost healed now. Alice says that they will leave scarcely a mark."

"I'll see to it that he suffers tenfold

for every hurt he gave you!" Adam said tersely.

"They don't hurt much except when they are touched roughly," Bella exclaimed, and shuddered at the memory of the pain she had suffered when Edward, uncaring, had forced himself upon her. "I can't — it doesn't — oh please, I can't!" she ended incoherently, and buried her face in Adam's shoulder.

He soothed her calmly, gently caressing her breasts and hips and thighs as she clung to him, avoiding the wounds on her back.

"I won't hurt you, my lovely one. Trust me," he urged, and slipped off the robe which was all he wore.

He drew her towards the bed but she resisted.

"No, Adam, please! I know you won't mean to hurt me, but it will, I can't do it!"

"Is it just your back?" he asked suddenly, and Bella nodded, her eyes frightened with the anticipation of renewed pain.

"He — forced himself on me — before they healed — the first time!" she gasped.

"I won't do aught to distress you," he

promised, as he sat on the bed and pulled her gently to stand between his thighs.

He took her face between his hands and pulled her closer towards him. Her arms slid over his shoulders as he kissed her lips, and then the hollows of her throat. Letting his hands slide down to her breasts he nuzzled them, rousing in her a remembered passion she had not known with Edward. Then his hands slid lower, his fingers moving lingeringly along her flanks, and when he lay back slowly she did not immediately realise that he had pulled her to lie on top of him.

He fondled and kissed her with growing urgency as she lay above him, his blue eyes smiling tenderly into hers. Gradually she discovered that there was no pain from her back and she forgot past horrors, abandoning herself to the exquisite delights only Adam could evoke in her.

Only once, when he penetrated her, did a flickering memory of Edward's insensitivity cause her to draw back, but soon Adam had coaxed away all such recollections, and as he led her on to a pulsating consummation she felt as though she was drowning in the ecstasy of it.

When their passion was spent, Adam gently cradled her in his arms.

"You'll stay with me, not run away to England?"

"Is it safe? Do we not break the law? Can Edward harm us?"

"He'll not dare try. Do you want to return to Clifford Manor?"

"I have no home there any more, and nothing to go to in England," Bella said slowly. Her thoughts were in turmoil again. Once the abandonment of love was over she wondered anew at her abject subjection to this man and the cravings of her flesh. She admitted her pleasure in their lovemaking, but afterwards despised herself, wondering why she yielded so readily to him and yet hated Edward's caresses.

He had not once said any words of love. He paid her compliments, and frankly admired her body, and as frankly demonstrated his desire to possess it. But he said nothing about any other need, and Bella firmly told herself that he was interested in her only as a companion and plaything in his bed, but had a far more subtle manner of achieving his aims than her husband.

However, she had spoken the truth

when she said there was nothing for her in England. Even if she could persuade Adam to send her back, what could she do once she arrived? Would it not be better to enjoy Adam's need of her while she could? No matter how she despised her own weakness afterwards, she knew in her heart that she would never be able to resist the exquisite joy of their lovemaking.

So she smiled at him and said that she was content.

8

WINTER in Virginia was milder than in England. Bella went with Adam all over his plantation, marvelling at all he had achieved in his few years in the colony. He proudly showed her his newly planted vineyard, and already flourishing orchard.

"We grow corn and vegetables as well as tobacco," he explained, "and I have brought animals from England."

"I haven't seen any other cattle," she said.

"Not many people can afford to ship them from England. There are more hogs and goats."

One day Adam took her with Thomas and John, who had readily accepted her equivocal position in the household, to visit his saw mill further up river.

"I'm also experimenting with the extraction of walnut oil," he told them as they toured the busy site where several men were employed.

"Is it worth it?" Thomas once asked. "The other things bring in far less than tobacco. Why, it fetches over five shillings a pound in England!"

"At the moment. We are producing so much here that the price must eventually drop, and then we shall not be able to afford to have a large part of our food brought from England. We must encourage the planters to provide more for themselves. Many of the craftsmen brought over by the Company have turned to tobacco planting instead in an attempt to make a quick fortune, and we are still short of skilled men."

"It's difficult to blame them," John put in thoughtfully. "Most of them have never before imagined having any spare money, let alone a fortune. It's probably the only chance they'll ever have."

"But it is short-sighted. If they work to establish good varied crops now they will benefit when the price of tobacco falls, as it surely must. Those who have made a fortune now will have to spend it again buying necessities at high prices."

John shrugged. "You are right, of course, but they will not see it that way. It is easy enough for us, who have always had enough and have families to help us in need, to be far-sighted. The poor devils the Company ship out here have never had any practice in looking further ahead than their next meal."

"One day they will learn. I pay my craftsmen high wages and promise them security, and they can see the advantage in retaining their skills. I want to persuade others to do the same."

"I'm with you," John said. "Better to do it by example than through the Assembly. What do you think of the land I saw yesterday near Charles City?"

"A good position, and plenty of room for expansion. Do you mean to buy it? Mistress Rawlings asks a fair price, and she cannot run it without a man."

"Did her husband die?" Thomas asked.

"Her son and daughter-in-law owned it. They both died of a flux. She wanted to keep the plantation for her grandson, but he is barely two and she has decided it is best to return to England where they still have some property."

"I have a fancy for some new land near Henrico," Thomas said slowly. "It would be a good place to set up mills."

"At the Falls? But I thought you wanted a quick fortune from tobacco?" Adam said teasingly.

"I do indeed, but perhaps I'll have both. You have inspired me with your talk of far sightedness," Thomas rejoined, laughing. "Seriously, if one intends to stay, there is need of more than tobacco plants."

"And we have the money to wait, to resist the temptation of a fast return. Our profits then will be to the benefit of the colony as well," Adam suggested.

Listening to such talk in the evenings Bella learned a great deal about the land she had come to. Occasionally she was persuaded to accompany the men on trips up the river, but usually she preferred to remain in the calm security of Adam's settlement, where she quickly became a favourite with his workpeople and their families.

There was always plenty to do. Meg was a competent housekeeper, but with so many people to cook for she had little time for anything else. Bella learned that the hangings in the parlour where she had been taken on that first night were some that Adam had brought from England. She found bolts of material stored away which were intended to provide more, and soon she was occupied with making and embroidering hangings, cushions, and bedcovers to add to the already considerable comfort of the house. She was quick with figures, and able to help Adam in keeping the increasingly complicated accounts, releasing him as the harvest season approached for work outside.

The tobacco harvest was the most critical because of its value in England. Bella had seen where the previous year's crop was hung to dry in the huge barns which Adam had built a year or so earlier. They would remain there for months until the leaves could be stripped off and sorted for quality, then packed in large hogsheads.

"Why does not everyone pack it the way you do?" Bella asked one day, after she had accompanied Adam to Jamestown to shop for stores and seen huge rolls of tobacco leaves lying on the wharfs waiting for shipment to England.

"Mine is the newer method. It bruises the leaves less, for they are not handled so much. Also, some planters, in their greed to make a swift profit, have stuffed the rolls with inferior tobacco. They care little that they damage the reputation of the whole colony. I and some others have begun to send our own marked hogsheads to factors in London, and soon we shall find our buyers relying on us for quality."

They were so busy that Bella was able to forget Edward for much of the time. Thomas and John left for their own newly acquired plantations, and Adam promised to visit them once the tobacco seedlings were planted in the sheltered beds in the forest. Several times he took Bella with him to visit his friends, and she was hostess when they came to Fairmile. They accepted her presence with him unquestioningly, although many of the men privately congratulated Adam on his good fortune in finding such a delectable mistress.

They were content apart from their shared reserve. Bella would not admit to herself that she felt any more for Adam than physical delight in his lovemaking, and he sensed that, despite her eager responses, she withheld the core of her being from him. That being so he could not bring himself to express in words his growing adoration of her, a feeling quite separate from his appreciation of her body. Adam had been independent for too long, and suspicious of the many who had merely tried to use him, to trust any women unreservedly.

Yet he wanted her to confess her love for him, and when she did not he began consciously trying to make her jealous by paying attention to other women.

Bella, hurt but unwilling to confess it, assumed that he was bored with her and told herself that this confirmed her opinion of men in general. She retaliated by flirting with the men, who were all too ready to encourage her.

At several houses they met Mary Bolton and her husband, now the owners of a small plantation near Charles City. Mary's jealous eyes soon discovered that while they appeared to be on perfectly amicable terms, Adam and Bella spent less time together than might have been expected. To her chagrin her attempts to attract Adam still met with polite rebuffs, and she concentrated on discovering which of Bella's many admirers received most encouragement. It was not long before she decided John Porlock was the most favoured suitor, and began a determined campaign to discredit Bella in Adam's eyes.

Bella's friendship with John had increased when she discovered that he knew Kent, and she frequently talked to him about it, finding that their reminiscences assuaged her loneliness and homesickness. John, while succumbing to the general admiration for Bella, was a perceptive young man and realised that although her relationship with Adam was far from perfect, she was unlikely ever to look seriously at another man. In unguarded moments the puzzlement and hurt could be seen in her eyes, as she watched him talking or dancing with other women. But then she would disguise her sadness with smiles and laughter and deliberately turn away to pay attention to someone else.

"I wonder what she sees in John?" Mary asked Adam one day. "They spent most of yesterday together and she has danced with almost no-one else tonight."

"They both lived in Kent," Adam replied shortly.

"So did her husband," Mary retorted. "She does not seek his company though!"

"Have you heard that Edward Sutton has been seriously ill?" she asked on another occasion. "A wound in a fight, I understand, but no-one appears to know how it happened, or who injured him."

"I'm not interested in Sutton."

"It seems surprising that Bella, who seems to be able to twist every other man round her finger, could not do as she wished with her own husband. Did she run away from him in a fit of temper when she could not get her own way?"

"You saw how she left," was all Adam replied to this and walked away.

The winter continued, cold, with a few flurries of snow and much rain. Several times Indians came to the house to trade, and Adam bought Bella a warm beaverskin jacket and soft moccasins. She found that the Indians, at peace with the settlers for the last five years, had acquired a few words of English. They were proud people, though gentle and friendly in their dealings with the strangers who descended on their tribal lands. They appeared strange indeed in their short fringed aprons, and

229

the curious leggings that they wore when it was cold, with feathered cloaks slung over their shoulders, and more feathers in the knot of hair which they made from what remained on the unshaven left sides of their heads. They prized white beads, which contrasted with their weather-browned skins, but cast longing eyes on the guns Adam and his men possessed, for the settlers were forbidden to trade guns with the Indians.

Their only weapons appeared to be knives, and the arrows which they always carried on their backs. They appeared to use these mainly for hunting, for they always had fresh meat, rabbits, venison, or wild turkeys when they arrived at the house.

Adam was often away for a night or so, but Bella refused to admit how desperately she missed him in the big bed on those nights. She would not tell him, nor would her pride permit her to let him see how his continued flirting with other women hurt her, but she lay for hours during those lonely nights and miserably thought of him in other beds. Firmly she tried to convince herself that it was less his lovemaking that she missed than the fear of her own loss of security and a home for Toby and Alice, should he tire of her.

In fact his absences were entirely to discuss common problems with other planters and leading men in the colony. He was trying to persuade them to develop more varied agriculture, and to relax some of the more puritanical laws passed at the first Assembly two and a half years before, when twenty-two burgesses representing eleven settlements along the James River had met for the first time.

"If men are permitted to drink and gamble in moderation, they need not do it in secret. Once something is done in secret it becomes a vice," he maintained.

"We must deter men from idleness and vanity," had been the reply from Governor Yeardley, whose period of office had just ended. "Bright apparel, wine and immodest behaviour lead to other sins."

Adam received the same reply from the new Governor, Sir Francis Wyatt after he took office in November, but still he hoped that his opinions would one day prevail.

Bella realised that while she remained quietly in Adam's house they would not be brought before the Council for their liaison. The Company needed Adam's support in new crops and industries. He was therefore too valuable to offend. But they could not flaunt their relationship, and so on visits to the colony leaders Bella had to remain at Fairmile. For Bella there were far too many lonely nights and when John appeared after Adam had left to visit the embryo ironworks at Henrico, the furthest settlement up river, she welcomed him eagerly.

"I was hoping that I could stay the night," he explained as he followed her into the parlour, "but if Adam is not here I had better not. I will go on to Jamestown."

"It is late and I do not see why you must," Bella replied. "Adam is not jealous," she added, a trifle wistfully.

They stayed up late talking, and in the morning Bella took John to the barns to show him the progress of the tobacco leaves which were being dried there, the windows opened and closed according to the weather. It was almost midday when Bella walked down to the landing stage with John to see him off. There were several small boats and canoes on the river, but by now Bella had ceased scanning each one fearfully in case Edward was there. He had made no move to reclaim or harm her, and she was beginning to feel safe.

"Is not that John Porlock, bidding Bella Sutton a fond farewell?" Mary Bolton asked her husband as they were rowed past. "I thought Adam was to be at the ironworks today."

"What of it? I should have been there also if you had not refused to come home and I had to fetch you," her husband replied gruffly.

"Well, we can go straight there and I'll come with you. At least you need not be afraid of showing me off to the men there, for I am honourably wed to you."

While John, unaware of Mary's presence, went in the direction of Jamestown and Bella returned to the house, Mary plotted her next moves. Her husband, pliable as wax in her hands, despite the knowledge that she would cuckold him at the slightest encouragement, agreed that she should accompany him to the Falls where the ironworks and the site of the proposed university and college for conversion of the Indians were. There she made certain that she gained Adam's attention.

"Oh, Adam, I quite thought that you had not come," she exclaimed.

"I wished to be at the discussions," he replied, moving to pass her.

"For the new improvements at the ironworks? How exciting! But when I saw Mr Porlock leaving Fairmile yesterday morning I made up my mind that you had remained at home, though I must admit I thought it odd that Bella was seeing him off alone. Oh dear, I should not have told you! I've no desire to make mischief, and perhaps he had just called in, although I do not see where else he could have spent the night!"

Adam surveyed her, his face inscrutable, but he reflected for a moment on what he would do to anyone who supplanted him in Bella's bed, even if it were as good a friend as John. With an effort to appear normal he bowed to Mary, smiling, and passed on.

Bella could bestow her favours on anyone she chose and he had no right to prevent it, he told himself fiercely. Yet he did not think that she was unfaithful to him, despite her flirting. That, he was sure, was a spirited retaliation against his own attempts to make her jealous. She was always infuriatingly cool and smiling, never showing the least sign of jealousy as he had hoped she might.

Mary fumed impotently. It was painfully clear to her that while Bella remained with Adam she had not the remotest chance of ensnaring him. She did not stop to consider why she had this desperate need to capture his affections, but in truth she had become so bored with her husband's pliant devotion that she craved the excitement of other men, and Adam's aloofness was a challenge that she could not resist.

Adam, however, continued to withstand her overtures, and she fretted with rage that he spurned her. She returned home vowing to revenge herself on Bella.

At the beginning of March a ripple of unease ran through the colony. On Ash Wednesday Mr Morgan, one of the planters had gone with a well-known Indian trader, Jack of the Feathers, to trade with some of his fellows several miles away. Two days later Jack had returned alone, wearing a cap of Mr Morgan's, and on learning that their master was dead two of Mr Morgan's servants had shot him. The Indian Chief, Opechancanough, sent threats of revenge, and these were duly reciprocated by Governor Wyatt, then all seemed to subside into its normal calm.

"I do not like leaving you," Adam told Bella a few days after Jack's killing, "but I promised Sir Francis that I would visit the ironworks again with George Thorpe of Berkeley Hundred."

"I shall be safe here, we are well protected," Bella assured him, and Adam, having arranged to double the guard he always kept at night, departed.

Mr Bolton, also interested in the success of the ironworks, was of the party, but this time he had left Mary with friends in Jamestown. While she was there she gossiped eagerly about everyone.

"I hear that Edward Sutton has recovered from his wound," said a friend who had come out on the *Virginian*. "That was odd. No-one seems to know how he got it. It's also said that his wife has disappeared, and there are rumours that she is with Mr Tarrant. Do you know the truth? I thought he favoured you."

Mary was thoughtful. On the following day, a Thursday, when a sermon was always preached in the chapel, she attended and afterwards lingered to waylay the minister.

"I am troubled in my mind," she told him, modestly lowering her eyes, "for I have condoned a sin. And yet I do not know if it is my business to report it."

"The eradication of sin is a sacred duty laid on us all," he replied. "It is a greater sin to conceal what you know."

"It concerns one who is well regarded, and important."

"All are nought before the Lord. Even though it be the Governor, you must speak."

Thus enjoined to reveal what she knew, as she had fully expected to be, Mary falteringly explained that the wife of a planter, Edward Sutton, was openly living as mistress of another man.

"Adultery is a grave sin. I will see them," the minister promised.

"Mr Sutton may not wish to take her back."

"It is his duty to chastise and then forgive her. I will see him first."

"What if Mr Tarrant defies you? He might hide the woman."

"He would not dare."

"He thinks he can defy the laws. But he is absent for a few days."

He looked at her sharply. "I will attend to it. Be satisfied that you have done your duty."

Concealing her triumph Mary retreated and gleefully awaited events.

Bella was walking in the forest with Sam on the following Monday morning, inspecting the beds where the young tobacco plants were sown until they grew large enough for transplanting, when one of the young workmen came running towards them.

"Ma'am, Miss Bella!" he gasped, and panted for breath as he halted before them.

"Adam? Is it Adam, Mr Tarrant?" Bella demanded fearfully, but the lad shook his head.

"Your husband!" he gasped eventually. "I was in Jamestown, I'd gone for the stores, and I heard some men talking. The Governor has authorised Mr Sutton to bring some men and take you back home!

They were just setting out. I managed to keep ahead of them, but they cannot be far behind!"

"Get the men!" Sam began to say, but Bella stopped him with a shake of her head.

"No. We are in the wrong, and to defy them would make it worse for Mr Tarrant."

"You can't mean to go with him?" Sam asked incredulously, for like the rest of Adam's servants he had heard from Alice of how Edward had ill-treated her.

"Oh, no, I shall go to Mr Porlock until I can reach Adam. Sam, get a couple of the strongest men to row us there, I will find Alice and Toby."

"You'll have to hurry, Miss, they're almost upon us!"

Unable to stop for anything, Bella ran to the cottage where Alice and Toby were to be found at that time.

"Come, Edward is here!" she gasped. Wordlessly Alice picked up the child and followed Bella.

The path to the landing stage twisted past a clump of evergreen bushes, low on the ground, and before they came into view Bella heard men talking there. She stopped, aghast. Sam was speaking loudly, demanding to know what was happening.

Edward replied curtly. "I am here on behalf of the Governor. Where is Mr Tarrant?"

"Quickly, we must hide!" Bella whispered, and took Toby from Alice, running as silently as she could back towards the cottages.

The lad who had brought the warning was still there.

"They've arrived, it's too late," Bella said swiftly. "We must hide in the forest; they will search every building."

"Come with me," he said. "I know a safe place."

He led the way swiftly across the cleared ground, and they had just reached the shelter of the trees when Edward and Sam, the latter protesting vehemently, came round the corner of Adam's house.

"Drop down!" the boy ordered, Bella and Alice followed his example and crouched behind some low bracken. When Edward had gone into the house they moved deeper into the shelter of the trees, and the boy led them swiftly in a half circle back towards the river. At last he stopped and took them towards an old tree, which leaned drunkenly on the bank of a small creek a few yards away from the main river.

"There's no hiding place there," Bella said in dismay, and looked over her shoulder. They were quite near the large barn, and voices could be heard approaching.

"You'd never guess, but the space is quite large," he answered, and took them round to the side, then parted some of the tangled, overhanging roots to reveal a small dark cave.

"Wait there, and when it's safe I'll get the canoe round to take you up the river."

Hastily Bella nodded, and she and Alice crawled into the dim, musty smelling cavity. Toby, bewildered, began to ask questions, but Bella quickly began to whisper a story to him, and he listened, enthralled, as she invented reasons for their strange behaviour.

They heard the crashing of footsteps through the undergrowth, and several men emerged onto the bank. Peering through a small gap in the roots Alice could see them as they looked along the creek. The boy who had guided them here was sitting some distance away, apparently intent on fishing.

"Have you seen any boats, or any women?" the searchers demanded, but he looked at them blankly.

"Why — who are you looking for? What women?" he asked slowly.

"Two women with a child."

"There's no boats here. The creek doesn't lead anywhere. And I've seen no women except at the plantation. Who are you?"

They ignored his question, and walked a little way up the bank. Almost on top of them one slipped, and clutched at the roots of the tree to save himself. Bella's heart lurched, she was sure that they would be discovered, and she quickly put her hand over Toby's mouth to prevent him from crying out. But the men noticed nothing unusual, and when they retreated to look in other places, the boy went with them.

Bella and Alice waited, cramped with cold, for another hour before he returned, saying that as the search was now all on the far side of the plantation, the canoe had set off, and was waiting for them at the junction of the creek and the main river.

He led them there swiftly, and they

thanked him as they scrambled into one of Adam's fastest boats, and the rowers sent it speeding up the river.

Bella realised that Edward had only dared come once he was confident that Adam was away. Why had the Governor supported him? Was it that he could do little else when Edward appealed to him? Adam's confidence had been misplaced. They were obviously answerable under the laws of the colony, however great Adam's importance.

They reached John's house late that night, and he promised to shield them. Bella was anxious to contact Adam and would not accept John's assurances that he would be bound to call on his way home and so find them.

"I must go to him!" she insisted. "If I leave Alice and Toby here can you spare a man to accompany me? I can manage a canoe, but I dare not go alone."

"I'll come with you, Miss Bella," one of Adam's own men volunteered. "Joe can row back alone, it's easier down-stream, and if we can borrow one of Mr Porlock's canoes we'll reach Mr Tarrant tomorrow."

This was agreed, and early on the

following morning Bella and Ned set out.

The river was peaceful, and there was less traffic on it here than closer to Jamestown. It wound through wooded banks, where lay the occasional plantation with its cleared acres, huddle of buildings, and fields, some of which were enclosed with zig-zag split rail fences. They glimpsed the occasional Indian village, usually in a clearing of the woods further from the river, and they met several Indian canoes from which men were fishing with both spears and nets.

Bella had leisure to think. She had flown instinctively to Adam's protection, but she began to wonder what he could do. Until now he had reassured her that the Governor would prefer to ignore them, but something had emboldened Edward to risk Adam's anger and obtain the Governor's assistance, in recovering his wife. Would she and Adam be able to defy the authority of the Governor? Would he listen to her accusations of Edward's ill-treatment? Somehow she doubted it. To the men who ruled Virginia their version of the Ten Commandments was inviolable, and a wife was totally subject to her husband.

For a moment she thought of claiming that the marriage did not exist, but she knew that Edward had papers to prove it, and the fact that she had had no option but to marry would count as nothing. The only solution she could see was for Adam to send her back to England before Edward could find her. It was a prospect that filled her with gloom. Not, she hastened to assure herself, because she would miss Adam, but because she would lose the security he provided. Yet the very idea of giving herself to another man in a similar way in order to provide for them all was somehow repugnant to her.

She was lost in these dismal thoughts when there was a sudden shout from the bank and she looked up in alarm. They were in an isolated part of the river, a sharp bend with no habitations or other boats in sight apart from a couple of Indian canoes, and to her horror she saw a group of savages, their bodies painted black and red in great circles and lines, standing on the river bank.

Ned began to row as fast as he could, begging her to lie in the bottom of the boat, but it was useless from the start. Hastily stowing their nets the men in the two canoes converged on them. Although Ned ceased rowing and threatened them with the gun he carried, there were too many of them and he was soon overpowered. Both he and Bella were carried to the shore.

They were bound securely, their arms behind their back, and with just sufficient rope left between their legs to permit them to walk. Bella could understand none of the savages' spoken commands, but the gestures made it clear enough what they wanted, and closely guarded on all sides, Bella and Ned were made to walk deep into the forest.

9

THEY walked for two hours or so, through country that was at first marshy beside a wide creek, the deep forest never far distant. As the ground rose slightly they left the marshland behind and passed under the dense trees, mainly pine and cypress, which shut out the faint spring sunshine. Later they moved into an area of oaks and maple and hickory, showing a faint gloss of green where the first buds were opening, with tangled undergrowth making their way more difficult. Occasionally they passed by clearings where the Indians tended their corn and beans, and once Bella caught a glimpse of an Indian village, the longhouse of the chief prominent amongst the smaller, neatly set out rows of lodges.

But it was a mile or so further before they rested a short while, and then resumed the march. Eventually they were met by another group of Indians who also had several captives, all young men, and after a short consultation the two groups went on together.

"Where are you from?" one of the other captives asked Bella. "We were coming from Henrico when they pounced on us."

"We were on our way there, from Mr Tarrant's plantation near Jamestown," she replied. "Do you know him?"

"Yes, we have met. You must be — " he paused, embarrassed.

"Bella Sutton," she answered quickly. "Was Mr Tarrant at Henrico when you left, do you know?"

"Yes, he still had to solve some problems with the new furnaces, and was detained for another day. Was he expecting you?"

"No. Why?"

"They won't know what has happened until someone realises we are missing, and that could be several days."

"What will they do to us?"

"That rather depends on who they are. Let us hope they are not great friends of Jack of the Feathers. You heard what happened?"

"Yes, but I thought it had all quietened."

"So did we. They might want us for ransom. Let us hope so, and that Mr Tarrant can organise a troop to come after us before — " he hesitated and came to an embarrassed stop.

"Before what?" Bella asked quietly.

"Before they take us too far away," he finished, avoiding her gaze, and she wondered what he had been about to say.

On her new friend's advice, Bella tried to note landmarks on their route which might help them if they could find a way of escaping, but the forest was all so similar that she knew she would never be able to find her way back to the river except by chance. But there were many small streams which they had to wade through, and surely, if they could only escape, they could follow one of them and must eventually get back to James River where there were habitations. The greatest difficulty would be to escape.

No plan had presented itself by the time they came to another, larger village, with several longhouses and a stockade surrounding the lodges, and fields of corn and pumpkins round about.

They were led in through the only

opening in the stockade, and naked children stopped playing to stare curiously at them. An elderly man wearing a cloak made of skins and decorated with beads emerged from one of the longhouses and harangued them incomprehensibly for ten minutes, then they were taken to a small lodge and thrown inside. Two guards remained by the door, armed with hatchets and clubs.

"Did anyone understand what the old fellow was saying?" someone asked.

They all shook their heads.

"He repeated Opechancanough's name several times, I think," one suggested.

"And Nenemettanan," another said gloomily.

"What is that?"

"Jack of the Feathers, his native name."

"Oh, God's death, that means revenge!"

"Not necessarily," the man who had first spoken to Bella replied stoutly. "This is Mistress Sutton, I am Nicholas Wilkes."

Thus reminded of a woman's presence amongst them they refrained from speculating on their possible fate, and began to plan an escape. They managed to release each other from the bonds, and when they were brought dishes of meal and fish their captors raised no objection.

In the afternoon they heard shouts and singing outside, and soon they were ordered out of their lodge with their hands again tied loosely behind their backs. A large fire had been lit in the open centre of the village and the Indian men were seated about it on woven mats. They could smell the tempting aromas of fish and turkey being roasted on hurdles and spits.

The captives were herded to a position before the main longhouse, outside which the old man, dressed in an even more elaborately embroidered cloak than the one he had previously worn, reclined against a raised hurdle covered in mats. He was smoking a long-stemmed pipe, and he totally ignored the prisoners as they were shepherded to a spot nearby and told to sit down. With a half dozen Indians standing behind them armed with hatchets they could do little but obey, and they watched the scene before them in some apprehension. For a considerable time nothing appeared to happen. Then the food was distributed in carved wooden bowls and meat, broth and fish eaten. The captives were offered nothing.

Suddenly they heard an unearthly howling from one of the longhouses and several men, painted red, emerged with quivers of arrows and clubs on their backs, and began to dance. It was unlike any dance Bella had ever seen. They shouted and howled continuously, and banged their feet on the ground, stamping and shrieking as they twirled about.

After a while the men fell back and girls took their places about the fire, dancing in an even more abandoned fashion. Their bodies, covered only with girdles of leaves, were also painted, and they wore headdresses made out of the horns of deer. Swaying, crying, working themselves up into a frenzy, they spun round and round and eventually cast themselves down before the old man who stared past them, oblivious.

Eventually he gestured with the hand which held his pipe, and they rose and fled towards the fire, mingling with the others sitting on the ground. A man who had been sitting quietly in the shadows rose and came forward. As he stepped to the side of the old chieftain, Bella realised with a shock that he was a European. His hair was light brown and curly and his skin, although burnt with the sun and wind, was much fairer than that of any Indian she had ever seen.

The chief spoke to him for a while, and the man turned towards the group of prisoners.

"I am ordered to say to you," he began, in a clipped fashion that seemed too precise and yet hesitant, as though, Bella suddenly thought, he had not spoken his own tongue for many years, "that you are here to pay for what was done to Nenemettanan."

"They killed Morgan first," a man beside Bella muttered, and the interpreter's eyes flickered over him. The chief spoke again, at some length.

"The Werowance says that for many years the Indian has lived at peace with the white men who had invaded his country and taken his best fields and fishing grounds, and used the forest clearings that he had made. They have suffered killings and injuries, but will do so no more. He proposes to make of you, each day, an example, until your leaders promise restitution."

"Who are you? What are you doing here

with these savages?" demanded the man who spoke before.

The interpreter ignored him, although his lips tightened and he blinked nervously. The chief suddenly pointed and two Indians stepped forward in front of the interpreter, who retired to the far end of the longhouse. The man who had been sitting beside Bella was hauled to his feet and marched off between the two Indians, towards a pole which was driven into the ground near the fire. Turning him round roughly his guards tied him against it and then stood back. The chief gestured again, and a younger man who had been sitting beside him rose lithely to his feet. He was painted more elaborately than the others, and adorned with many ropes of beads. In his hair he sported a bird's wing, spread and stiffened somehow so that it rose proudly from the crown of his head.

He strolled languidly across to the bound man, spoke a few words to the guards, and then proceeded to walk round the captive several times, bending down frequently as though he were placing something on the ground, all the while chanting in a monotonous tone. Two other Indians,

254

painted black, silently joined him in this ritual, and the other prisoners watched nervously.

"The black ones are their priests," one of the men whispered. "It looks horribly like a sacrifice!"

Bella heard him and turned her head round.

"Can't we *do* something?" she demanded. "Have none of you guns?"

"They took them when we were caught. Best not interfere, or we'll all suffer. As it is help might come before they get around to us."

She slumped down again, and in horrified fascination watched the perambulations of the Indians. After what seemed hours, when the last of the daylight had gone and the scene was lit only by the glare of the fire, the three of them halted before the victim.

One of the priests stretched out a hand and forced the prisoner to spread out his foot, splaying it against a carved piece of wood held by a second priest. The young man had produced a knife and as Bella watched, rigid with shock, he slowly brought down the knife and chopped off one of the prisoners's toes.

The man jerked convulsively and an agonised scream burst from his lips. Bella clutched at her throat to prevent herself from crying out, and watched, horrified, as the prisoner struggled against shock and pain, his pale lips drawn back in a parody of a grimace. His leg, although tied at the ankles to the post behind him, twitched and twisted, but he could find no ease for the mutilated limb.

It was several minutes before Bella realised that the Indian priests had moved away from their prisoner. She looked for them and saw that they had placed the severed toe on a small carved wooden platter, and were carrying it in procession towards the chief. When they reached him the priest carrying the grisly object bowed low, then took another pace forward and knelt, holding the platter towards the chief as he reclined, his eyes half-closed, in an attitude of boredom.

The chief glanced at the priest, and languidly stretched out his hand, contemptuously flicking the toe with a long bony finger before dismissing the priest and his acolytes, who then moved ceremoniously across to the prisoners and held the platter with its hideous burden before them. Bella closed her eyes and turned away her head to ward off the nausea that attacked her, and glanced towards the prisoner again. He was totally neglected, no-one had attempted to bind the wound or come to his relief in any way, and even at the distance which separated them she could discern his trembling, and the efforts he was making not to give way to the terror which gripped him.

The priest moved back to the victim, laid the severed toe to one side and began the ritual once more. Realising their intention, Bella gasped out a protest, staggered to her feet and tried to run towards the chieftain, crying out to him for mercy. She had moved only a couple of yards before his servants had seized her, and thrown her back amongst her fellow prisoners.

The chief had taken no notice of the slight disturbance, and neither had the celebrants of the ghastly sacrifice, who had continued with their monotonous circling of the victim. Again a toe was chopped off, this time from the other foot, and again presented solemnly to the chief.

The unfortunate victim could no longer control his screams of agony, and tears ran unheeded down Bella's cheeks as she watched, unable to turn away from the horrid spectacle.

The mutilation went on, toe by toe, alternating with a grim harmony from one foot to the other. A pool of blood had formed on the ground below the victim and was continuously replenished by the drips from his crippled feet. Long before all his toes had been rent from him he had succumbed to the shock, and now hung unconscious and helpless against the ropes which bound him to the stake.

When all was done there was no relief, for after a more prolonged spell of chanting and circling, the priests began to hack away at his fingers. Two of his fellow captives had succumbed to the fear and nausea which had gripped them, and were retching miserably, hiding their faces. Bella tried to force her eyes shut, realising that there was no help they could give to the sufferer apart from praying for a speedy death for him, but again and again she found her gaze reverting to the stake where he was undergoing the torture.

Then there was a change in the chanting which had all the time been going on softly in the background, and another priest, taller than the others, stepped forward. Bella's stomach heaved as she realised that, with a knife he held ceremoniously before him as he in turn circled round the pole several times, he was cutting the skin of the victim's shoulders and peeling it from him.

"God save us! They're skinning him alive!" someone muttered, and Bella found herself pulled roughly round and her face pressed against a serge doublet.

"Don't look!" Ned ordered.

Bella shuddered as she clung to him. The cries and chants of the Indians gradually increased, and erupted in a crescendo of triumph, all the spectators rising to their feet and howling their glee as, with a final flourish, the sacrifice was concluded. The head of the man was severed from his body and hoisted onto a pole which had been waiting.

"I am ordered to tell you," the shaking voice of the interpreter spoke as the howls died away, "that each day one of you will suffer that fate and his head shall be sent to the Governor until reparation is made for the death of our brother."

The captives were hauled to their feet and Ned's arms, which he had somehow contrived to release from his bonds, were tied again behind his back. They were all forced to follow their late companion's head as it was borne in a shambling procession round the perimeter of the village. At last they were led back to the lodge where they had previously been held, and the men were pushed inside. Bella, to her dismay, found herself held back, and when the men had all been disposed of she was taken back to the chieftain's longhouse.

The old man gestured to her to come closer, and shivering, she obeyed. The interpreter was standing a short distance away, and he averted his eyes as the chief looked Bella up and down, then stretched out his hand to prod. She flinched away from his touch, which was more like that of a cattle dealer than a man seeking lascivious satisfaction, but as soon as she did so her arms were held firmly and she was forced to stand still.

The young man who had taken part in the sacrificial ceremony was once more reclining at the chief's side, and his lecherous gaze embarrassed Bella far more than the chief's examination. When he spoke, gesturing to the longhouse behind them, Bella stiffened. Was she to be handed over to him for his enjoyment? An argument ensued between the young man and the chief, and to Bella's relief the young man eventually stormed off into the longhouse, plainly angry and thwarted. Bella breathed a sigh of relief, but then the chief spoke to the interpreter, and he turned to her. She thought she saw a look of sympathy in his blue eyes, but he swiftly lowered them and translated what the chief said in a low monotone.

"The chief's favourite son wants you, but it is not allowed. The chief will spare you the punishment of the others, for he wishes to keep you to entertain important visitors, other chieftains or their envoys. He says that they do not often have the opportunity of sampling a white woman, and you will be a great asset to him. You are to be housed alone until he needs you, which will be tomorrow night when a minor chief of the Pamunkey tribe is expected. I am ordered to tell you that he is reckoned a lusty man, and regularly satisfies ten or more of his concubines each night. If the Pamunkey chieftain is pleased with the entertainment you offer him, you will be treated honourably here, and given only to the most esteemed visitors. If you are unco-operative, then the son of the chief will be permitted to do as he wishes with you, and afterwards the men of the village can have their turn."

He glanced once more at her, then swiftly away. Bella shivered. His words painted a dire picture; she thought she might even prefer the painful but certain death which awaited her fellow prisoners.

She was dismissed and the guards holding her arms led her away to a small lodge nearby. They pushed her inside, and she heard them making themselves comfortable against the doorway, chatting and laughing quietly together. At least it was empty, Bella thought numbly, as she felt her way to the woven mat which served as a bed, and sank down on it to rest her head against the embroidered leather pillow. After a while the cold penetrated her awareness sufficiently for her to reach out and pull a covering of furs over her, but she could not sleep. The horrors she had been forced to witness made sure of that.

Some hours later, rousing from her torpor, she became aware of a scratching sound on the wall behind her head. She thought of rats, recalling the many she had seen running about the streets of Jamestown, and shivered, but then a whisper came to her.

"Mistress, are you awake?"

"Who is it?" she responded after a moment of stunned surprise.

"Quietly. There are guards at the door. My name is Walter, I was the interpreter. I came to warn you. Be ready to escape in a few minutes. I am going to set fire to the chief's longhouse and in the confusion you should be able to escape. When you come out of the door turn left, and the opening of the stockade is straight ahead. Your friends will be going there too and I will join you. I can lead you to safety. Do you understand?"

"Yes, but how — "

"No more, it is not safe. Be ready."

He was gone and Bella rose to her feet, her blood racing with renewed hope. It seemed hours before anything moved, then she heard one of the guards outside her lodge shout, and an answering call came from further away. The sound of running feet went past, then more shouts, and a scream from a woman. Cautiously Bella lifted the skin which hung down in the doorway and peered out. Some distance away one of the longhouses was already ablaze, and another had flames licking up the walls. Her guards had disappeared.

Trying to keep in the shadows Bella slipped out and turned left as she had been instructed. Everyone else appeared to be running towards the flames, and she quickly reached the stockade.

"This way!" a voice called softly, and she saw an arm waving to her round the edge of the fence where the opening was now visible.

As she approached Ned ran up behind her and swept her onwards, his arm about her waist. Outside the other captives waited, and Walter their rescuer, who came up after Ned, nodded swiftly and led the way across the fields, into the shelter of the trees.

They did not halt for some time until Walter held up his hand. As they crowded round him with thanks and questions, he had difficulty in making himself heard, but they soon quietened.

"There is no time for explanations. We must go silently, for the Indians have ways of tracking unknown to us. I am making for a small river which leads to the Chickahominy, and there we might find canoes. Follow me, but in silence, if you please."

He turned and led the way, and they fell into step behind him. It was difficult to match the pace he set, for they were tired after their ordeal and the forced march earlier that day, but none wanted to pause.

The dark forest appeared trackless, but Walter, helped only by the faintest gleams of starlight, went unhesitatingly forwards, leading them round obstacles, warning them of patches of swampy ground, or shallow streams, and somehow negotiating the thick undergrowth so that they followed without stumbling into barriers or pitfalls that they would never have been able to avoid on their own.

At intervals Walter stopped and permitted them a brief respite while he himself lay with his ear to the ground listening for the sounds of pursuit. He warned them not to talk and they obeyed unquestioningly.

Bella found that her petticoats hampered her, and very soon she kilted them about her waist, leaving her legs free to the knees. The air was cold but the exercise warmed her, and she found that she did not need Ned's proffered help very often in order to keep pace with the others.

Dawn came, but the light merely spurred Walter to go faster and pauses he permitted became less frequent. When they stopped beside a small stream to drink thirstily, he urged them on again almost at once.

"You look worried, man. Have we lost our way?" Ned asked softly.

Walter shook his head.

"No fear of that. I've travelled this road many times in the past few years."

"How do you come to be living with the Indians?" one of the others asked.

"I ran away," was the laconic reply. "Seven years ago, living in Jamestown was worse than being imprisoned. We were marched out to work in the fields, marched back to pray, and never permitted a moment's peace and solitude. That was not what I had come across the ocean for. I found a place with the Indians — until last night."

"But surely there must previously have been sacrifices?"

"Not of fellow Englishmen, and not with such cruelty," Walter said slowly. "We have been used to peace for some years. I enjoyed the freedom of their ways of hunting. I had a woman, she was very beautiful. But last night, no! I could not watch that happen again, but there was nought I could do to save him then."

They went on again in silence, dragging their feet, for it was now four and twenty hours since they had slept and the fear and exertion were beginning to slow them down. Every few minutes Walter put his ear to the ground, and at last he confessed they were being pursued.

"I have been uncertain, but now am sure. A large band of men are only a short way behind us."

"How far is it to the Chickahominy?"

"Too far. A march of several hours. Have you any weapons?"

"No, they took them all. But we could

FL18

fashion clubs from tree branches," Ned suggested.

Recognising that the Indians would be fleeter than they, and that the only chance was to wait and fight them off, the men swiftly organised themselves and broke off stout branches. Walter found a place well amongst the trees where the Indians would not be able to use their bows effectively, and where only a few at a time could approach. There they erected a makeshift barrier with swiftly interwoven branches, and made themselves a small triangular fort.

Bella worked alongside the men, refusing to think of what would be her fate if she were recaptured, until Walter ordered them all behind the barrier, saying that their pursuers were only five minutes away.

In the silence following there was nothing to be heard apart from the rustling of the branches and the fluttering of the occasional bird. Bella was just beginning to hope that Walter had been mistaken when she saw an Indian appear, speedily but utterly soundlessly, from behind a tree some yards distant. Then another, and a third, and yet more, until the small group of fugitives seemed surrounded.

"Keep your heads down!" Walter ordered softly, and Bella crouched behind the pitifully sparse barrier, peering through a gap as the savages approached.

Walter's choice of defensive position was soon seen to be a good one, for there were too many trees and overhanging branches for the Indians to be able to shoot accurately. They did not appear to wish to harm their prey, however, for although they held their bows ready, no hail of arrows such as Bella had been expecting struck them. Instead, with a gradual but certain inevitability, the Indians closed in. The defenders could do nothing with the paltry weapons they had provided themselves with until the Indians were within reach of the clubs.

The end came with terrifying suddenness. At some signal unperceived by the fugitives, the savages broke out into a howling and leaping frenzy, and after a minute of this rushed on the puny defences and by sheer weight of numbers overwhelmed their former prisoners. There were a few injuries inflicted, but the Indians were greatly superior in number. Having cast aside their bows as they ran to the attack, they used sharp hatchets to beat aside the branches protecting Bella and her companions.

The colonists fought furiously but they were overwhelmed, smothered and tied up before they could inflict a great deal of harm themselves. Then began the long dreary march back to the village. At midday a halt was called, and the leader of the Indians spoke to Walter who translated what he said to the others.

"They say they do not wish to hurt us, since they intend to carry out their previous plan of killing one each day. I am to be the victim tonight, and then lots will be drawn."

They listened in silence. Bella wondered wearily whether she would be included in the sacrifice this time, or whether she would be returned to the separate lodge and the other part planned for her.

Eventually they came in sight of the village. Over the stockade Bella could see that several of the lodges had been severely burned, and the main longhouse was still smouldering, a thin spiral of smoke rising lazily into the sky. The captives and the

Indians emerged from the trees and wound their way along a narrow path between two fields of maize. They were about half way to the outskirts of the village when a lone figure suddenly burst from the trees to the side, and ran as fast as he could towards them, converging on them and shouting, waving his arms urgently.

"What is it? What is he saying?" Ned asked Walter.

"It is not clear, but it appears that the village has been captured while they have been away! He was the only one to escape!"

"Who? From Jamestown? Is it help?"

"It could be. But it is more likely to be one of the other tribes. There is always rivalry, and this has happened before."

As he finished, from the village in front of them a line of men filed through the gateway and stood, guns raised. Aiming at the returning group.

10

ADAM finished his business at the
ironworks earlier than he had
expected, and decided to set off
towards home that afternoon. He missed
Bella as unbearably as she missed him
when they were apart. But their liaison
could not be continued for much longer.
Already he had received strong hints from
some of the older men in the colony that
the Governor could no longer ignore his
flouting of authority.

George Thorpe, the overseer of the
college lands had made this clear to
Adam. A deeply religious man, he had
been considered in the colony as a likely
successor to Sir George Yeardley, but had
been passed over by the Company in favour
of Wyatt. Thorpe, who was busy trying to
improve the ironworks, and had planted
thousands of vines for the proposed college,
firmly pointed out to Adam that it was his
duty to marry and provide heirs for his
own extensive acres.

"You cannot take the part you should in the affairs of the land while you continue your present way of life," he said severely.

This was undoubtedly true. Never having met a woman he wished to marry, rather than enjoy a brief flirtation with, Adam had taken it for granted that eventually he would agree to accept a suitable bride. Many had been suggested, both by his Virginian friends and his family in England, but so far he had always evaded the issue. He could not for ever put off the unpalatable fact that he needed to marry. If Bella had been free he would have married her, so sure was he now that no-one else could ever again rouse in him the feelings she did. But she was married. He could not marry her, nor could he expect her to remain with him if he married some other more eligible woman. One day they would have to part, and it was this depressing thought that sent him hurrying away from Henrico, to enjoy Bella's company as much as possible before the inevitable separation came.

It was dusk when he and Daniel came to John Porlock's plantation, and since he could not reach his own before the middle of the night, he decided to ask for John's hospitality and leave again at dawn.

John welcomed him gladly and then looked past him. "Where is Bella? Did you not meet her?"

"Bella? She has been here? When? Why?" Adam demanded.

John explained. "Edward somehow obtained Wyatt's support, and he went with the Governor's men to remove Bella from your protection. She fled here with Alice and Toby."

"Then where is she?"

"I thought she would have met you. She was so anxious to prevent you from going past unknowingly that she set off with Ned early this morning."

"We could not have failed to meet unless something had happened!" Adam declared. "John, will you lend me all the men you have? I must begin at once to search for her. God knows what will happen to her if she has been taken by the savages! They are seeking revenge for Jack."

"It is too late tonight," John protested. "Of course I will do all I can, and so will my neighbours, but we cannot work in the dark. Sleep for a few hours, and I will send a message to your own men, they can set off at first light with all your guns and join us. That will be far more effective than exhausting ourselves to no avail during the night."

Impatient, but recognising the sense of this, Adam went to bed, but lay tossing restlessly all night, unable to dismiss from his mind visions of Bella drowned, injured, or, worst of all, in the hands of the savages. Long before dawn he was up and fretting to start and John was helping him organise the distribution of every gun and other weapon they possessed.

They set off as soon as it was light, taking two of the canoes, and leaving instructions with Daniel to send the other men after them as soon as possible. For some distance they saw nothing, and none of the few people who were out on the river so early could help them. They were paddling along a quiet stretch when Adam, who had been scanning the banks closely, gave a shout and turned his canoe towards the north bank.

John followed, and soon saw what he had.

"It is my canoe," he said quietly. "What happened?"

"It was not overturned, so they have not drowned. Look, here is a thread of silk caught on the seat where it is rough. Did Bella wear a green gown?"

"Yes. Then it looks as though there was a struggle."

"It could hardly have been Edward Sutton. He would not have known where she had flown to."

"Indians!" John exclaimed despairingly. "How can we follow them? They could be anywhere in this vast forest."

"With prisoners they would have left tracks. There is a trader I often deal with who lives a short way up river. He will help me. Stay here and intercept the others while I go to fetch him."

It was an hour before Adam returned, and he had more news.

"Joshua here says that another attack took place yesterday and several men were captured. He had not heard of this one, but it is probable both attacks were made by the same group. I'll go ahead with him, you can follow when the others arrive. We will leave marks."

Joshua was old but still active and nimble. He soon picked up the Indian trail, and assured Adam that there had been a white man and a woman with them. Just before John and his reinforcements caught up with them Joshua was explaining that many more Indians, with half a dozen white men, had been added to the original group.

At last Joshua motioned them to stop, and Adam came up alongside him at the edge of a clearing and saw an Indian village before them.

"I do not like it!" Joshua said quietly.

"What is wrong?"

"There are too few women in the fields. And almost no children playing outside the stockade. I would suspect that the men are not there."

"Could they be out hunting? Or are they the ones we seek? Might they be out searching for others to take prisoner?"

Joshua shook his head. "It is impossible to tell. Wait here, and I will try to discover what it is."

Without further ado he went off, keeping well inside the shelter of the trees so that within a short time they could no longer see him. It seemed an age before he reappeared silently beside Adam, having circled the whole village.

"Well? Did you discover aught?"

"They are the ones we seek. But the prisoners are not there. I think they escaped during the night and later the Indians pursued them."

"How can you possibly tell that?" John asked, amazed.

"I can tell by the way the grasses lie," Joshua replied. "I also can see from the far side that several of the lodges have been set on fire. That smoke you can see is not all from cooking fires, a longhouse is still burning."

"So they contrived to escape," Adam murmured. "Is there much chance that they can evade pursuit?"

Joshua shook his head. "It is unlikely, the white men will not know the country. They will be caught."

"Then let us go on," John urged.

"Wait. What will be done to them when they are recaptured?" Adam said quietly.

"It depends what they are wanted for. They might be killed at once, but it is more probable that they will be brought back. I would think that if they are not killed during the fighting that is what will happen. The chief will want to take revenge for the destruction of his longhouse."

"Then we will take the village and wait for them."

Swiftly Adam gave orders and they began the attack on the village. Apart from the women and children, only a few old men were left to guard it, and the resistance was weak. Adam's two dozen men, armed with guns, were soon in control, and only one man amongst the Indians had been slightly hurt as a bullet grazed his leg. The villagers were herded into one of the longhouses which had not been burnt, and Adam set a guard at each end. Then the anxious wait began.

At last the lookout signalled the approach of the Indians, and Adam's men crouched near the entrance to the village, where the stockade overlapped to form a short, narrow passageway. They planned to permit the Indians to come as near as possible before declaring their presence. Adam hoped that the total absence of women in the fields would not warn the Indians that something was wrong, but before that could be tested he saw a figure racing across the fields towards the returning group. He could now see that several of the men were tied together, and to his immense relief Bella with her skirts kilted about her waist to permit greater freedom of movement, there and apparently unharmed.

The Indians stopped as the gesticulating figure approached them, but Adam gave rapid orders and his men filed out of the stockade, threatening the Indians with their guns before they could retreat to the cover given by the forest. Adam, with Joshua beside him, walked forward until he was well within reach of their arrows, but he did not hesitate. He held his gun aloft as a peace sign, and the Indians stood sullenly watching his approach.

"I come in peace, to bargain with you," he said, and Joshua swiftly translated. "Release the prisoners you have and we will take no further action."

"They are our captives, to do with as we please," the chief's son replied haughtily,

"We have prisoners too," Adam responded coolly. "Your old men, your women and your children are in our power. You would not wish it known that you permitted them to die for the sake of a few white men."

"You killed Nenemettanan. We will have revenge."

"Neither I, my men nor the ones you hold there were responsible for killing Jack of the Feathers. This is foolish talk. Are you willing to trade your prisoners for ours? Or must we act to convince you that we will show no mercy if you refuse?"

The young man still protested, and at a sign from Adam John, waiting inside the stockade, led out the old chief, his hands bound behind him.

"He will be the first to be shot," Adam said calmly. "Your young son will be the second."

Another of the men led out a four-year-old child to stand beside the old man.

"There is no need to shed blood," Adam said quickly. "Give us the prisoners and we will depart in peace."

There was some muttering from the crowd of Indians surrounding the captives, and the young leader replied angrily at first to their remarks, then he grew quiet and sullen, and eventually shrugged his shoulders.

"It will serve you little, a respite of but a day," he retorted, and walked forward to bow before his father, while his companions released the prisoners.

Bella ran forward to meet Adam and collapsed into his arms, trembling now that the ordeal was over. The other prisoners crowded round asking eager questions, but Adam held up a hand for silence.

"Are you all here?" he asked quickly.

"They killed Jacob yesterday," one replied. "The rest of us are here."

"They tortured him. They deserve to be shot, all of them!" another protested.

Adam shook his head. "We cannot take revenge. We still have to escape, and that is no simple matter. If we kill more Indians after Jack's death, there would be a full scale rising. We must concentrate on getting away ourselves."

Under Adam's careful leadership they soon left the village well behind. The Indians followed them only for a short distance, apparently to ensure that they were really departing.

When they reached the river and the place where they had left all the boats Joshua slipped away, proudly refusing the reward Adam offered.

"Thank you, but no. I am ashamed that my people have behaved so. Especially to a lovely young lady, and glad that I could help."

Without any further words he vanished, and Adam helped Bella into a boat. They all set off for John's house, where there was much-needed food awaiting them and they could sleep without fear.

Lying in Adam's arms that night Bella shudderingly recounted to him details of the horror she had witnessed, while he held her tightly.

"How could they be so cruel?" she cried, weeping at the memory and clinging to him.

"There are tortures just as bad carried out in Europe's dungeons," he replied. "We have progressed as far as to perform them secretly. One day, perhaps, these horrors will no longer exist. We must do what we can to prevent them. You are safe, thank God, and with me again!"

"It was so dreadful," she whispered, unable to stifle her sobs. "I want you to turn over, my darling," he said gently, and disengaging her clinging arms, he carefully repositioned her so that she was lying face down on the bed.

Then, with his hands warm and strong on her skin, he began to stroke her, massaging the knots of tension between her shoulder-blades, drawing gentle fingers down the hollows of her spine, caressing away the shudders which still shook her frame. Gradually she felt the numbing cold of her remembered fear being replaced by a glow of longing until every sensation in her body seemed to be concentrated in his fingertips. As he stroked the soft curves of her buttocks and began lazily to trace the contours of her thighs, she gave a half-articulate cry and turned to face him, her legs parting involuntarily in a gesture of surrender.

He knew at once that her need had changed, and took her quickly, not prolonging as he usually did the slow langorous awakening, but thrusting fiercely, almost roughly, carrying her on his own violence to a forgetfulness of the ordeal through which she had passed. Several times during the night she cried out at her dreams, but his caresses soothed her and she slept peacefully again.

When they rose in the morning John told Adam that the man Walter wished to speak with him urgently.

"He is the man who helped us escape, he had lived with the Indians for several years," Bella explained.

"Shall we talk as we eat?" Adam asked. "I would like to set out for Fairmile as soon as possible."

"Edward!" Bella recalled suddenly. "What are we to do?"

"We'll discuss that on the way home. Let us now hear what this man has to say. He may wish to be reassured that he will not be punished for running away."

But that was not what Walter was concerned about.

"I am worried," he told Adam when he had been sent for, and awkwardly seated himself near the table. "I would not have you think that the men I lived with were always like that. They rarely used torture in all the years I was there."

"You cannot be blamed for that," John reassured him.

"No, that is not what I am concerned about. For years we have all lived in comparative peace, but there have been

285

mutterings of late, and it is my suspicion that something is being planned. Nenemettanan was well respected, but his death could have been an accident, and there have been many other deaths that were no such thing. It has served as a spark for a discontent that has been growing for some time."

"We shall have to take stronger precautions, then," John said.

"I think it is more. It has been clear to the Indians that many people have been coming to the settlements during the last few years, and they are afraid. Also they do not like what they have heard of the plans to convert them by force. They think their children will be taken from them and imprisoned in the college."

"Do you know anything more definite?" Adam asked quietly.

"I cannot be certain. They have been preparing for something. They have been collecting together more trading goods than is normal, and there has been much toing and froing amongst the various tribes. I do not know what is planned, but I am uneasy."

"I must go to Jamestown tomorrow to

report what has happened to the Governor. You had best come with me and tell him all you can. He will wish to thank you for what you did in helping the captives."

They set off soon afterwards, and John decided to travel with them, to make his own report to the Governor and collect some stores that he needed from Jamestown. Alice was fretting in case Edward was waiting for them at Fairmile, but Adam tried to reassure her.

"He will not have waited for three days. My men told me yesterday that after his men had searched the plantation and all the houses on it they went back to Jamestown. Bella is safe for the moment — at least until we can make plans."

Bella, still weary from the long marches and loss of sleep, made no demur. Obviously Adam would have to send her back to England, but that would not be difficult to arrange. She was for the moment too exhausted to worry about Edward or even the impending, necessary parting from Adam.

She slept during the journey, and was considerably refreshed by the time they reached Fairmile. News of the attack and rescue had already reached the people there through the men who had made the journey earlier in the day, and Bella was congratulated many times on her escape. Smiling and laughing, she thanked them and eventually she and Adam reached the house where Meg had a meal waiting for them.

They were up early the following morning.

"There's a wretched savage waiting to see you," Meg announced disdainfully as she served breakfast. "He came a couple of hours ago, and he would not go whatever I said to him."

"Do you know him?" Adam asked quickly.

"I've seen him before, many a time. He says his name is Joshua."

"Joshua! Bring him straight in, Meg."

Joshua was grey with fatigue, Adam pulled a chair up to the fire and made him sit and eat some meat before he would listen to what he had to say.

"Are you hurt?" he demanded, when the colour began to return to the old man's wrinkled cheeks.

Joshua shook his head. "Just tired. I learned of it when I got back to my village yesterday, and have been coming by secret ways all night to warn you of the trouble."

"Trouble? With the villagers who took the captives?" Adam asked.

"With everyone. There is a plot to wipe out the white men, all of them. This morning, it is arranged, traders will come everywhere as if in peace, and then they will seize weapons and kill all they can. All along the river they plan this. I think the towns will be safe, they cannot attack them. Get to Jamestown! Go as fast as you can. Save yourselves."

Adam shook his head slowly.

"You do not believe me! It is true. They are coming!"

"I believe you, Joshua. You are my friend and we trust one another. The fact is there are not enough boats to take all the women and children, and I doubt if we would have time. We shall have to stay here. You must stay too. Bella, fetch everyone from the cottages into the house. It is the easiest building to defend and everyone can be together. I will collect everyone from the fields."

He was gone and Bella, her energy

revived in the face of this new threat, ran hastily outside and shepherded all the women and children from the cottages, telling them to bring whatever guns they had, and food and blankets. By the time Adam returned she had them established upstairs, with the weapons assembled on the parlour table.

Men were soon stationed at all the windows on both storeys, with guns loaded and waiting. If they could keep the Indians at a distance they would be safe. The Indians very rarely possessed guns, and Adam doubted if they would challenge such a well defended position. It was too late to send warnings to other plantations; he was thankful that John had not yet set out for Jamestown, and was still there to help take charge.

For some time there was an eerie silence, broken only by the soft voices of the watchers, or an occasional wail from one of the children, frustrated at being crowded together so strangely. Bella, helped by Alice and Meg and a couple more of the women, began to gather groups of children about them and told them stories of the early years in Virginia, or of life back in

England, of the magnificent Queen Bess who had ruled when they were children and had defied the might of Spain and her invincible Armada.

Outside the birds sang, the farm animals snuffled and grunted and rooted about for delicacies in places from which they were normally excluded. Rabbits grazed unhindered, and even a deer was seen speeding across the field which was being prepared for the young tobacco plants when they were transplanted from the sheltered beds in the forest.

After the excitement of the preparations the waiting became tedious. For a couple of hours nothing happened and then, quietly and apparently normally, a couple of Indians loaded down with game and rolled mats walked out of the forest. They hesitated slightly when they found the fields deserted, but then walked on along the track towards the houses. Adam permitted them to come within range of the guns and fired a warning shot above their heads. They stopped, turned as if to run, and then looked back, puzzled.

"Go in peace and you will be unharmed," Adam called to them from the nearest window. They dropped their trading goods and spread wide their arms as if to show that they were weaponless.

"How did they intend to kill us all?" Alice muttered.

"The plan was to take whatever weapons were to hand," Joshua, who was sitting beside the kitchen fire, explained. "White men would have been suspicious if they had carried clubs and bows, but there are always weapons to be seized when the opponent is unwary."

The men outside had not moved and Adam called to them again.

"We do not care to trade today. Go back."

As he spoke he saw that there were several more Indians emerging from the forest. Leaving John to guard that window he made a swift survey of the other windows, and saw that two other Indians were approaching from the direction of the river. Again he shot to warn them, and repeated his order. They vanished behind one of the cottages and reappeared some time later making towards their companions at the back. A hurried consultation took place, then the Indians fanned out, and using whatever cover they could began to creep towards the house.

"Shoot to wound, they must be driven off!" Adam passed the order round and his men swiftly obeyed, firing spasmodically when they had an opportunity of aiming at one of the attackers. Two Indians appeared to receive minor wounds, for they could be seen being helped away from the vicinity of the house and out of range, but it was some time before the rest, about ten of them, drew away.

After another hurried consultation they dispersed, and Bella cried out in anger when she saw two of them with hatchets chopping down the young fruit trees in which Adam took such pride. Others could be seen further away hacking at the young vines, and those animals which were penned in were soon squealing as the Indians cut their throats.

"Adam, we must attack them, drive them off," John protested.

"To what avail?" Adam replied, grim-faced. "We cannot protect the entire boundary; we would only put ourselves in worse danger. If we spread out they could attack us singly, while we could not prevent more than a tenth of what they are doing!"

"But it's the work of years they are ruining!"

"A fortune is not easily made," Adam replied, shrugging.

"Look!" shrieked one of the women suddenly.

Smoke was pouring from one of the cottages. As the watchers looked on helpless more smoke poured from several other cottages, and then the barn which still had last year's tobacco harvest in it, burst into flames.

It was as much as Adam, John, and the cooler-headed men could do to restrain some of the others from rushing out in vain attempts to save what represented their worldly wealth.

"It's useless!" Bella pleaded with one woman, struggling to get past as she screamed that her home was destroyed. "You'll be killed yourself. See, they are shooting arrows towards the house to prevent us from leaving it!"

Weeping hysterically, the woman was led away and Alice went with her, but another, more cunning, flung herself out of one of the downstairs windows, her sudden push unbalancing the man stationed there with his gun. She ran across to one of the further cottages, and Adam had to prevent her husband by force from following her.

"Stay! She'll come back when she realises how hopeless it is," Adam tried to reassure him, but at the moment a howl of triumph rose from the throats of the savages, and Adam saw them pounce on her.

They fired warning shots, but the Indians dragged her, screaming in terror, behind one of the cottages. Suddenly the screams were cut off short, and in a few moments they saw the woman, held between two of the Indians, being dragged out of the range of the guns. Then it was Adam who had to be restrained from rushing after them, and it took Daniel, John and three other men to prevent him from hurling himself out of the house.

Safely out of range the Indians threw the woman to the ground and, while the others danced around her and canted in horrible glee, took it in turns to rape her. When they had finished their vile sport, watched in helpless fury by Adam and the others, they used one of the hatchets to cut off her head, and after setting it up on a pole, finally disappeared amongst the trees of the forest.

Adam turned from the window and sank onto a stool, groaning.

"We should have gone after them!" he exclaimed.

"They could have held us off, there was nought you could do," Bella declared, kneeling beside him and putting her arms about his waist, hiding her own tear-stained face against his chest.

"It was her own fault, she was told not to go out," Alice said bracingly. "Master Adam, there's no point in repining, it was not your fault. But for you we'd most of us have been killed. Here, drink this."

She had poured out a generous helping of a potent drink which was brewed from maize, and Bella took some and persuaded Adam to drink it. He had recovered himself within minutes, and went round talking to the others, reassuring them that they would soon be able to rebuild the houses and replace the trees and the vines.

Some of the men ventured out when all the Indians had vanished, to see whether they could douse the fires. Only two cottages were completely destroyed, and three others had partially lost walls and roofs. When it was considered safe work was begun in transferring the undamaged possessions into other cottages or Adam's house, and after organising a strong patrol for the rest of the day and night, everyone sat down for a belated dinner.

That night it was Bella who sought to comfort Adam with her body, holding him in her arms as he berated himself for not having saved the woman and more of the plantation.

"You did all you could," she insisted. "Even her husband said so. You cannot be blamed for someone who disobeys you and acts foolishly."

Gradually she persuaded him to forget, and with a primitive, instictive skill, roused the fierce passion which always lay dormant in him. Kissing him, her lips soft and inviting, withdrawing so that he followed her to seek their comfort again, and then becoming fiery and demanding, she tantalised him into forgetfulness. Soon she was able to entice him, with murmured words and gentle caresses, into oblivion as he held her closely, forgetting all the anguish in her loving acceptance of him.

As he lay afterwards, spent and peacefully asleep, Bella knew that she felt more than gratitude towards him; more than mere physical delight in his love-making. No longer did she wish to think of their liaison as a means of achieving security for herself, of using a man as they had used her. She knew that it was something far deeper.

"Adam, I love you," she whispered in quiet, happy wonderment and fell asleep.

Early on the following morning they were awoken by a frantic hammering on the bedroom door. Adam was instantly awake and out of the bed with a robe about him while Bella was struggling into consciousness.

Adam opened the door and revealed Alice, her hair awry and a puzzled yet anxious expression on her face.

"What is it? More trouble?" Adam asked swiftly.

"Trouble? Aye, I've no doubt! You're needed. The men are bringing in some poor devil they found on the banks of the river. He's badly wounded, they think left for dead in a canoe which beached just above our landing stage."

"Bring him into the kitchen. Bella, find bandages and salves. I'll get a pallet."

Bella had pulled a robe over her nakedness and was finding strips of linen for bandages when she heard them bring the wounded man into the house. She ran down the stairs and into the kitchen. The man, naked apart from a badly torn shirt, was covered in blood oozing from a dozen different wounds. One leg lay crookedly, and a fearful hole in his side made her catch her breath in horror. Then she looked at Adam staring down at him with a blank look in his eyes, and she gazed herself into the injured man's face.

His eyes were open and he was conscious, although his mouth was twisted in pain. It brought into sharp relief the scar across his left cheek, a pale streak across darker, bruised and bloodstained skin. Bella stared down at him and then looked slowly at Adam.

"It is Edward Sutton," she whispered, holding out her hand to him blindly and stumbling slightly so that Adam put his hand about her to hold her. "Edward! What is he doing here?"

11

DURING the whole of that day, after Bella and Adam had tended Edward's wounds, washing and bandaging the cuts, and Daniel had set the broken leg between a pair of narrow boards, news and fugitives trickled in from the other plantations. The Indians had struck everywhere at the same time, and very few places had been prepared.

"They had traded with me the day before, and came back early, sitting down to breakfast with my family," one man recounted indignantly. "Then suddenly they took up the knives and threatened us. Some of us managed to hide or to escape to the forest, but they killed two of my servants and set fire to the house."

"We were out in the fields and they fell upon us," another said. "I was the only one to escape. They killed all the animals too!"

"I hid in the branches of a tree, and watched them as they cut the bodies to pieces and threw them in the river, then set fire to the crops," a young lad reported, still shaking with horror.

Meg provided them all with food, but they would stay only a short time.

"Jamestown was spared. It is the only safe place. They might come back!" they explained as they hurried nervously away.

Adam himself, after giving instructions about the patrol that was to be maintained, had gone with Ned and Walter to Jamestown. He had not referred to Edward, apart from instructing Daniel to do what he could for the man. When he returned late that night Edward was delirious, having been unable to tell anyone what had happened.

"It was a concerted attack all along the river," Adam reported. "A few people had warning and were able to reach Jamestown in safety."

"Will they return?"

"Possibly. These isolated habitations are impossible to defend properly. Those who have survived are to go to the towns. We have not yet heard from Henrico or the further plantations near the Falls, so we cannot estimate the losses there."

"We must all go to Jamestown?"

"Yes. I am sending the women early tomorrow, then the boats can come back for the men. Preparations are being made for our housing. It will be crowded, but the Governor considers that better than risking other attacks."

"But that will leave all the plantations and the stores for the Indians to take or destroy!"

"Until we have a better method of protecting ourselves, or can rely on peace with the Indians, it is safest. Some of the cattle are being driven into the town already. Will you be ready to leave at dawn?"

"You are sending me? Can I not stay with you?"

"You must attend to your husband."

"Edward! But Adam, I cannot! You could not force me to go back to him!"

"We must, Bella. In Jamestown we cannot defy the law as we have done here. With your husband injured they would never forgive you for remaining with me. Besides, who else is to care for him? I met one of his neighbours who said everyone else on his plantation had been killed. Don't be afraid. He's in no state now to harm you."

He was tired of her. There was no other explanation, Bella thought wearily. This was merely a convenient pretence to be rid of her. That night, for the first time since she had given herself to him, she turned away and pretended to be asleep when he came to bed. Adam shielded the candle flame and looked down at her thoughtfully. She had changed from the moment she had seen her husband. Shocked, as she would have been at the sight of any man with such ghastly wounds, she had subtly withdrawn. What did she feel for Edward Sutton? Could she, despite what she had told him, still have any soft feelings for him? The very fact that she had now turned her back indicated some reluctance or embarrassment at remaining in Adam's bed while her husband lay in another room in the same house.

If that were so he could not bring himself to make love to her now, on what might be the last opportunity for them. Edward was severely injured but Daniel reported that he was not likely to die. Many men had recovered from much worse wounds. In Jamestown Bella could not be with him, but she would be safe for the moment with her husband where there were many people to whom she could turn for help. Edward would not be in a position to illtreat her as he had done before. When he recovered Adam could see him and make his own threats known, and he thought Edward would pay heed to them. If Edward died it would be another matter.

Adam could not, however, permit himself to dwell upon the possibility of his own gain through another man's death. If it came that was fate, but he must not begin to wish for it since that would be as bad as trying to bring it about. He lay beside Bella, resisting the urge to taste her sweetness just once more, and rose quietly the next morning before she was awake.

Edward, who seemed to be rather better, was sent off in one of the first boats and Bella, cool and unsmiling, prepared to accompany him. On the journey she eased his discomforts as well as she could, and when they arrived in Jamestown followed the men who carried his improvised stretcher towards a small, one-roomed house that had been obtained for them by Adam the day before. Alice and Toby soon joined them.

"Some of Mr Tarrant's people are in the next house," Alice informed Bella. "They will give help whenever we need it."

For several days all was confusion, both in Jamestown and in Bella's emotions. The people who had escaped the massacre on the settlements along the river poured into Jamestown with their news. Thomas Wray had been killed near the Falls, and so had the Bidwells who had been living near the ironworks. Mary Bolton's husband had died on his plantation. Mary herself had been visiting friends and had thus escaped. Bella soon saw her in Jamestown, ostensibly mourning her husband but gleeful, Bella was sure, that as a widow there was a real chance of capturing Adam's affection. Some of John Porlock's men had escaped, and he and Adam were fully occupied in travelling up and down the river searching for survivors who might be hiding in the forests or the ruins of houses. A further gruesome task was that of burying the dead and often mutilated bodes they found.

When the final count was made almost three hundred and fifty people had died, most of them horribly. George Thorpe and a dozen others on the Berkeley Hundred had been killed, and the ironworks had been destroyed. Once the numbness of the shock was over the colonists began to talk of outright war with the Indians, and the need to subdue them if the settlers were ever to live at peace in Virginia.

The cattle and stores were brought into Jamestown and half a dozen other main settlements, and gradually some sort of order prevailed. During this time Edward hovered on the brink of death. The less serious wounds had begun to heal but he was still delirious for much of the time, and when rational he feebly cursed Bella.

"I've had no luck since I set eyes on you!" was his constant cry. "What good have you brought me?"

"Some land and money," Bella once retorted, irritated beyond endurance at his implacable hatred, and the necessity which bound her to him.

"And what use are they now? My fields will be forest again before I can tend them."

Two weeks after the disaster Edward seemed to improve, and fretted at his inability to do more than pull himself from the pallet where he lay to a stool beside the fire. Occasionally friends came to visit him, staring curiously at Bella before settling down to play cards and dice with him.

Daniel came every day to help tend Edward's wounds, and it was mainly from him that Bella heard of Adam's doings. Adam had called once the day after they had been installed at the house, and thereafter carefully kept away. Alice frequently went to visit Meg and some of her other cronies, but Bella nursed her hurt and bewilderment in solitude, driven out of the house and into the town only when Edward's friends were with him and their admiring looks and bold comments could no longer be borne.

One morning in the middle of April, Alice came running back to the house only a few minutes after she had taken Toby with her to visit Meg.

"What is it? Toby?" Bella demanded.

"He's fine, Miss Bella, he's gone with the older children to the quay. There's a ship in from London."

Infected by her excitement, Bella ran

with Alice to watch the ship sail the last
few hundred yards towards Jamestown and
anchor in the deep water which came right
up to the walls of the town. For a while
there was pandemonium as new settlers
disembarked, thankful to have reached
land safely after a journey of eighteen
weeks. The established settlers eagerly
described the terrors of the massacre, and
amidst it all the sailors tried to unload the
cargo. In the middle of the chaos Adam
suddenly appeared at Bella's side.

"How go things with you?" he asked
quietly, and she turned to look up at him,
wildly attempting to mask her welcoming
smile with a cool nonchalance.

"I am well," she replied. "I hear that you
have been very much occupied of late?"

"Yes, there has been a great deal to do."

"I heard about Thomas. I am sorry," she
said, feeling very inadequate.

"We lost many good men," he replied
soberly. "But John is to be wed, had you
heard?"

"No, but I am pleased. He was so kind.
Who is she?"

"Rachael Marsh, who was on the same
boat as he was, with her parents. They

were both killed and she is now alone, so John hopes to wed her immediately so as to have the right to take care of her. She will be a good wife for him."

"Yes, she seemed very sensible," Bella replied, recalling a quiet, but very self-possessed young woman who had been at some of Adam's parties.

"How is your husband?" Adam asked after a pause.

"He seems better. Thank you for sending Daniel to help, he has been a great support to me."

Adam smiled bleakly. "Pray ask him for anything you need. Have you made any plans yet?"

"What sort of plans?" she asked bitterly. "Edward will be unfit to work his plantation for many weeks yet, even if it were safe to return there. I would like best of all to get on that ship and go back to England."

"Then why do you not do so?" he asked coolly.

Bella bit her lip and turned away. He did not want her! She was undoubtedly a great embarrassment to him. But she could not face a future with Edward, and only remained with him now because of the unsettled state of the colony and the fact that there was nothing else to be done while he was ill.

"I think I might. Would you give me a character?" she asked, her voice brittle. "Do you think I could occupy the same sort of position in London as I did with you? I cannot think what other future there would be for me now."

"Naturally I will arrange for you to have an allowance," he answered abruptly. "It can ge paid through my family in London. I will put pressure on your husband to send you money too."

"I neither want nor need your money," Bella said furiously, and turned away, hastening back towards the house where Edward was greatly excited and demanding to be told all about the ship's arrival.

On the following day a letter from the ship was brought for Edward, and he read it avidly, then lay back thoughtfully watching Bella as she moved about the house preparing dinner.

"Was it good news?" she asked at last, made uncomfortable by his gaze.

"Of a sort," he replied, and suddenly grinned. "Where's that brat?"

"Toby? He went with Alice. Why?"

"He's almost three, is he not? A sturdy lad."

Bella looked at him curiously, but he relapsed into silence. He had never before shown any interest in Toby, and she could not understand why he should now think of the little boy.

"Is there any news from England?" she asked to break the uncomfortable silence.

"Not a great deal. The war in Europe continues, but it is all much the same. I've a mind to try my fortune there. I could be a good soldier once this leg is healed. Help me to the stool now."

She stared at him, aghast, then moved to take his arm as he rose.

"You mean to return to England?"

"Why not? There is nothing for either of us here, is there?" he asked, watching her closely. Bella recovered herself.

"I could not care," she shrugged. "Here, sit down."

"I'll make you, damn you!" he suddenly shouted, and lurched towards her instead of dropping to the stool which was near the fire.

"Take heed!" Bella cried, and instinctively

moved to catch him as he swayed precariously. He almost fell, and then grasped at her arms.

"Aha, my beauty, you'll not evade me for ever!" he cried in sudden triumph as he pulled her to him.

He was surprisingly strong despite his recent wounds, and Bella had to struggle furiously to evade his grasp, for he clung tenaciously to her. As she pulled away to escape him he lost his balance, and although he fell to the floor with a thud he retained his hold on her and they went down together.

He attempted to roll on top of her, tearing at her skirts in a frenzy of lust, but she held him off. She was unable to wriggle free of his grasp, for he held one arm as if in a vice and by exerting all his strength dragged her bodice away from her breasts. He struggled to clutch them, but Bella shrank away and manged to slither from him, fending him off as he puffed after her.

The fight was fierce but short, for Edward's strength could not last, and Bella was soon able to break away from his hold. She stood up, looking at him as he lay spent, groaning at the pain, and with trembling fingers tied her laces and straightened out her bodice.

"You're no better than a beast!" she told him disgustedly, and went towards the door.

"Bella, you're not leaving me!" he cried out in sudden alarm. She turned back, surveying him in contempt.

"So you have another use for me, do you?" she asked sharply, and ignored his cries as she went out.

She made her way slowly to the wharf, hoping that the cool air would calm her and help her to think. It was clear now that she had to get away from Edward. The utter revulsion she had felt when his hands had pawed at her only confirmed what she already knew: never again could she submit to him. Or to any other man, a small persistent voice told her, but she tried to ignore it, for, without Adam, what else was open to her apart from becoming the plaything of another man? Not Edward, never Edward Sutton! Some other man might be bearable, but what he might be like she could not envisage. In time, she tried to convince herself, she might even forget Adam Tarrant. After all, less than a year ago she had not even been aware of his existence.

Was Edward serious when he had suggested returning to England? The very idea caused her to look about her in panic. She wanted to return herself only as a means of escaping him. If only he would go and leave her here with Adam. She pushed the wayward thought aside. She would still be married to Edward wherever he was, and Adam had shown that he no longer wanted her.

The ship which had arrived the previous day was still being unloaded, and Bella stood on the wharf, watching it but for a long time not aware of the activity. Then, because there was nothing else she could do, and no-one (for she refused to consider Adam) to whom she could go, she slowly wended her way home.

Inside it was getting dark and she was blinded for a moment. She almost fell as she moved to the table to search for a candle. As she regained her balance and took another step her foot encountered something soft and warm, and Bella became frightened.

"Edward!" she exclaimed, but there was no reply. Hastily she lit the candle, and then drew back in horror. Edward lay sprawled across the floor, his arm outstretched towards the door, and beneath him, oozing from the wound in his side, was a sticky pool of blood.

He was still breathing but she dared not move him. Anxiously she ran for Daniel and was fortunate enough to find him immediately. He returned with her at once and competently heaved Edward onto the pallet, stripped his clothes from him, and rebandaged the wound. He did not ask her how it happened and Bella was too conscious-stricken to offer any explanations.

"He'll do, Mistress Bella. I'll send Alice in now. You look as though you could do with a drink."

Bella thanked him distractedly, and sat beside the fire, oblivious of Alice when she came in and bustled about getting a meal. Alice was consumed with curiosity but took one look at Bella's face and worked in silence. At last she persuaded Bella to retire to the loft where they slept as soon as she had eaten.

315

During the night Edward lapsed into delirium, and it was clear the next day that his exertions had retarded his recovery. He tossed and raved and Bella, full of remorse for deserting him, devoted herself to his care. He was far from grateful and spent his lucid hours berating her for disregarding his wishes.

"But it'll not last once I'm recovered!" he stormed at her. "We'll leave this God-forsaken place and in England I can keep you in your place! There's no reason for staying where life is hard when we could live at ease and in comfort."

"How can you do that in England any more than you can here?" she asked, but he smiled and shook his head.

That night he lapsed once more into delirium. Bella sat with him and listened to his ramblings. They seemed to refer to the cards he so much enjoyed playing. After a while he slept and Bella rested her head on her arms. She was woken by a sharp laugh, and when she looked across at Edward his eyes were open, gleaming in the flickering light from the low fire she kept in all the time.

"They thought they'd beaten me!" he

was saying. "Accusing me of cozening him! Ha! He wasn't worth the trouble, but I held such damned bad cards! And as for you, Henry Martin, you'll regret fobbing me off with so small a share! You getting all of Clifford Manor! I'd have been content with half and now I'll get the lot!"

"Edward, what are you saying? What was that about Clifford Manor?" Bella demanded, rising and standing beside him.

He ignored her, and she realised that he was still in a state of confusion and did not know she was there.

"Henry Clifford, indeed! What a jest! But you'll be sorry!"

He rambled on for some time, and then suddenly closed his eyes and slept. Bella sat and puzzled over his words. She had known that Edward had been forced to leave England in a hurry immediately after their marriage, and from what he had now unwittingly revealed it could have been because of an accusation of cheating at cards. It was clear from the few remarks his friends had made in the past few days that he gambled often. How was it, then, that he now felt safe in returning to England? And how was her brother Henry involved?

She suddenly recalled the letter he had received and, after a brief struggle with her conscience, in which she concluded that she had herself been forced into this marriage and had a right to know the truth, began to search for it. There were few enough hiding places in the house, and fewer still that Edward could reach. She recalled that he had been lying on the pallet when he had received the letter, and it had not been on him after he had injured himself again. She soon discovered the single sheet of paper pushed into a gap where the primitive mud plaster of the wall had dried and parted from one of the wooden posts of the frame, just behind Edward's head.

The only part of the letter which could have had any bearing on Edward's flight from England, and present freedom to return, was a reference to Mr Carter. 'Old man Carter died of apoplexy last month, you'll be interested to learn. His wife fell into a decline when her precious Benjamin fell into the Thames, and has been dead these six months. He'd have blamed you if you had still been in Kent, but was forced to admit the impossibility, much to his chagrin. It was rumoured that he meant to wed a girl of sixteen to provide a much-desired heir — though dear Benjamin had lost most of it at the tables. But it was not to be, and the King is the richer.'

If the man Carter had been the one Edward feared, and he, and apparently all his family, were dead, that would explain why Edward could plan to return to England. But why had he railed against her half-brother? It sounded as though Henry had in some way cheated him, but how?

When Alice appeared and sent her to rest for a few hours, Bella gave up trying to resolve the puzzle, but later that day she told Alice what she had discovered.

"You say he called him Henry Martin? Why?"

"He called him both Martin and Clifford, he was raving; he did not know what he said."

"Could Henry have duped him? How can he talk of getting more from Henry unless he has some way of forcing him? What does he know to Henry's disadvantage?"

Bella shook her head. "I could believe much of Henry! If we are right and Edward cheated at his gaming, Henry could have known it. Could Henry have done the same?"

"It's possible, he frequented taverns all the time."

Before they had discovered a way of forcing Edward to tell them the truth, he grew much worse. Daniel shook his head doubtfully and said that the reopened wound in Edward's side was festering. Although she knew that he had brought it on himself by trying to attack her, Bella blamed herself for having left him lying on the floor. It was pointless to remember that she had thought him capable of moving back to his pallet, she had not made sure of it. She wore herself out caring for him, and Adam, hearing of her constant attention to her husband, was torn with jealousy he had never before experienced.

Bella avoided him. Daniel reported that she accepted the aid he could give, and rejected neither his visits nor the food he took, but never spoke of Adam. Has she forgiven the brute of a husband, he wondered, frantic at the thought? Had she, as he had half suspected all the time, merely been using him in her quarrel with Edward? Or had she resented living in Jamestown under false pretences? Surely she could not expect him to defy the conventions of the small community by taking her away from her husband when he lay seriously wounded. She must understand that when the present crisis was over they could return to Fairmile and all would be as before. He never met her to suggest this. She rarely left the cottage, and he would not intrude on her there.

Her remarks about wishing to return to England seemed to imply that she wanted neither him nor her husband, and although there was some consolation for Adam in this suggestion that she did not love Edward, it seemed that she did not love him either. Whether she remained with Edward or went to England, he had lost her.

Mary Bolton, watching anxiously, knew that he did not see Bella. She hinted at her own readiness to console him, but Adam was more brusque with her than ever before. He knew that she would be the last woman to help him forget. But someone else might, someone new who had never previously been compared with his lost love.

His opportunity came with a red-haired beauty who had arrived on the latest ship. She was encouraging, but cautious, seeking promises before submitting to him. The gossips of Jamestown were delighted and made certain that Bella heard the rumours.

She gritted her teeth and tried to wish him happiness, while her heart cried out in pain. She had no right to care, he had cast her off, and she knew his reasons were sensible, but had he forgotten so soon? They had never spoken words of love, but he had been both passionate and tender. Had even that meant so little to him that he could brazenly flaunt his new mistress before her? Men, she decided yet again, were faithless, heartless creatures whose baser needs governed them to the exclusion of all else.

One night, soon after dusk, when Alice had retired for a few hours until she relieved Bella of the task of watching over Edward, he woke from a restless sleep and lay looking at Bella who was sitting hunched up on a stool by the fire.

"Bella," he said softly, and she turned in some surprise. Usually, when he was rational he spoke to her sharply or cursed her unremittingly. "Bella, please come here."

"What is it?" she asked, moving to stand beside him.

"I'm dying," he said, calmly but with bitterness. "I'll never see that lying brother of yours squirm. You must do it for Toby!"

"Toby? What do you mean? How can he lie? He's still a child."

"I don't mean Toby. Henry Martin. What he said was false."

He stopped and closed his eyes. At that moment a gentle tap came on the door and Daniel, who never stood on ceremony, entered.

"How is he?" he asked.

"Talking strangely," Bella whispered. "He says he is dying."

Daniel nodded and went to look down at Edward. Edward's eyes opened and Daniel knelt beside him, offering him a drink of the tisane he often used to dull the pain.

Edward began to speak again, slowly, his speech slurred.

"He forged the papers. He wanted Clifford Manor and the rest of Toby's inheritance. His mother was never married to your father. She could not have been, she was already wed. She died some years ago, but he still lives."

Bella stared at him in amazement. "You knew this all the time?" she asked in horror. "It can't be true!"

"It is, that is why he wanted you out of England. His mother left her husband and came back to her village. That was when she met your father and Henry was born. Afterwards, because your father lost interest in her, she went to London and found another protector. Henry told me she died ten years ago. But her husband lives. He will tell you the truth. He lives in Greenwich. His name is Flowers, Peter Flowers. Don't let Henry steal it. He cheated me, because I dared not wait, and he took advantage. Go to England with Toby. I was going to. Henry must not win."

"I have no money to get to England!" Bella exclaimed, accepting the amazing

324

truth of what Edward said, and realising that it explained many things.

"My gold, I buried it. Before the Indians came. Under the landing stage. I was returning to the house, but I was too late. They saw me and gave chase. They caught me before I reached the canoe, and attacked me. Then they threw me in it. Henry was there. He killed Toby. With an arrow. He told them to kill me. He came after me with a hatchet. He's afraid of me. I won't tell them. It's mine."

"He's rambling again," Daniel said quietly, and persuaded Edward to drink some more, which quieted him so that soon he slept.

Daniel looked up at Bella who was staring past him dazedly.

"Do you think he knew what he said earlier?" he asked. "About your brother and the gold?"

"Why should he lie? He thinks he is dying. And he wanted revenge on Henry. I want justice! Daniel, will you help me? I must go to England to claim what is Toby's by right, and with that gold I can pay for our passages. When does the ship leave?"

"The day after tomorrow, if all is loaded. Are you sure you want to go, Mistress Bella?"

Bella closed her eyes for an anguished moment. "I must, Daniel, for Toby's sake. He is our father's heir, and has been cheated by Henry. This man Flowers must be old, he might die. Daniel, I must not lose time. I cannot afford to waste time! Will you stay here with Edward while I go and beg the loan of one of Adam's canoes?"

"Mistress Bella!" Daniel exclaimed in sudden alarm, but she shook her head at him and whisked out to run the few yards towards the house where Adam now lived.

Daniel cast a harassed look at Edward and decided that he was in no danger. He hurried after Bella and was in time to see her knock on Adam's door. Without waiting for him to answer she opened it and walked in.

The room was softly lit with candles and the glow from the fire. A small table was drawn up near the fire, for the April nights were still cool. Adam was standing beside it, leaning forward as he poured wine into a goblet, and the red-head, the bodice of her gown unlaced and pulled off her shoulders, held Adam's free hand as it rested on her breast. She had her head tilted backward and was laughing up into his face. In the split second before he turned to see what the interruption was, Bella saw him smiling down at her.

For a moment the room swayed before Bella and she grasped at the doorpost, then with a moan of anguish she turned and fled, evading Daniel's outstretched hands as she ran back to her own house, slammed the door and bolted it. Then she cast herself down before the fire and wept uncontrollably.

Gradually her senses returned. What right had she to expect that Adam would not pay attentions to other women, she demanded fiercely of herself. Why should she care that he made love to other women? At least it was not Mary Bolton.

Eventually she returned to the problem of what Edward had disclosed. It was out of the question to ask Adam to help her now, and as soon as it was light she went to find John Porlock. He willingly agreed to take her upriver to Edward's plantation, and they had no difficulty in finding the small chest from which, once before, Bella had taken some gold.

Back in Jamestown John sought out the captain of the ship and booked a cabin for Bella. She returned home to find Alice had been packing feverishly all day, delighted at the unexpected events, but apprehensive at the thought of another long and uncomfortable voyage. Recalling their difficulties on the first one, she had also been making arrangements for food and wine and a crate of hens to be taken aboard. Daniel had promised to care for Edward, although he predicted that he was too weak to live more than a few days.

As Bella hastily packed the last of her clothes, for they were to go on board that evening, ready to sail on the tide, the door opened. It was Adam.

"Bella, I must speak with you."

She stared at him, her heart suddenly racing. She had both longed for and dreaded the possibility of seeing him again, and was weakly refusing to prepare what she would say. Now she shook her head slightly.

Adam looked round. The boxes stood

ready. Edward, sleeping but tossing restlessly, lay in one corner, and Alice was trying to persuade an excited Toby to eat some supper.

"Come outside for a moment," he said, and Bella moved towards him as if in a dream. He took her arm and guided her outside.

"Must you go?" Adam asked quietly. "Daniel told me what Edward said. Do you believe him?"

Bella nodded. "It must be true."

"Daniel says he is dying. Would you not wish to wait?"

"I must lose no further time. This man might be dead, then there would be no proof."

He nodded, understanding. After what she had seen the previous night he did not expect that he could persuade her to stay with him in Virginia, even with the prospect of marriage to him once Edward was dead. Even had it been possible to propose to her in the circumstances he knew that she would consider it her duty to fight for Toby's inheritance.

"Shall I come with you?"

Bella looked at him in surprise. "There

is no cause for you to feel in any way responsible for me," she managed to reply with tolerable composure. "I have learned a great deal this past year. Alice has made suitable preparations this time, and we can provide for ourselves on this voyage far better than on the previous occasion."

"That was not what I meant," he began, but Bella, afraid that if he asked her again she would succumb to the intense desire to feel his arms about her once more, broke in hastily.

"I would prefer to say farewell now. I have no claim on you, and you are needed here to work for the reconstruction of the colony. John was explaining to me how much there is to do, how few settlers there are who have been here for very long, and know the Indians."

"Have you a place to stay?" he asked, certain now that she had never felt more for him than gratitude, and thinking that her present coolness was a desire not to be more beholden to him.

"John has given me a letter to his sister and assures me that I will be welcome there. Now, I still have much to do, and I beg that you will excuse me. I will leave money with Daniel to pay for anything that Edward might need. Thank you for all you have done for us."

She turned and left him. Her eyes were red with weeping and so full of tears when they sailed from Jamestown early on the following day she did not see Adam standing at the gate of the town to take his last longing farewell of her.

12

THE voyage took three months. It was far less eventful than the previous one, and even Alice, soon becoming used to the motion of the ship, felt little discomfort. There were only a dozen or so passengers, those who had decided to abandon Virginia after the Indian massacre, and this time Bella had few problems with amorous advances.

This might have been due to the fact that she rarely emerged from her cabin, coming on deck only when she could no longer endure Alice bullying her to take the air. She spent many hours making new clothes for Toby, who was growing apace and had needed few in the free and easy life of the plantation. Much of the time when she was supposed to be engaged in stitching, however, her needle was still while her thoughts were busy.

The past year, from her father's death and her hated forced marriage, then her submission to Adam, eventual acceptance of her love for him, and final disillusionment, seemed a dream. Yet in other ways it was still vivid. Bella could still feel the tingling of her flesh where his hands had caressed her, and recall the heady delights of his kisses. Every night she longed for his hard, supple body against hers, and was desolate in the knowledge that she would never again experience the ecstasy of lying in his arms.

Somehow the voyage was endured, and when they disembarked they went straight to Lady Rowe, John's sister, who welcomed Bella eagerly as soon as she heard that Bella had news of her brother. Elizabeth Rowe was some years older than John, already had several children, and absorbed Bella and Toby into her own family with calm friendliness and efficiency. Alice was more than content to be back in a comfortable, well-run English mansion, and spent her time happily in the nursery where Toby was already fast friends with the two youngest Rowe boys. Sir Francis Rowe had many friends at Court, and when he heard Bella's story immediately set about presenting her petition to Chancery.

Their family and acquaintances regarded

Bella with a great deal of awe when they discovered that she had actually been across the ocean to Virginia and been captured by the savages there. A few had friends or relatives who had emigrated, and she was able to give news of them. Too many, she thought, had known Adam, and she was for ever being asked about him. She was certain that no-one knew of her relationship with him, for the enquiries were all innocent of any innuendo, but the constant reminders kept raw the pain of her loss.

She frowned therefore when two of Adam's former friends were announced one afternoon, and would have left the room if there had been time. They came in, however, and greeted lady Rowe solemnly.

"I've sad news," the husband reported, "just brought from Bristol. Cawston is dead of an ague. He sickened only three days before, poor man."

Elizabeth regarded him closely. "Poor man," she echoed. "He was to have been married in October, I think?"

"Yes, indeed. Poor young lady."

"I wonder how this will affect Adam?" Elizabeth mused, turning to Bella, who was staring at their informant incredulously.

"He'll come home. Already they're saying that the King will forgive him that stupid quarrel if he weds my Lady Jane," the wife said.

"She is a ward of the King's, is she not?"

"Yes, and very wealthy. He wants the title for her, and since Roderick is dead, poor fellow, he must look to Adam. There was no entanglement in Virginia, was there, Mistress Sutton?" he added suddenly, turning enquiringly to Bella.

"He was — was not promised to anyone that I knew of," she stammered.

Elizabeth laughed. "Not Adam! I'll warrant there were plenty of women who would have taken him, marriage or no, but he's plenty of wild oats to sow yet. I vow he'll be none too pleased at having Lady Jane thrust upon him."

"Not pleased at a fortune? My dear Lady Rowe! Even Adam could not refuse, rich though his brother was, and now Adam himself of course. Particularly when it would mean freedom to return to a civilised life here. And the chit is lovely, they say. Black hair and creamy skin and a tall shapely figure all the men admire. Even Philip here licks his lips when he sees her."

Her husband protested, but she laughed at him and shook her head.

"Adam will be back in England and the King's favour as soon as letters can be sent. He'll not cavil at marrying a lovely fortune to attain it. Besides, he must provide an heir now, and it's about time he set about it."

Desperately though she longed to see Adam again, Bella prayed that she would have been able to settle Toby's affairs and be back at their home in Kent before Adam reappeared in London. She missed him as deeply as ever; time had not soothed the agony of their parting, and no good could come of another meeting.

It was a month since she had arrived in England, and Bella had been with Sir Francis to see some of the lawyers handling the case one afternoon. The business took longer than they had expected and when they returned home it was to discover the house in an uproar.

Alice came running down the stairs as Bella came through the door, and flung herself at Bella's feet.

"Miss Bella, forgive me! I left him for just a moment, I swear that was all. I thought he was safe. I never dreamed aught could harm him, for he was with the other children."

Bella paled. "Toby?" she gasped. "What has happened to him? You mean Toby, do you not?"

Alice nodded, suddenly overcome, and Sir Francis moved quickly forward as if he feared Bella was about to swoon. His wife, who had been following Alice down the stairs, came forward and took Bella's cold hands in hers.

"Mistress Sutton, it may be some mistake. He was taken from the garden this afternoon while he was playing with the other children. Pray come and sit down, and we will tell you all we know."

She led Bella to a chair and gently forced her to be seated.

"I must search for him," Bella protested, but Elizabeth was firm.

"Do you imagine we have not had all the servants and neighbours searching since it was discovered? You can do nothing. Let me tell you what happened."

Bella nodded, and with Alice and one of her own maids standing by occasionally confirming what she said, Elizabeth told Bella all they knew.

"Toby was with three of my children, and James from the next house. They were all in the garden, where as you know there are high walls and the gate is always fastened. They could not open it and get out themselves. James fell and cut his leg, and so Alice brought him into the house to attend to it."

"But I did not stay, Miss Bella. Joan here took James from me and I went straight back."

"Aye!" Joan corroborated. "It were a nasty cut, but not deep, and he'll come to no harm."

"When Alice returned to the garden," Elizabeth continued, cutting in firmly, "Toby was not visible. She thought he had hidden and called to him, but then the other children told her that a man had climbed over the wall from the lane at the back and taken Toby out through the gate, which he had unfastened. They wanted to follow, for Toby was crying and struggling, but the man shook his fist at them and told them that a lion had escaped from the Tower and would gobble them up if they put their noses outside."

"What was he like? Who was he? What did he want?" Bella demanded urgently.

"We cannot be certain. At first the children said he was tall and dark, but now they are so frightened that they say all manner of things, agreeing with whatever we ask them. Did anyone know that you were here? Anyone who wished harm to your brother?"

Bella shook her head. "The only person he is a menace to is Henry Martin, but I do not see how he could have discovered that we were here."

"He is aware that the claim is being examined, for he had been questioned," Sir Francis said quietly. "He might have seen Mistress Sutton in the City and followed her here."

"That is possible, I suppose," his wife agreed, "although Bella has been out very little. There is another possibility, though, and that is that Toby was taken in mistake for one of our children, by someone who hoped to hold him for ransom. When they discover their mistake they will probably return him."

It was said to comfort, but Bella knew that any desperate man who had taken the wrong child by mistake would be more likely to abandon him, if not kill him, to rid himself of evidence. It must have been Henry. Would he harm Toby? Throughout a sleepless night Bella thought of all the terrible possibilities. Henry might kill Toby, but that would not gain him the inheritance even if he escaped from a charge of murder. Yet he would kill Toby rather than abandon him, or place him in a foundlings' home, for by now Toby knew his name, talked a great deal, and could reveal something of the people he had been with. Perhaps Henry wanted to bargain with her, Bella suddenly thought, and finally dropped into an exhausted doze on this faint hope.

It seemed more than a hope the following morning, however. As Bella listlessly tried to eat a portion of mutton pie, an excited maid ran into the room with a crumpled sheet of paper clasped in her hand. She thrust it towards her master.

"It were found in the garden, sir, old

Reuben found it beneath the apple tree, wrapped round a stick. He says it must have been thrown over the wall for it's near the gate!"

Sir Francis was anxiously reading what was written on the paper. He looked up and smiled at Bella.

"From this I think Toby is unharmed, but we must proceed carefully. Whoever it is wishes you to negotiate for the safe release of the child. A further message will come, it says."

He showed the paper to Bella and it was exactly as he had said. She could tell nothing from the writing, and there was no hint of who had sent the letter, but it gave hope and she smiled tremulously at the maid.

That day and another night passed with no further news. Sir Francis had arranged for a watch to be kept on the lane behind his house, and Bella wondered if Henry, for she was certain it was Henry, had been frightened away be seeing the watcher.

"Will he be angry, and harm Toby for revenge?" she asked fearfully.

"I doubt it, my dear. My man watched from the coach house opposite, from a small window there, and could not have been seen. No, it is more likely that your half-brother, if he is intelligent, would expect us to keep some sort of watch, and he will devise another way of getting in touch with us. And he will not harm Toby, for to do so would destroy any hope he has of making a deal with you."

Bella permitted herself to be comforted, and even agreed to accompany Sir Francis on another visit to the lawyers to discuss the latest developments with them. As they left the Temple chambers an elderly clerk hurried after them.

"Sir Francis, pray wait. My master saw you leaving, and he wished to consult you about the sale of your house in Norwich. He knows of someone who might purchase it."

"Who is your master?" Sir Francis asked suspiciously, but the clerk named a well-respected lawyer known personally to him, and he turned apologetically to Bella.

"It should not take long, my dear. Do you object to waiting? Or would you prefer for me to escort you home first? It is not far."

"The young lady can wait in a private

room," the clerk offered, and Bella, who was already full of gratitude to Sir Francis for the time he had spent on Toby's concerns, would not hear of any delay.

"I will wait, and indeed you must not hurry on my account," she assured him. The clerk, with an obsequious smile, led her into a small room on the ground floor and nodded approvingly.

"You will not be disturbed," he said. "This way, Sir Francis."

Bella sat down, but the door had scarcely closed behind the clerk when a small door almost invisible in the panelling near the fireplace opened, and a small man slipped silently through.

"Who are you?" Bella demanded, rising to her feet.

"Hush, Mistress Sutton. Do you wish to see Toby alive again?"

"Of course I do! What have you to do with him? Where is he?"

"You must come with me and I will take you to him. This way, we can get out of the house at the back."

"No, I must wait for Sir Francis!"

"If you do, I am instructed to tell you that by nightfall your brother will be another of the bodies that float in the river. You will not be harmed if you are sensible, my dear. But my master does not want Sir Francis foiling him of his reward, does he?"

Bella knew that she would be sensible to refuse, but if she did, and Toby were harmed she could never forgive herself. She had to take whatever risk there was to herself. She nodded, and the man turned, led her through the doorway and along a narrow passage. At the end he let them out of an insignificant doorway and went through Fountain Court and Garden Court until they came to the gate opening onto the river bank where a boat awaited them by the landing stage. She was carried swiftly across the river to the Southwark side where horses were waiting them. The small man helped her to mount and clambered onto his own horse.

Bella was so certain they were going back to her old home in Kent that she did not bother to ask where he was taking her until, after several miles, she realised that instead of following the road nearest the river shore they had turned southwards into the higher folds of the hills.

"Where are we going?" she asked sharply then, but her companion, who had said nothing to her since they had left the room in the Temple, shrugged and did not answer.

They travelled for several miles along narrow rutted lanes, and eventually turned into what was little more than a cart track leading into a wood. At the end of it was a clearing beyond which the ground fell sharply towards a widening valley through which a river could be seen winding its silvery way. A farmhouse, wooden-framed, with lath and plaster walls, sturdy but neglected, stood at the edge of the clearing, it's jetted upper storeys overlooking the valley.

"Here we are," the small man said, and Bella looked about her nervously. It was an isolated spot, no other houses in sight apart from those scattered over the valley. This house looked neglected, weeds smothering what had once been a herb garden, and no dogs or fowls inhabiting the clearing or the small stable to one side. She permitted the man to help her down and found that she was stiff from the unaccustomed exercise.

The man remounted and rode back along

the track, leading Bella's horse. Bella, aware of the isolation of the spot, shivered. She began to walk hesitantly towards the door of the house, set in the centre of the long side facing her, and as she drew nearer it slowly opened. The hall inside was dark, and a shadow was cast across the doorway by a large oak tree, so Bella glimpsed only the outline of a man standing there. Then there was a squeal of joy and Toby ran out of the house at Bella.

"Bella! You've come! You've come!" he cried excitedly, and then burst into tears.

Bella knelt to gather him into her arms, and gasped with relief to find that he was unhurt. She did not look up until a scornful laugh came from the man in the doorway.

"Very touching, my dear. But do come inside."

Incredulously Bella looked at him. He had moved out of the shadow and was standing a few feet away from her. She rose slowly to her feet, holding Toby's hand so tightly that he cried out to her not to hurt him.

"Edward!" she breathed. "How did you come to be in England?"

"The same way as you, my dear wife, by ship. How else?"

"You are recovered," she said slowly.

"Did you hope that I should die?" he asked mockingly. "I am no weakling, as you will learn."

"You thought you were about to die," Bella retorted, stung into a response. "I care nought!"

"A pity for you that you did not wait to make certain that I did," he sneered. "I began to improve as soon as you had left. I got rid of that fool Fletcher, and my own friends cared for me. I wonder why yours did not poison me while they had the opportunity? Was it on the instructions of Mr Adam Tarrant? Did they not want you free to plague him?"

"No-one did aught but good for you," Bella said coldly. "It is your good fortune that you recovered. But enough of that. What do you want? Why have you followed us?"

"Come in," he repeated. "We can discuss it in comfort. I even have a meal prepared for you."

He turned and led the way in. Bella noticed that he limped slightly, but it did not appear to inconvenience him. She followed slowly into the large hall and found it almost bare of furniture, although the beaten earth floor had a thick covering of old dried rushes. Edward went through into the kitchen, where there was a table, some stools, and a cauldron simmering on a hook over the fire. A pile of newly chopped logs lay in one corner, their fresh scent mingling with the aroma of herbs and pork. A loaf of bread and some cheese stood on the table, and some ale was already poured into a mug.

Bella sat down and held the still sobbing Toby on her knees while Edward ladled some of the stew he had been cooking onto platters, and cut manchets of bread. Toby wriggled off Bella's lap and began to spoon his portion hungrily, and Bella realised that it was a long time since she had herself eaten. Edward watched in silence, his lips curling.

"Well, what do you want?" Bella repeated.

"You are my wife," he answered. "What more can I want? What did you discover when I was in delirium that sent you hotfoot to England?"

"You told me the truth about Henry,"

Bella answered, "and I came to claim Toby's inheritance."

"Yes, Henry Martin took it by a trick and has benefited by a year's possession. We must hope that he has not sold too large a part."

"We?" Bella asked coolly.

He smiled sardonically. "Of course. You and I, Bella. I've no mind to risk my life in Virginia or as a mercenary in Europe when there's a good home waiting for me in Kent."

"It is not your home," she stated quietly. "It is Toby's."

"Come, my dear. I am trying to be reasonable. How can he manage it for himself? You must be there, and where you are I will be. It is as simple as that."

"I'll never agree to live with you again," Bella said, but her heart was beating unnaturally loudly, and she was afraid that he would hear it.

"You have no choice. We are wed. And I hold both you and Toby. Do you know what will happen to him if you ever disobey me again? Or if you ever refuse to come to my bed, and do as I wish?"

Bella looked at him as bravely as she

could. "Do you threaten me?"

"Not you. I am sure that you have learned some pleasing tricks from that whoremaster of yours, and can satisfy me now as you did not when you were a timid virgin. If you do not — well, a child's life is uncertain, is it not? I am surprised Toby has survived the hazards of such a voyage and the conditions of that hellhole. But children die easily, and then you would inherit Clifford Manor. As my wife that means I would own it. I am sure you understand me."

Bella knew that for the moment she was trapped. Until she could secure some protection for Toby she dared not anger Edward, for there were so many ways in which he could kill a child, and if Toby died he would be able to claim everything in her name as he had threatened.

"You will have to permit us to return to London to challenge Henry's claim," she said as calmly as she could.

"I have my own attorney who will work on our behalf. There is no further need for you to be in London. I shall act for you, and take Toby when it is necessary to produce him. You will stay here, my dear, under close guard. I do not intend you to escape from me again."

Bella shrugged. There must be some way out, and in the meantime she must appear to accept the situation to safeguard Toby. Then she shuddered. Edward would probably expect to exercise his husbandly attentions, and she would not dare risk angering him by resisting.

Her fears were soon confirmed when he ordered her to put Toby to bed in the innermost room upstairs. When she took the child up the steep staircase she found three rooms leading out of each other. Toby had clearly used the furthest one, for a rough pallet of straw was in one corner and a torn blanket covered the makeshift bed.

In the centre room, Bella saw with a shiver of apprehension, was a larger straw mattress, and Edward's spare clothing was hanging on nails in the beams. Before she had finished telling Toby his favourite stories, Edward had followed her upstairs and was waiting for her. A candle illuminated the room, where he had closed the shutters to keep out the chill wind which had suddenly sprung up.

"Get undressed," he said brusquely. "I've no more gowns for you, but if you prefer to spend the rest of your time here in rags, I'm willing to tear your clothes off again. That is sport in itself, and if you go about the house half naked I might pleasure you more often, not just at night."

Attempting to control her revulsion, knowing that he was fully restored to strength and could force her if she resisted, and that this time she had no knife with which to protect herself, Bella slowly unlaced her bodice. Edward lounged, still dressed, on the mattress. His gaze burned into her as he enjoyed her reluctance. Slowly Bella slipped off her gown and chemise, feeling totally humiliated as she finally stood naked before her hateful husband. His hot eyes inspected her slowly, travelling up and down her body, lingering at the luscious curves and making her want to scream with fury and mortification.

"Methinks you've grown more enticing since I last sampled your charms," he commented. "Now, you can show your appreciation of me by acting the valet. Take off my clothes."

She could not refuse. He lay there, and

as she approached, nerving herself for the hateful task, he stretched out his hand and viciously pinched her thigh. She winced, and he laughed.

"That's just a taste of what you'll get if you do not co-operate. Show me what Tarrant taught you. Go on, stop prevaricating! I've not been so desperate for women, or short of them, these last few weeks, that I'm anxious to get it over with quickly. Let me see how you have learned to tempt a man. If you don't know how I'll have to teach you, but I had heard that your paramour had some skill. Make use of it for my pleasure now."

13

SIR FRANCIS came down the stairs considerably ruffled, and in great alarm when he discovered that his eminent lawyer friend had neither known he was there, nor sent for him. The helpful clerk had vanished after showing him into the lawyer's anteroom and was, he discovered, unknown to his friend. He almost ran into the room where he had left Bella, but it was empty. Swinging round on his heel he did run out of it, and collided with a tall blond man dismounting from a powerful looking chestnut horse just outside the door.

Hastily Sir Francis apologised and stepped back, trying to look round the man and the horse to discover whether Bella was in sight, but he found his arm grasped firmly. Distractedly he tried to shake off the man, who laughed.

"Francis! I implore you, is this the way to greet a friend who has travelled across the ocean to see you? Or have I changed beyond all recognition?"

"Adam!" Sir Francis gasped. "What the devil are you doing here? But I've no time for that! Here, you knew Mistress Sutton in Virginia, didn't you? Did you see her come out of there?"

Adam's grasp on his arm grew even firmer. "Bella? No! What has happened? Elizabeth told me about the child being taken, and that you were visiting lawyers, which is why I followed you. Where is she?"

"I don't know, but I'm afraid we were duped!" Ruefully he explained. "Her brother was too clever for us. We were to await another message, but he has separated her from her friends."

"It may not be her brother," Adam informed him tersely. "Her husband recovered enough to sail on the next ship from Jamestown. I discovered from some friends of his that he planned to kill Toby and claim the inheritance in Bella's name. That is why I came to England. I was fortunate to get a ship soon afterwards which had a swift crossing. Her husband's ship arrived ten days since, however, so he has had ample time for plotting."

"Then how can we start to look for her? It might have been possible to trace her brother, but where did her husband come from? Who were his friends? She never spoke of them, or even said where he lived before they were married."

"Henry Martin might know, and he is most likely at Clifford Manor. Daniel is with me. I'll go and fetch him from the tavern where he's waiting, and we'll ride into Kent. You had best go home in case we are wrong. I'll come back to you there."

He was mounting as he spoke and had gone without waiting for a reply. Sir Francis, distracted, set off for home to explain the strange turn of events to his wife.

Adam rode swiftly through the crowded streets and on to London Bridge, thrusting his way through the crowd of people and carts that blocked the narrow roadway between the houses. Having gained the far side he and Daniel were able to ride together past the White Hart, and Tabard Inn and the Marshalsea Prison, until they reached the open country, where Adam set a punishing pace.

The manor house where Bella had lived

was a large, commodious building standing in a formal garden. There were stables to one side where outhouses surrounded a courtyard, and as Adam reined in to take stock of the house a horseman rode hurriedly from this yard and, without a glance in their direction, spurred his horse into a gallop and past them. Adam looked after him.

"I have seen Henry Martin but the once, and briefly," he said urgently, "but I am certain that is he. Daniel, follow him and see which road he takes. If he goes away from the London road, wait for me. Off you go, or you'll lose him!"

He dismounted as he spoke, hitched his horse to the gatepost, and strode up the path between the formal flower beds to the front door. An elderly man answered his firm knock and peered up at him.

"What is it?" he muttered irritably.

"I need to speak to Henry Clifford. Is he here?"

The ancient shook his head.

"You missed him," he wheezed, and started to close the door.

"That was him, riding away?"

"Aye, likely."

"Where has he gone?"

The old man stared curiously at Adam and shook his head.

"Why should I tell you? You're a stranger. Mr Clifford might not want it known."

"Did you live here when Miss Bella was here, and Master Toby?" Adam asked, putting his booted foot in the way so that the old man could not close the door. He looked up, startled.

"What has it to do with my little Miss Bella? She's gone far away."

"No, she's back in England, and in some danger. I think your master has gone to find her. Where has he gone? I am a friend of Miss Bella's."

"Miss Bella? In England? No, she be in Virginia or some such outlandish place. She's not been in England for a year or more. I'll never see her again, poor little maid. A sweet lass she was, too!"

Adam restrained his impatience.

"She has come back, and is in danger. Please help me find her. Where has Henry Clifford gone?"

"The Pilgrim's House," the old man eventually informed Adam. "That's what he said, anyway."

"Where is it?"

"Take the road through Cobham, and it's up on the Downs, it looks over the Medway Valley. Anyone in those parts will tell you."

"My thanks," Adam rapped out, handed the astonished old man a crown piece, and turned to run down the path. He was soon galloping back along the road after Henry Martin.

Some miles further on he found Daniel waiting for him.

"He's only ten minutes ahead, but he's riding as though the devil were after him, and my horse went lame a hundred yards back," the man explained. "It was fortunate he turned off here."

"There is a village nearby, get the horse stabled, and get yourself somewhere to stay until you can bring him back to London," Adam ordered, and Daniel watched reluctantly as he followed the narrow lane along which Henry Martin had ridden.

The lanes soon degenerated into a tangle of small tracks, so Adam stopped in a village and found a young lad who seemed confident that he could show him the way to the Pilgrim's house.

"Though no-one's lived there for the past year or so," he informed Adam, "since Mr Carter left."

"Come pillion behind me," Adam said briskly and the lad, awed at the opportunity to ride on such a fine horse, scrambled hurriedly up onto the horse's back.

"It's only a couple of miles," he volunteered, and soon he was pointing along a narrow track through thick woods. "It's at the end of that, there's no other house," he said.

"Thank you. You'd best go home now," Adam said, presenting him with a silver sixpence, and so stern did he sound that the lad, who had been determined to creep after this elegant stranger to see what he wanted at the long-deserted Pilgrim's House, decided that he might be wiser to return home as directed.

Adam turned along the track and came out of the trees to find a sweating horse standing, his head drooping, a few paces from the open front door.

Bella had, with trembling clumsy fingers, started to unfasten the buttons of Edward's doublet as he ordered, trying to control her instinctive flinching as he stretched up one hand and grasped her breast. Then his hand slid down her thigh and round her leg to pull her down on top of him.

"You're not very expert," he jibed, and then suddenly pushed her away and sat up, listening.

Bella heard it too, the drumming of a horse's hooves outside the house, and as Edward rose and crossed to the small window, peering through a small slit between the shutters, she reached for her gown and dragged it hastily over her head.

"Stay here while I attend to it!" Edward ordered, and went through into the next room and down the stairs. He was half way down, Bella anxiously peering after him, when the door was thrown open and she heard a loud voice.

"Come out, you rogue! Where the devil are you hiding your miserable carcass?"

"Henry!" Bella whispered, and shrank back. It would not do to let Henry know that she and Toby were in the house, for he had a powerful reason to wish them both dead.

She saw Edward snatch a knife from the

kitchen table as he went towards the hall and then, curiously overcoming her fear, went down a few steps. She kept well into the shadows, but she could see a part of the hall through the open door.

Henry stood, legs astride, in the other doorway, a short sword in his hand.

"Well, what have you to say for yourself?" he demanded as Edward appeared.

"Henry, my old friend, what a surprise," Edward responded calmly. "I was proposing to visit you as soon as I had made this place habitable. It has been sadly neglected since I left England. Won't you come and sit in the kitchen?"

Bella swiftly and silently retreated back up the stairs, but she could see Henry with his back to her, as he accepted the invitation and sat on one of the stools. He prudently kept his sword by his hand, however, and Edward seated opposite him played nonchalantly with the knife he held.

"What are you doing back in England?" Henry demanded. "Our agreement was that you would remain in Virginia."

"That was what you thought I would do," Edward replied. "I had little choice at the time, for as you know I had to leave England in something of a hurry. But things have changed. Life is too uncertain in that fiendish place. I prefer England."

"Where is the girl?"

"Is it the girl you are concerned with?" Edward asked sneeringly. "Do not trouble yourself, she is safe."

"And contesting my inheritance for that brat. I might have known you were not to be trusted, Edward Sutton! I thought that you were behind it when the claim was first made, and then I heard that you had been seen near here. Well, we will soon show you how unhealthy it is for such lying dogs in England!"

So saying he leapt to his feet, kicking away the stool on which he had been sitting, and thrust his sword across the table at Edward. But Sutton had been expecting the attack, and sprang aside, dodging round the table and hurling one of the pewter mugs at Henry as he did so.

It caught Henry a glancing blow on the side of the head, and for a moment he was caught off balance. It was enough for Edward to leap forward, beating Henry's sword arm out of the way and striking at him with his knife. At the last moment Henry realised his danger and gave ground, but he slipped on the loose rushes and fell backwards, crashing to the floor with Edward on top of him. Abandoning his sword, which was useless at such close quarters, Henry fought desperately to disarm his assailant. He hung grimly on to Edward's arm, attempting to twist it and force Edward's fingers to relax their grip on the knife.

Agonisingly, slowly, Edward felt his hold slackening and he brought his knee viciously up to catch Henry in the groin. With a gasp of pain Henry released Edward's hand, and as Edward drew back, ready to strike with the knife, Henry rolled aside, conscious even in his physical anguish of the need to evade his opponent. He rolled towards the fire and knocked against the cauldron, setting it swinging wildly on the hook.

Edward thrust with the knife, but the blow merely scraped Henry's shoulder, tearing his doublet and producing a small spurt of blood. As Henry attempted to stagger to his feet Edward jabbed him in the stomach with his elbow. Henry collapsed onto the ground again, clutching at the cauldron as it swung towards him and bringing it crashing to the floor. Edward coolly bent down to retrieve Henry's sword.

"I'm sorry, my dear Henry, that you will not live to see me take your house," he sneered. "It is quite an attractive one, worth far more than that miserly sum you gave me to take your inconvenient sister out of your way. And the brat does have a valid claim, as you must know."

Gloating he watched as Henry, still suffering excruciating pain, attempted to crawl out of his way. He followed and when Henry hauled himself to his knees, kicked him contemptuously. This sent Henry sprawling headlong through the doorway into the hall. Edward followed, the sword raised and stabbed Henry in the back.

Bella heard Henry give a scream which was cut off abruptly, but she had spied Edward's knife lying unheeded amongst the rushes, and she ran swiftly down the stairs in an effort to secure it. She reached it as Edward, the sword dripping red with blood, came back into the kitchen. As she straightened up and backed away from him he gave a grunt of laughter.

"Were you proposing to assist me, my dear?" he asked sarcastically. "Come here."

Bella remained where she was.

"Have you killed Henry?" she asked quietly.

"Of course. Could you doubt that I would? Do you wish to make certain, my dear wife? He'll not come creeping up to us when we resume our interrupted activities."

Bella bit her lip. He was stronger than she was and Henry's sword was a better weapon than the knife. It was most unlikely that she could fight him off. Fleetingly she thought that to die from a thrust of that sword would be preferable to submitting to Edward's lusts. But for Toby's sake, peacefully asleep upstairs, she had either to agree or discover a way of escape.

Aware of her hesitation, Edward began to walk towards her. Bella tried to strike him with the knife, but it was to no avail, for he parried it with the sword and then, grasping her hand in his, forced her to drop it.

Throwing down the sword he held Bella to him and ruthlessly, despite her struggles, removed the gown she had so short a time before put on again.

"So you prefer to fight do you?" he demanded, panting somewhat for she was putting up a spirited defence and it was all he could do to hold her.

Bella fought desperately, but he gradually forced her backwards against the table, and tried to bend her arms up behind her back. When she twisted away so that he could not he suddenly lost patience. With a sudden push he threw her to the floor and before she could recover her breath had thrown himself across her.

"If you'll not submit peaceably I'll take you here!" he snarled, and while he held her down with his own body he began to wriggle out of his clothes. It was difficult, for Bella struggled with a strength born of desperation, scratching his face and clawing at his flesh whenever she could get her hands free, and once managing to bite his arm. Edward had wriggled half way out of his breeches and Bella's strength was failing as she shrank away from the hateful contact with his nakedness, when a cool voice addressed them.

"My dear Mr Sutton, you are hardly

appropriately dressed to receive visitors."

Startled, Edward tried to rise to his feet, reaching out for his abandoned sword at the same time, but the breeches descending about his ankles impeded him and he stumbled, falling to his knees.

"What are you doing here?" he demanded in a tone of utter loathing as he tugged at his breeches and hastily fastened a few points.

"I think I arrived just in time, sirrah."

"Adam!" Bella exclaimed, rising to her feet and staring at him in relief and bewilderment. He smiled comfortingly at her.

Naked, flushed, and with her hair dishevelled, she had never looked so desirable. But he noted the bruises and reddened marks where Edward had gripped her too tightly, and his lips tautened as his glance moved back to Edward.

"She's my wife. You've no right to interfere and I'll thank you to leave my house!"

Adam slowly shook his head.

"There is a small matter of a dead man out there," he said softly, "apart from your wife and the child. Where is Toby?"

"Upstairs, and safe," Bella said, then, as Adam smiled at her again, realised her undressed state. She blushed fiercely and thankfully espied her gown, somewhat torn but better than nothing, on the floor behind Edward. She moved to pick it up and slipped it over her head before turning to face the two men again. Edward was blustering angrily and suddenly stooped to pick up the knife by his foot. As he straightened and flung it towards Adam, Adam stepped swiftly aside and closed with him, grappling firmly and forcing him to give way. They swayed perilously for a moment, and then crashed to the floor. Breaking away from each other they both swiftly regained their feet and began circling warily Bella retreated to the stairs.

Then Adam moved, feinting to the right and as Edward parried, he drove his left fist with shattering force into Edward's face. Edward staggered back and Adam followed up the blow with another, and a third, before Edward fell to his knees. As he grovelled on the floor, half dazed with the battering he had received, his hands came into contact with the sword and he began to swing it wildly round so that Adam was forced to stay out of range while drawing his own sword from the scabbard.

As Sutton stumbled to his feet Adam stepped backwards and Edward, dimly perceiving that his opponent was moving away from him, took a fumbling step forwards. Adam circled him and Edward staggered to hold the table, still preventing Adam from getting near him by wildly brandishing the sword. Then, with a tremendous effort he heaved up one end of the table, flinging it towards Adam. It was a wasted effort, for as the heavy table smashed down on the hard beaten earth floor, crushing one of the stools beneath it with a splintering sound, Adam moved to one side and, before Edward had recovered from the strain, moved in and delivered the *coupe de grace* with his fists.

At that moment Toby, waking and hearing the sounds of the fight below, cried out, and Bella turned and ran up the stairs to comfort him. She was sitting on his bed, rocking him in her arms, when Adam appeared from the adjoining room.

"Hello, young man," he said easily. "I

thought you were too old to cry now."

"I am!" Toby said indignantly, and then gave a crow of welcome. "Adam!" he exclaimed, and struggled free of Bella to run and clasp Adam about the legs. "Where've you been?" he demanded imperiously, his fright and his tears forgotten.

"Oh, on a ship, like you were," Adam said. "Now be a sensible fellow and go back to sleep. Bella and I have a great deal to say to one another."

With a trusting smile Toby slid back under the blanket, and closed his eyes. Adam retreated and after a few moments Bella followed. Adam was waiting for her in the next bedroom and without a word held out his arms. She gave a sob and ran to him, clinging and shivering in reaction to the terrors of the day.

"What of Edward? Is he — ?" she paused.

"He's not dead," Adam said gently, "but he will no longer be a danger to you. He is unconscious, I hit him very hard."

"But if he recovers, he might come up here. He is wicked, Adam, and cunning."

"I am aware of that. I have tied him up

and he cannot move. You have no need to fear."

"He killed Henry. Henry is dead, I suppose?" she asked.

"Yes, there is no doubt of that, he must have died immediately. Did that brute hurt you?" he asked, looking closely at her.

She blushed adorably. "Not — not much," she replied hurriedly. "But Adam, why are you here? How did you find us? Why are you in England at all? Oh, there are so many questions!"

"There is plenty of time to answer them. Do you feel strong enough to ride to the nearest inn? You can use Henry's horse. I put it with mine in an outhouse. Once I have you and Toby safe I will bring a cart to take Edward somewhere until he can be charged with the murder."

"Will — will they hang him?" she asked slowly.

Adam looked at her closely. Surely she could not still have any tender feelings for the man, he thought in dismay.

"If it can be proved, and I do not think there will be any doubt. Do you regret it?"

Bella shook her head in quick denial.

"No, no, apart from not wishing anyone to suffer! If he had never known me it might not have happened."

"His quarrel was with Henry; he used you only as a pawn. He is the sort of man who would have been bound to get himself hanged one day, or killed by someone he had cheated. Will you mind?"

"I should never again feel safe if I thought that at any moment he could have found me," Bella declared, and shivered again.

"You are safe now. Oh, Bella, my love. I should never have let you go back to him. I should have defied the authorities in Jamestown, or taken you somewhere else. We could have made a life together in some other country. Bella, when I discovered that he had left Jamestown and followed you I was in terror that I might be too late. He planned to kill Toby and claim your father's lands for himself."

"You came after me, to help me?" Bella asked in wonder, and then, a coldness sweeping over her, she remembered that he was no longer Adam Tarrant, a rich but simple Virginian planter, unwelcome in the England of King James, but Lord

Cawston, possessor of a vast fortune, and able to regain the approval of the King if he married the lovely and wealthy Lady Jane.

"Of course, my love, for I realised when you had gone how much I needed you," he replied, taking her into his arms.

"How did you follow us here?" Bella asked, trying to keep her voice calm.

"I met Sir Francis Rowe outside the Middle Temple, just after you had disappeared. I had just arrived in England and I went straight to his house. Elizabeth told me where you were, and about Toby. I decided that Henry would be the most likely person to know where Edward was, and so I rode to Clifford Manor. He had just left, but I followed him. An old man gave me the name of this house and I found a lad in the village nearby to show me the way. Is it Edward's house?"

"I do not know. Did you know that he had been forced to leave England? I think it was because of some deception to do with gaming. I suspect from what he said once that he might have won this house before he left England."

Adam nodded. "As he won his plantation,

and most likely by foul methods. But you will soon be free of him, my love. Will you come back to Virginia with me, or have you been given a distaste for it?"

He kissed her before she could answer and Bella, overwhelmed by the knowledge that he did apparently love her and had followed her from Virginia, raged inwardly at the cruel fate which must again part them. It was clear that he did not know of his brother's death, or he would not talk of returning to Virginia. When he knew he would have to accept the marriage which the King and his friends expected him to make. A great longing to lie just once more in his arms overcame her, and she suddenly decided to forget for this one night that he must afterwards belong to another woman.

When Adam drew her to the bed she went willingly, and trembled with remembered joy at the touch of his fingers and the flame which consumed her as his kisses grew harder, more sensuous and demanding. Her gown slipped unheeded to the floor. Adam soon disposed of his own clothing and drew her into his arms, thinking with wonder that never with any of the beautiful women he had known before had he found such delight.

Gently he caressed her and Bella, with a bitter sweet knowledge that this was the last time she would ever experience such rapture, responded with an ardour she had never before shown. Fiercely quelling his own need, Adam prolonged his slow exploration of her body, rediscovering every inch of it tenderly and lingeringly while Bella, anxious to be able, in arid future years, to recall every detail of him, passed her hands over his lean muscular frame, marvelling in his strength and tenderness, the warm hard body that elicited such a passionate answer in her own blood.

At length, when Bella was almost swooning, they came together in a fervent climax which left both of them breathless yet langorous. Warm and relaxed, all the tension of the past weeks drained out of her, Bella slept peacefully. The candle was almost finished and Adam leaned across Bella to blow it out, smiling tenderly down at her as she reached out sleepily to catch his hand and hold it against her cheek. He took her in his arms and closed his eyes, breathing deeply, content that he had at last found her again.

It was some hours later when he woke, immediately alert in the knowledge that there was danger around them. Then he rose swiftly from the bed, calling to Bella. From the doorway leading towards the end bedroom and staircase he could see a rosy glow, and hear the ominous crackling of flames from the room below.

14

THE staircase, rising out of the kitchen, was already a charred wreck. As Adam reached it and looked down he could see that the fire had been started because some of the dry, brittle rushes covering the floor had been pushed into the embers of the fire when Edward had overthrown the table. The flames had crept along these rushes, and gradually the table and the pile of logs and the other furniture in the room had been set alight. Probably the fat from the overturned cauldron had fed the flames.

As Bella came to join him he held her back, for he had just seen Edward, his clothing burned and his flesh charred, sprawled in the centre of the floor where he had left him after the fight. Briefly Adam hoped that he had still been unconscious when the fire had reached him. Surely he would have cried out and given warning if he had known of the danger to himself.

"We cannot get out that way. But the

other side of the house will still be untouched," Adam said calmly.

He took her hand and led her through into the central bedroom.

"Get dressed and then see to Toby," he said briefly, pulling on his own shirt and breeches. Bella was soon dressed and went to rouse and dress Toby, who sleepily protested at being disturbed.

While she was persuading him to co-operate, Adam came through and inspected the windows in the gable end. He pulled aside the sliding shutters and tried to force the mullions away from the frame, but they were thick and sturdy. He looked about him, then pulled the straw pallet towards the window. Smiling confidently at Toby, who was beginning to ask why there was a bonfire downstairs, he tore a strip off the blanket and went through the other room. When he came back the blanket was smouldering, and Adam sent Bella and Toby into the central room. Then, packing the straw round the bottom of the mullions, he set it alight, feeding more straw from the mattress and the one from the centre room until the mullions were charred through sufficiently for him to wrench them out of the window aperture. Throwing the blankets over the edge of the opening he doused the fire, and using other pieces of blanket to protect his hands, he worked at the charred wood until he had made an opening large enough for them to squeeze through.

Coughing because of the smoke which now filled the room, he called to Bella and Toby.

"Come, we must hasten."

Bella, who had been watching apprehensively as the fire spread from the stairs and up into the rafters, went through thankfully, choking at the thickness of the smoke in the end room.

"I will lower you as far as I can, then you must drop," Adam explained. "I'll lower Toby to you afterwards."

"And you?"

"I will manage. There's nothing to use as a rope, and no time, but the drop is not far. Can you climb through? I'm holding you; you will not fall."

She scrambled through the aperture and then, twisting about so that she could clasp Adam's hands, slid off the window sill and felt herself dropping until she was fully stretched.

"Are you ready?" Adam asked above her, and she let go her hold on his hands to fall a short distance to the ground, stumble, and roll over.

"Bella, are you all right?" Adam called.

"Yes, and I'm ready to catch Toby," she called up to him, then stood braced beneath the window as Adam lifted a suddenly terrified little boy and pushed him through the window.

"No, no!" Toby screamed, struggling to hold on to Adam.

"Toby, be brave, I'm already down here and I will catch you," Bella called up. As Toby looked down at her, Adam managed to turn him so that he could not hang on, and leant as far as possible out of the window before releasing him.

"There, that was not difficult, was it?" Bella asked as Toby, arms and legs flailing wildly, dropped into her arms and she staggered a few steps backwards under his weight.

"Keep clear," Adam called, and a moment later Bella saw him swing out of the window, turn round to lower himself, hang by the hands and drop lightly down the last few feet to the ground.

Then she spared a moment to look at the building. The whole of one end was now a raging inferno, and the flames could be seen through the ground floor windows beneath the room they had escaped from. A little while longer and they would not have been able to get down.

Putting his arms about her, Adam led her further away and when they were a safe distance from any flying sparks stopped and looked back.

"Edward — is — still inside?" Bella asked quietly.

"There was no hope for him, he must have died very quickly," Adam said gently.

"Henry too. His body was still there, I suppose."

Adam nodded. "We might all have perished. I was careless, I should have realised the rushes might have caught fire."

"No! You must not blame yourself!" Bella exclaimed, and at that moment a terrified whinny came from one of the horses as it scented the fire.

"I'll go and get them out of the outhouses. Edward had a horse there too."

She moved towards the track away from the house, lit up eerily by the glow of the fire. Adam went to calm the horses and bring them to where Bella waited, less nervous as they saw that they were being taken further from the fire. Bella hitched her skirts so that she could ride astride, and Adam lifted her onto the back of one of the horses.

"Would you prefer to take Toby in front of you, or lead the spare horse?" he asked.

"Toby rode with me in this fashion when he was little more than a year old. Do you remember?"

The child nodded and stretched up his arms to her. His fright had gone and he chattered excitedly as they carefully picked their way along the dark track. Adam laughingly said that he was more accustomed to steering by the stars at sea than on land, and turned northwards.

Fortunately it was a warm September night and dawn was not far distant. As the sky brightened they came into a small village and outside the inn a sleepy-looking man was standing yawning. As they approached he stared in surprise and

Adam laughed ruefully as he dismounted from his horse.

"We're confoundedly dishevelled," he said. "We've escaped from a fire. Can you provide a room for the lady and some meat and ale?"

The man called loudly to another who came and took the horses. Soon Bella was installed in a small, pleasant room overlooking the garden, and a lavish breakfast was being set before them.

"Afterwards I must go and inform the nearest Justice," Adam said as they began to eat. "Then what? Do you wish to return to London or go to Clifford Manor? There will be formalities, no doubt, but Toby's claim should soon be established. And then, my love, we can arrange for a steward to look after him until he is old enough to take charge for himself. Will you come back with me to Virginia, or would you prefer to forget that and make a home with me somewhere new?"

Bella took a deep breath.

"Adam, do you know about your brother?" she asked abruptly.

"Roderick? What about him?"

As gently as she could Bella told him

what she had heard.

"So you are Lord Cawston now. I am sorry, Adam, that I had to tell you in this way."

He was silent for a moment.

"Poor Roderick," he said at last. "But that makes no difference to us, Bella."

"Oh but it does. They are saying, Lady Rowe's friends in London, that now King James would pardon you if you married Lady Jane. You would be able to live in England again and you must, you have responsibilities to your name. They said that she was lovely too. I expect you know her? You must have done so when she was betrothed to your brother."

A slight reminiscent smile curved Adam's lips and Bella's last hope that he would reject this heiress disappeared.

"I met her," he answered slowly, "but it was before she was betrothed to my brother. It was when I last came to England to see my mother. It was mainly my mother's wish that Roderick married. I do not think either of them were in love."

"Then that makes it easier, does it not?" Bella managed to say lightly. "She will not object to you." Not that any girl would, she added to herself.

"Do you prefer to go to London?" he asked again, and Bella quickly shook her head.

"Pray give my most grateful thanks to Sir Francis and Lady Rowe. I hope to see them again soon but now I would prefer to go home. Can you arrange to send Alice to me, if you please?"

"Of course. She will no doubt be frantic with anxiety by now. Do you wish to sleep here for a few hours or shall we ride straight for Clifford Manor?"

"Let us go," Bella said, realising the futility of lingering, and after she had washed and tidied herself they set off.

Bella received a rapturous welcome from the servants at Clifford Manor, for most of them had served her parents and knew her well. They did not seem unduly perturbed by Henry's death, and a bevy of maids swarmed about Toby exclaiming at how much he had grown. They took him away to renew his acquaintance with Cook and her gingerbread men. Bella was left alone with Adam in the comfortable parlour overlooking the front garden.

"Thank you for all you have done for

me. Toby and I owe our lives to you more than once. I do not know how to thank you enough."

"Come with me," he said, trying to take her in his arms, but she evaded him and shook her head vehemently.

"Adam, I cannot. You are important and must marry well. You must obtain the King's pardon. I cannot prevent you from doing that."

"Bella, you have never said it. I know now that you have never loved Sutton but do you not love me just a little? Last night I thought you did, although before I have always wondered. Do you, Bella?"

Bella ached to tell him that she loved him, that all her former doubts and suspicions about men had evaporated in his arms. She knew now that their physical love, while it might have begun as something else, was as different from the casual lust of temporary liaisons as land from water. The one was solid, fruitful, dependable, the other insubstantial, treacherous and barren. But if she did she would bind him to her, and he would lose the opportunity now granted to him of taking his rightful place in England. If she asked him to forego that he would resent it in the end. They would have to return to Virginia, to the heartbreaking task of rebuilding what the Indians had destroyed, to the dangers and problems that beset the planters, when Adam could remain in peace and safety, luxury and in influence here in England.

It took but a few minutes for these thoughts to flash through her mind. Taking a deep breath she turned away so that he would not see the truth in her eyes, and spoke lightly.

"Adam, do not disappoint me after all by being intense. I have never loved, nor could love, any man," — apart from you, her heart cried out. She contrived a slight laugh. "I thought you understood that? After what Henry and Edward did to me, how could you expect it? Oh, I know that you have been gentle and kind and risked much for me, and I am truly grateful, but I think I have — paid my debts."

"Then you wish me to go?" he asked quietly. "After all we have been to one another, Bella?"

"I hope that I will see you again some day, perhaps at Court when Toby is grown," she added, "and you have heirs of your own."

"Goodbye, Bella," he said, and raised her hand to his lips.

Kiss me properly, once more, her heart pleaded, but he merely brushed the back of her hand with his lips, cool and unemotional, and with a slight smile bowed and left her.

She longed to run after him, to cling to the stirrups and beg him not to go, to retract all she had said, but somehow she refrained. For his sake she must not. It was for the best. She stayed at the door where she had walked with him until he had ridden out of sight. Then, thankfully aware that no further dangers threatened Toby, she shut herself in her old room, telling the maid who was busy sorting out the clothes she had left behind when she had been unceremoniously packed off to Virginia, that she was too tired to eat and did not wish to be disturbed.

She remained in her room, pleading exhaustion, for the next two days, sending even Alice away when her faithful maid arrived, escorted from London by one of Sir Francis's grooms.

When Bella finally emerged she was pale and listless, and permitted Alice to organise her days. She ate, played with Toby, inspected the linen room and the stillroom, brewery and buttery as Alice instructed, and sat in the parlour with a piece of tapestry on her hands. She set stitches only when Alice was by, however, and for the rest sat silently remembering.

One morning Alice remarked that she was too pale, and drove her to sit in the orchard behind the house. Unresisting Bella had permitted Alice to help her dress in a pale yellow taffeta gown, but as she sat on a rug and watched Toby playing with a puppy from the stables, she reflected that it was not a gown suited for work, even for such tasks as needlework or supervision of the maids. Did Alice expect her to spend the rest of her days sitting in the orchard or the parlour, she wondered? And a faint stirring of self-disgust animated her. Adam was gone; she had herself driven him away, and brooding over him would not bring him back. She could not for ever remain in this dream-like state, holding at bay the pain of her loss. She was afraid that once she permitted herself to feel the agony would be unbearable, but trying not to feel was very little better. The sooner she busied herself with work the easier it might be to drive to the back of her thoughts the memory of Adam, his laughing eyes and tender smile, his gentle tutelage in the delights of love, and his passion and bravery.

Determined to start at once she recalled that Alice had brought out a basket for blackberry picking, so she rose, took the basket and walked purposefully to the bramble hedge at the bottom of the orchard where she picked industriously for a few moments.

Then she paused and closed her eyes in brief annoyance. Such activity did not banish the recollection of Adam at all, it brought the memory of him even closer; she even imagined that she heard his voice. Angrily she shook her head and stretched to reach a succulent berry on a high branch, and then exclaimed in annoyance when her skirts caught on another branch. She dragged at the skirts, heard the material tear, and then froze in amazement.

"Keep still, I will untangle you."

It could not be! For a moment Bella was

incapable of moving, the basket slipped from her nerveless grasp, and then, as she felt a warm breath on her cheek and arms about her, she knew that it was Adam himself and no dream. Slowly she turned to face him as he smiled down at her, his arms holding her tightly.

"You! How? Why? I do not understand! Why are you here?" she stammered.

"I've come to tell you that I'm sailing for Virginia again next week."

The momentary desolation in her eyes told him all he wished to know. She opened her mouth, tried to speak and achieved only a faint moan, and then shook her head as if to clear her thoughts.

"The — the King!" she managed at last.

"Yes, I've seen the King. He has forgiven me."

"Then you — you will marry Lady Jane," she whispered.

"No. She does not care for the notion of Virginia. To be perfectly truthful I did not ask her if she wanted to come with me. I was afraid, you see, after what you said about my irresistible charm that she might take up my offer. And that would not do, for I had other plans."

"I do not understand!" Bella exclaimed, knowing only that if he took away his supporting arms she would sink to the ground.

"I saw King James when I went back to London. I explained everything to him and asked for his advice. The King, you must understand, likes to think he is the wisest man in his kingdom. He told me it was unthinkable that Toby should be left alone in England. Yet I could not return to Virginia without my wife, and she needed to look after her young brother. In the end he suggested that Sir Francis could oversee a steward for Clifford Manor until Toby was old enough to decide whether he wanted to return to England or remain in Virginia. I wonder which he will choose?"

"Your wife! You are returning to Virginia? Why do you not wish to remain here? What about your own estates?"

Adam shrugged slightly. "I would feel stifled here after the life I have led. I could not mince about the Court, paying vapid compliments to the ladies, waiting for the King to notice me. We came to an arrangement satisfactory to us both. There are likely to be changes in Virginia and James needs men of substance, men he can rely on there. I convinced him that it would be possible to establish a flourishing community, and since he deplores tobacco so much, he welcomed my insistence that other crops should be grown and industries established. He is to take charge of my brother's lands, and use the income to send out to me each year horses and cattle, tools and skilled artisans, plants and seeds. But I cannot do everything out there myself. Will you help me?"

"Adam, I can scarce believe it," Bella whispered. "I am surely dreaming."

"Bella, my dearest love, I know that what you told me was untrue. You do care for me a little, do you not? Could you come to love me enough to marry me, to share my life and the dangers of it in an inhospitable land?"

"Are you doing this for me? There is no need, Adam, you could remain in England."

"I could remain in England with you if I wished. The King would have agreed now that I am Lord Cawston. But he will be happy for me to use my new wealth in Virginia. We'll found a fortune and a new family there. Bella, my dearest one, we have a week. Will you wed me tomorrow or the day we sail? Can you leave Alice to pack for you and Toby here, and come with me now to London? I want to show my English friends that I have been the most fortunate of men to capture you. Elizabeth begs me to take you back to her. I have booked the passage and there will be room for any more of the servants you wish to bring from here. Or any favourite furniture, or a horse, or what you will."

"Adam, I cannot believe it. Oh, my beloved! I was only half alive when I thought I would never see you again!"

Their kiss was long and satisfying, and only broken when Toby, chasing his new puppy, suddenly saw Adam and rushed at him, demanding to be kissed too, and then that Adam should admire his puppy.

Later, when supper was over, Bella sat before the small fire Alice had lit in the parlour, holding Adam's hand.

"It is all so different," she sighed contentedly. "I was terrified before that other hateful wedding, even though I had not seen Edward. Then I tried so desperately not to love you, for I could not bear to be hurt."

"I'll do the utmost in my power to save you from the slightest hurt again," he vowed. "But it is late and we are to be married tomorrow."

"I am so pleased it is to be here. I would not care for another London wedding. Come."

She rose and led the way upstairs. Although Alice, suddenly aware of the proprieties, had ordered a separate room to be prepared for Adam, he did not even glance at the door as he followed Bella through hers.

Slowly, lovingly, they helped one another to disrobe, and joyfully they clung together.

"I suspect it will be a lifetime's task to tame such a wildcat!" Adam murmured mockingly.

"I'm not a very conformable wife," she warned him, and evaded his grasp as he came for her.

He advanced purposefully and she dodged to the other side of the bed, wrapping the curtains about her and giggling as he tried to disentangle them. At last he picked her up and tossed her onto the bed where she lay, peeping through half-closed eyes as she feigned sleep.

Adam tickled her feet and she shrieked, rolling over and trying to pull the covers about herself. He dragged them away from her and suddenly, as their bodies touched, they paused and stared deep into one another's eyes.

"My most precious love!"

"Adam, my darling."

Bella discovered that night, as they laughed and loved, that there were many delights that she had never previously imagined for two people united in heart and mind as well as body. Their passion was greater than ever before, and together they reached heights of ecstasy never yet attained, but a deeper, more tranquil emotion gripped them both as they afterwards lay quietly entwined in one another's arms.

"You are so deliciously perfect already," Adam whispered in her ear, "yet it is going to be even more wonderful when we are married."

Other titles in the
Ulverscroft Large Print Series:

TO FIGHT THE WILD
Rod Ansell and Rachel Percy

Lost in uncharted Australian bush, Rod Ansell survived by hunting and trapping wild animals, improvising shelter and using all the bushman's skills he knew.

COROMANDEL
Pat Barr

India in the 1830s is a hot, uncomfortable place, where the East India Company still rules. Amelia and her new husband find themselves caught up in the animosities which seethe between the old order and the new.

THE SMALL PARTY
Lillian Beckwith

A frightening journey to safety begins for Ruth and her small party as their island is caught up in the dangers of armed insurrection.

THE PLEASURES OF AGE
Robert Morley

The author, British stage and screen star, now eighty, is enjoying the pleasures of age. He has drawn on his experiences to write this witty, entertaining and informative book.

THE VINEGAR SEED
Maureen Peters

The first book in a trilogy which follows the exploits of two sisters who leave Ireland in 1861 to seek their fortune in England.

A VERY PAROCHIAL MURDER
John Wainwright

A mugging in the genteel seaside town turned to murder when the victim died. Then the body of a young tearaway is washed ashore and Detective Inspector Lyle is determined that a second killing will not go unpunished.

DEATH ON A HOT SUMMER NIGHT
Anne Infante

Micky Douglas is either accident-prone or someone is trying to kill him. He finds himself caught in a desperate race to save his ex-wife and others from a ruthless gang.

HOLD DOWN A SHADOW
Geoffrey Jenkins

Maluti Rider, with the help of four of the world's most wanted men, is determined to destroy the Katse Dam and release a killer flood.

THAT NICE MISS SMITH
Nigel Morland

A reconstruction and reassessment of the trial in 1857 of Madeleine Smith, who was acquitted by a verdict of Not Proven of poisoning her lover, Emile L'Angelier.

THE SONG OF THE PINES
Christina Green

Taken to a Greek island as substitute for David Nicholas's secretary, Annie quickly falls prey to the island's charms and to the charms of both Marcus, the Greek, and David himself.

GOODBYE DOCTOR GARLAND
Marjorie Harte

The story of a woman doctor who gave too much to her profession and almost lost her personal happiness.

DIGBY
Pamela Hill

Welcomed at courts throughout Europe, Kenelm Digby was the particular favourite of the Queen of France, who wanted him to be her lover, but the beautiful Venetia was the mainspring of his life.

LEAVE IT TO THE HANGMAN
Bill Knox

Dope, dynamite, guns, currency — whatever it was John Kilburn and his son Pat had known how to get it in or out of England, if the price was right. But their luck changed when one of them killed a cop.

A VIOLENT END
Emma Page

To Chief Inspector Kelsey there was no shortage of suspects when Karen Boland was murdered, and that was before he discovered that she stood to inherit substantially at twenty-one.

SILENCE IN HANOVER CLOSE
Anne Perry

In 1884 Robert York is found brutally murdered at his home in Hanover Close. When, three years later, Inspector Pitt is asked to investigate, the murder remains unsolved.

BALLET GENIUS
Gillian Freeman and Edward Thorpe

Presents twenty pen portraits of great dancers of the twentieth century and gives an insight into their daily lives, their professional careers, the ever present risk of injury and the pressure to stay on top.

TO LIVE IN PEACE
Rosemary Friedman

The final part of the author's Anglo-Jewish trilogy, which began with PROOFS OF AFFECTION and ROSE OF JERICHO, telling the story of Kitty Shelton, widowed after a happy marriage, and her three children.

NORA WAS A NURSE
Peggy Gaddis

Nurse Nora Courtney was hopelessly in love with Doctor Owen Baird and when beautiful Lillian Halstead set her cap for him, Nora realised she must make him see her as a desirable woman as well as an efficient nurse.

SEASONS OF MY LIFE
Hannah Hauxwell and Barry Cockcroft

The story of Hannah Hauxwell's struggle to survive on a desolate farm in the Yorkshire Dales with little money, no electricity and no running water.

TAKING OVER
Shirley Lowe and Angela Ince

A witty insight into what happens when women take over in the boardroom and their husbands take over chores, children and chickenpox.

AFTER MIDNIGHT STORIES,
The Fourth Book Of

A collection of sixteen of the best of today's ghost stories, all different in style and approach but all combining to give the reader that special midnight shiver.

MORNING IS BREAKING
Lesley Denny

The growing frenzy of war catapults Diane Clements into a clandestine marriage and separation with a German refugee.

LAST BUS TO WOODSTOCK
Colin Dexter

A girl's body is discovered huddled in the courtyard of a Woodstock pub, and Detective Chief Inspector Morse and Sergeant Lewis are hunting a rapist and a murderer.

THE STUBBORN TIDE
Anne Durham

Everyone advised Carol not to grieve so excessively over her cousin's death. She might have followed their advice if the man she loved thought that way about her, but another girl came first in his affections.

THE LISTERDALE MYSTERY
Agatha Christie

Twelve short stories ranging from the light-hearted to the macabre, diverse mysteries ingeniously and plausibly contrived and convincingly unravelled.

TO BE LOVED
Lynne Collins

Andrew married the woman he had always loved despite the knowledge that Sarah married him for reasons of her own. So much heartache could have been avoided if only he had known how vital it was to be loved.

ACCUSED NURSE
Jane Converse

Paula found herself accused of a crime which could cost her her job, her nurse's reputation, and even the man she loved, unless the truth came to light.

THE TWILIGHT MAN
Frank Gruber

Jim Rand lives alone in the California desert awaiting death. Into his hermit existence comes a teenage girl who blows both his past and his brief future wide open.

DOG IN THE DARK
Gerald Hammond

Jim Cunningham breeds and trains gun dogs, and his antagonism towards the devotees of show spaniels earns him many enemies. So when one of them is found murdered, the police are on his doorstep within hours.

THE RED KNIGHT
Geoffrey Moxon

When he finds himself a pawn on the chessboard of international espionage with his family in constant danger, Guy Trent becomes embroiled in moves and countermoves which may mean life or death for Western scientists.

NURSE ALICE IN LOVE
Theresa Charles

Accepting the post of nurse to little Fernie Sherrod, Alice Everton could not guess at the romance, suspense and danger which lay ahead at the Sherrod's isolated estate.

POIROT INVESTIGATES
Agatha Christie

Two things bind these eleven stories together — the brilliance and uncanny skill of the diminutive Belgian detective, and the stupidity of his Watson-like partner, Captain Hastings.

LET LOOSE THE TIGERS
Josephine Cox

Queenie promised to find the long-lost son of the frail, elderly murderess, Hannah Jason. But her enquiries threatened to unlock the cage where crucial secrets had long been held captive.

CLOUD OVER MALVERTON
Nancy Buckingham

Dulcie soon realises that something is seriously wrong at Malverton, and when violence strikes she is horrified to find herself under suspicion of murder.

AFTER THOUGHTS
Max Bygraves

The Cockney entertainer tells stories of his East End childhood, of his RAF days, and his post-war showbusiness successes and friendships with fellow comedians.

MOONLIGHT AND MARCH ROSES
D. Y. Cameron

Lynn's search to trace a missing girl takes her to Spain, where she meets Clive Hendon. While untangling the situation, she untangles her emotions and decides on her own future.

THE WILDERNESS WALK
Sheila Bishop

Stifling unpleasant memories of a misbegotten romance in Cleave with Lord Francis Aubrey, Lavinia goes on holiday there with her sister. The two women are thrust into a romantic intrigue involving none other than Lord Francis.

THE RELUCTANT GUEST
Rosalind Brett

Ann Calvert went to spend a month on a South African farm with Theo Borland and his sister. They both proved to be different from her first idea of them, and there was Storr Peterson — the most disturbing man she had ever met.

ONE ENCHANTED SUMMER
Anne Tedlock Brooks

A tale of mystery and romance and a girl who found both during one enchanted summer.